'No, I sha  **e
annulled,'** **e
suddenly** **l**

The sound of it sent shivers down her spine
and she looked at him, startled by his change
of mood.

'I've had enough of gossip and of being laughed
at behind my back, Lucinda. You are my wife,
and you will accept your duties as a wife.'

'Justin…' She faltered, her throat tight with
emotion. Tears gathered in her eyes but she
held them back. 'I know how angry you must
feel…'

'If you cared for me you might have trusted
me, Lucinda. I would have given you a fair
hearing. Do you not think it was your duty to
tell me before you accepted my proposal?'

'Yes. I think now that I should have told you.
I—I was afraid you would not wish to marry
me if you knew that I had such a terrible secret.'

THE DISAPPEARING DUCHESS

Anne Herries

MILLS & BOON

All the characters in this book have no existence outside the imagination of the author, and have no relation whatsoever to anyone bearing the same name or names. They are not even distantly inspired by any individual known or unknown to the author, and all the incidents are pure invention.

First published in Great Britain 2011
Paperback edition 2012
by Mills & Boon, an imprint of Harlequin (UK) Limited.
Harlequin (UK) Limited, Eton House, 18-24 Paradise Road,
Richmond, Surrey TW9 1SR

© Anne Herries 2011

ISBN: 978 0 263 89222 2

Harlequin (UK) policy is to use papers that are natural, renewable and recyclable products and made from wood grown in sustainable forests. The logging and manufacturing process conform to the legal environmental regulations of the country of origin.

Printed and bound in Spain
by Blackprint CPI, Barcelona

Anne Herries lives in Cambridgeshire, where she is fond of watching wildlife, and spoils the birds and squirrels that are frequent visitors to her garden. Anne loves to write about the beauty of nature, and sometimes puts a little into her books, although they are mostly about love and romance. She writes for her own enjoyment, and to give pleasure to her readers. She is a winner of the Romantic Novelists' Association Romance Prize. She invites readers to contact her on her website: www.lindasole.co.uk

Previous novels by the same author:

Prologue

Justin, Duke of Avonlea, looked round at the sea of faces. They were all staring at him expectantly, believing that he was about to make a speech of welcome and cut the cake with his bride. His mouth was dry, his chest tight with a kind of suspended agony, as he struggled to come to terms with what was seemingly going on.

Lucinda, his beautiful bride, had gone. She had left him almost immediately after the wedding ceremony. They'd returned from the church together in the carriage to his beautiful home, where the lavish reception was being held. She'd excused herself to him, saying that the flounce on her wedding gown was torn.

'I shall be no more than ten minutes, Avonlea,' she'd said with that shy smile he found so attractive. 'Please make my excuses to our guests. I shall join you as soon as I can.'

'Of course, my love.' He'd taken her hand to kiss the

palm. 'You look beautiful, Lucinda. Have I told you how much I adore you?'

'Yes, Justin, several times. I am very fond of you, too,' she'd said, smiled and left him to run lightly up the stairs.

That was more than an hour ago and since then no one had seen anything of her. Concerned after thirty minutes or so that she was keeping their guests waiting unduly, he'd gone up to her rooms to ask what was causing the delay. He had found only her maid, Alice.

'Where is your mistress?' he asked. 'We must not keep the guests waiting any longer.'

'I have not seen Lady Avonlea since you left the church, your Grace.'

'But she came directly up to have the flounce mended on her wedding gown. How can you not have seen her?'

'I have been waiting for her,' the maid said and looked nervous. 'Truly, she has not been here, sir.'

'Lucinda told me her gown was torn...' He looked around the room, which had been recently refurbished in the colours his young wife loved: creams, various shades of rose and gold, blending perfectly. No expense had been spared and he had imagined her being happy in the luxury he had provided. 'Is there no sign of her gown? Did she change into something else?'

The maid could not meet his eyes as she shook her head. 'Forgive me, sir. I was gone but a few moments and only to make sure that my lady's bags were safely stowed ready for your journey. When I returned I thought a few small things might have disappeared, but I was not certain.'

Avonlea strode over to the armoire and opened it, but the shelves were full of the gowns and beautiful silks he had purchased for his bride's pleasure.

'I cannot see that anything has been taken.' He frowned at the maid, feeling stunned. How could his bride have disappeared from her home on her wedding day, and more importantly, why? 'Make up your mind, girl—this is important. Surely your mistress would not leave without taking anything—or leaving a message?'

'There was an old gown—and some trinkets that my lady valued, which *have* gone from the dressing chest, but all her good jewels are here, your Grace.'

'Your mistress must be in the house or gardens,' Justin said, refusing to believe that what the maid was implying could be right. Why on earth would Lucinda leave him? He could think of no possible reason for they had been on good terms; there had been no quarrel, no dispute between them. The marriage might not have been a love match, but there was respect and affection on both sides—at least he had believed so when Lucinda accepted his suit. What could have changed her? What had he done that she must flee from him without a word?

He took a turn about the room, trying to find an answer to his questions; discovering no clue, he turned back to the anxious maid.

'Search your mistress's room thoroughly and make

certain whether there is a letter left somewhere. Also, please make a list of what has been taken. I need to know whether this was planned or an impulse. In the meantime, I shall have a search made for her.'

The search had begun, but as yet no sign of the new duchess had been found and no one seemed to have seen her.

The guests were getting restless, beginning to gossip amongst themselves. Justin could see concern, intrigue and some exchanged knowing looks; his true friends would be anxious, but some of his slight acquaintances might be amused if they learned that his bride had left him—not at the altar, it was true—but before the wedding reception had been held. It was a lowering thought and one that hurt his pride. Accustomed to homage, and with his good looks and vast wealth, sought after by every matchmaking mama in England, he had thought long and hard before asking a lady to be his wife. Lucinda might be a virtual nobody from the country, but her modesty and shy smile had convinced him that she would be the perfect wife for a man in his position.

Since childhood Justin had been taught his duty. He was born to a family of impeccable lineage and respectability. There were no skeletons to hide in his family closet, no scandals or acts of dishonour.

'Always remember your honour,' his father had told him as a young lad. 'No matter how much it hurts, no matter how hard, you must always do your duty, Justin.

A gentleman's honour and his family name come first. Promise me you will never forget, my son.'

Justin promised. His first offer of marriage to a lady of whom he knew his father to approve had been refused; slighted, it had taken Justin a long time to select another lady. He had believed Lucinda perfect in every way—and now she had run away, making a fool of him before his friends on his wedding day, hurting him in a way he would not have imagined possible until this moment. Looking round the room, he drew a deep breath, squashing the anger and disappointment that raged inside him.

'Forgive me,' he announced and the voices were silenced, faces inquisitive, eager for news. 'I am distressed to tell you that my wife has been taken ill. She will not be able to attend the reception. Please, enjoy the food and wine provided. I want to thank you all for coming and beg you to excuse me.'

He saw from their faces that they guessed he was lying. They had sensed something was wrong. He cared not to speculate on what they imagined was going on, but nothing could be stranger than the truth.

Chapter One

'You have no idea where Lucinda went or why?' His good friend and neighbour Andrew, Lord Lanchester, looked at him thoughtfully.

'I've had no word from her in almost two months,' Justin replied morosely.

Andrew had just returned from a tour of duty as the Duke of Wellington's aide in Spain. Wounded at Salamanca, he was now recovered, with only a slight limp to show for his suffering.

'I've searched everywhere. I've spent weeks looking for her, but although one or two of the tenants think they may have seen her walking near the estate on the day of her disappearance no one knows where she has gone.'

'What else have you done?' Andrew frowned. 'Have you employed an agent to trace her? Offered a reward for any information regarding her whereabouts?'

'I have thought about employing an agent secretly. I did not wish to offer a reward, because it would cause such a scandal. If—when—Lucinda returns, I do not want vicious tongues to destroy her.'

'You cannot hope to keep this brushed under the carpet?' Andrew raised his eyebrows. 'My sister Jane was here for the wedding and she told me as soon as I returned home from Spain that she felt something was amiss. She is not a gossip, but she was fond of Lucinda and is naturally worried about her, especially since she's heard no word since that day. The tale of Lucinda's disappearance has got about and people will talk, however discreet you are.'

'Your sister has been both considerate and kind,' Justin said, turning to look at his long-time friend and close neighbour. 'I know that she is Lucinda's good friend and I have been able to voice some of my concerns to her. However, she has no idea of what might have caused Lucinda to run away.'

'Are you certain she *has* run away?' Andrew asked gently. 'Couldn't there be another reason for her disappearance?'

Justin ran his fingers through his thick hair. There were dark circles beneath his eyes, proof of his sleepless nights, and a new harshness about his mouth. He seemed not to hear his friend. 'What made her do it? I have racked my brains to try to think if I did or said something that distressed or frightened her. If she did not wish to be my wife, she could have sent me a note before the wedding to break it off. Why marry me and then leave without a word? Surely I am not such a monster that she feared me?'

'I have no answers for you,' Andrew said. 'Had I been at home I should have advised employing an agent immediately, as it all sounds very suspicious to me. You are certain there was no letter? She left no word for you?'

'Her maid had not seen her and there was nothing that either of us could find anywhere.'

'Why not search her room again? Something may have been missed. I remember meeting Lucinda once when she and Jane were at the Raddlit Academy for young ladies. She did not strike me as the type of girl to behave badly. Jane liked her a great deal and my sister is usually a fine judge of character.'

'Lucinda is the sweetest creature I have ever met,' Justin said and the look he gave Andrew was one of despair. 'I cannot believe she would hurt me like this— yet perhaps you are right, maybe there is more to this story than meets the eye.'

'If you will permit me, I shall find an agent for you. I think we should give him Lucinda's maiden name. She will hardly be using yours, Avonlea.'

'Lucinda Seymour,' Justin said. 'She was such a quiet girl, but her smile attracted me from the beginning. When her aunt brought her to Harrogate I knew she was the one I wanted as my wife from the first moment I saw her—but she resisted me. She was polite but reserved, keeping me at a distance. It was not until she came to stay with Jane and we met again at your home that she let down her guard enough for me to have hope.' His eyes reflected his anguish. 'She told me she was very fond of me just before we parted. Why did she say that and then leave me? What could she hope to gain?'

'My guess is that there is some mystery here,' Andrew said. 'I cannot solve it, but I am certain that when Lucinda is ready she will return and explain everything.'

'If she cared for me even a little, she could have told me what distressed her so very much.'

'Forgive me, Avonlea—are you in love with her?'

'Naturally, I care for her…but I am not certain I know what love is in the sense you mean—there was precious little of it in our house when I was a lad.'

'Then it was not a love match.' Andrew looked thoughtful. 'Perhaps she felt that you might wish her gone if you knew the truth about her.'

Avonlea stiffened. 'What do you mean, pray?'

'How well did you know her? Was there some secret in her past, perhaps?'

'Nothing that she could not tell me. I would have listened and helped her if I could.' Justin frowned. 'Do you know of something?'

Andrew hesitated, then, 'I remember she left school quite suddenly and Jane did not hear from her for some years. She was very distressed about it at the time.'

'You do not know why she left?'

'I have no idea. Of course, it may have no bearing on this matter.'

'I do not see how it could.'

'Then perhaps she will return when she is ready.'

'I pray that you are right. I fear for her. I think she has very little money with her. I gave her some guineas for use while we travelled, but it was hardly enough to live on for the past two months, though she may have some jewels and a little money of her own, I suppose.'

Justin's mind was torn between distress, anger and bewilderment. He had searched every day for the past few weeks, but there was no sign of his duchess. In his heart he had begun to think that she might be dead—why else had she not told him where she was or why she had gone? Had someone abducted her—or, worse, murdered her to be revenged on him? He could not think of anyone who hated him that much—but why else would she have been taken?

'So, you would take her back—no matter the reasons for her disappearance?'

'She is my wife,' Justin said and looked at his friend, as if surprised at the question. He was a gentleman and a man of honour—what else could he do but take his wife back if she came to him in trouble? 'I've been in hell these past weeks. Besides, it is my duty to care for her. If she is in distress, I shall help her, no matter what. I should thank God for her safe return and pray that I could make her happy.'

'Then I shall go to London in the morning and

employ an agent for you,' Andrew said. He reached out to lay a hand on Justin's shoulder. 'Do not give up hope yet, my friend.'

Lucinda looked around the small kitchen and sighed. She had scrubbed the floor that morning before it was light; it was much cleaner than it had been when she first arrived, but nothing would make this hovel the kind of home in which she could bear to live. However, it was all she could afford, because she had spent the guineas her husband had given her as pin money.

If she had not run away, she might have been at Avonlea now. Lucinda felt her throat catch and a tear slid down her cheek. She brushed it away impatiently. Her husband must be so angry with her. When she'd discovered the blackmail letter lying on her dressing chest on her return from the church, she had fled in panic, taking only a few things rolled into a paisley shawl. How could anyone know her secret? It was more than five years since that terrible time when the shame had come upon her.

Her first thought had been for her husband's good name. Avonlea was such a well-respected man and the realisation that she had brought a stain of dishonour to that proud family had almost overpowered her. She knew that he had married her because he'd believed her a girl of blameless past, modest, her reputation beyond reproach.

How she had deceived him! What a wicked thing she had done by marrying him without confessing the truth.

She ought to have been resolute in refusing his oblig-
ing offer; at first, she had managed to keep a distance
between them, but, as she became more attracted to
him, she had found it too hard to resist the prompting
of her heart. In the end she had fallen so desperately in
love that she could no longer refuse Avonlea—yet she
sensed he did not love her as she loved him. He spoke
easily of love, but she thought it merely liking: the kind
of feeling that might grow to warm affection with the
years and the coming of children—but the spiteful letter
would destroy his respect for her. He would hate her,
wish to be free of the burden she must become to him
when he learned the terrible truth.

Lucinda closed her eyes and sat down in the rocking
chair by the kitchen fire, trying to control her thoughts.
She had tried to block out the memory of that evil night
when as a young girl she had been raped in her own
room by a man she had thought her father's trusted
friend.

Warned that unless she kept silent her father would
be ruined, Lucinda had said nothing until her condition
had become noticed. It was a terrible misfortune that
she had fallen with child so easily. When she tried to
explain that she had been raped, but would not give the
name of her seducer, her father had refused to listen.
He had banished her to live with her strict grandmother in seclusion; when her child was stillborn, she
had remained in seclusion until her father died. It was
her punishment and he would not allow her to return

home. Her mother had relented after her father's death and allowed her to visit Harrogate with an aunt. It was there she had met Avonlea and begun to fall in love. She had kept her distance, because her shame was so terrible that no decent man would wish to marry her if he guessed that she had borne an illegitimate child.

'Your father told you that you had forfeited the right to happiness,' Mrs Seymour had told her when she mentioned the duke's attentions. 'I do not wish to deny you all the pleasures of life, Lucinda, but you must surely see that you can never marry?'

Because of her late father's strictures and her mother's doubts, Lucinda had kept Avonlea at a distance in Harrogate, but then, when they met again at the home of her great friend Jane Lanchester, she had taken the bold step of confiding in Jane, who had advised her that she must follow her heart and marry him.

Lucinda sighed as she looked around the cottage. It had hurt her so very much these past weeks to stay away from Avonlea, but the blackmail letter had told her something she had needed to confirm. Now she knew the truth and she was going to do something so daring that it frightened her.

She had fled from Avonlea in panic, not knowing what she meant to do, conscious only that she was not ready to confess the truth to a husband who had married her believing her beyond reproach.

In a state of absolute shock, she'd hardly known what to believe. Not only had the blackmailer known all of her intimate secrets, but also surprised her with the revelation that her infant hadn't perished at birth, but was in fact even this day alive.

The blackmailer had threatened to reveal her shameful secret to the world unless she paid ten thousand pounds, but he or she had also offered to tell her where her child was living—in poverty and danger, the note had said, the words sending icy shivers down her spine.

At first resentful of the babe growing inside her, during the months of her confinement Lucinda had grown to love the idea of a child coming to life within her womb. Rejected by her family, with no one to love or care for her, she had talked to the babe, believing that when the child was born she would no longer be alone, but then after hours of pain and suffering she'd been coldly informed that the babe was dead. Lucinda had grieved for the child, but come to terms with her grief, banishing all the tainted memories to a tiny corner of her mind. She had told herself that the past no longer mattered to her—and then, suddenly, on the morning of her wedding to the duke, to learn that her child was alive!

Her mother had lied to her. The distress of learning the extent of her parent's cruelty had completely overset her. Instead of going to Avonlea and throwing herself on his mercy, as she might had she been certain of his feelings, she had thought only to run away. Better that she simply disappear than bring shame to him.

At first the shock had been so great that Lucinda

could hardly take it in; then, seized by sudden panic and the need to know the truth, she'd taken an old gown and some trinkets and fled through the gardens. In confusion, with only a vague idea of what she meant to do, she set out for her family home. She was weeping, in terrible confusion and pain as she fled, unable to think coherently. It was only in the long lonely days and nights that followed that she'd begun to think about what she was doing—to discover her feelings about the child she'd believed dead.

Lucinda had arrived at her mother's home some ten days later, having begged lifts for some of the journey, but walking much of it. After first making her escape, she'd changed into her old gown. She'd hidden her beautiful silk wedding gown behind some hay bales in a barn at the edge of the Avonlea estate; carrying only a small bundle, she had continued her journey wearing a plain grey gown more suited to a governess than the duchess she'd become. No one had given her so much as a second glance. When she finally arrived home, her mother had greeted her with a sour look. Mrs Seymour had refused to attend her daughter's wedding on the grounds of ill health, though her true reason was that she did not approve of Lucinda marrying anyone.

'So you've come to your senses. It was a stupid thing to do, Lucinda. I suppose he threw you out?'

'Avonlea knows nothing,' Lucinda replied. Shaking with anger, she had thrust the letter under her mother's nose. 'Where is she, Mama? Where is my daughter?

The child you stole from me—the child you told me was dead?'

Her mother's face had turned pale. At first she had continued to refute her daughter's accusation. For ten days she had tried to deny all knowledge of the child, swearing it had died at birth and that she knew nothing. Lucinda had questioned her relentlessly, never giving her a moment's peace, and in the end she'd broken down in tears.

'Your father would not let you keep the babe. He took it to a workhouse and…I believe she was adopted by a childless couple.'

'Tell me their names, Mama.'

Mrs Seymour shook her head. 'I know no more. I swear he told me nothing.'

'Very well, give me the name of the workhouse.'

'It will do little good after all this time.'

'Tell me what I wish to know and I shall leave you in peace. Deny me and I shall continue to question and demand. I am no longer the frightened child I was when I was so cruelly abandoned by you.'

'It was not my wish—but your shame had to be hidden.'

'Why? Had you loved me as a mother should, you could have taken me away, perhaps abroad, and let me keep my babe. We might have found an honest living somehow.'

'Why do you care about the child if you were raped, as you claim?'

'How could you doubt me?' Lucinda looked at her sadly. 'The man who used me so cruelly was a monster and if my father had stood by me, he might have been punished—but Papa preferred to believe his friend's lies. He, I hate—but my child is innocent. Mama, can you not see that I need to see my child? The knowledge that she lives is tearing at my heart. I shall never be at peace until I know how she is.'

'What will you do if you find her?'

'I am not certain—but I must know she is well and happy. Can you not see that I should never rest easy if I simply left her to her fate?'

'I do not…' Mrs Seymour's eyes dropped in shame.

In the end she'd given her daughter all the details she had. Lucinda had left the house that same day.

It had taken her two weeks of travelling, often on foot, to find the workhouse and another week before she could persuade the woman in charge to tell her the names of the couple who had taken her daughter.

'You understand that I told you nothing,' she said and looked at the silver locket and ruby brooch lying in her hand. 'Your father told us to have the brat adopted and Mrs Jackson had none of her own then.'

'She has other children now?'

'Aye, they come like that. She has four of them under the age of four and more than she can manage. She'll likely be glad to get rid of Susan.'

'You called my daughter Susan?' The woman

nodded. 'Thank you, madam. Now will you kindly tell me where to find my daughter?'

'You'll find the family at the sign of the Cock's Spur.'

'Mrs Jackson and her husband run a hostelry?'

'Aye, you might call it that, though some round here would have other words—'tis a den of thieves if you ask me.'

'Thank you for the information. I hope you have told me the truth. If not, I shall return—and then you will be very sorry for lying to me. My husband is a powerful man and he will punish you.'

'You don't look like the wife of a powerful man.' The warden sniffed.

'What I choose to wear is my business,' Lucinda said proudly.

She had walked away, her heart beating frantically.

It had not taken long to discover the inn of which the warden had told her. She had ventured inside, hoping to find a reasonable woman with whom she might bargain for the return of her daughter. However, she had soon discovered the innkeeper's wife to be a filthy slut who harangued her husband and her customers and screamed abuse at any provocation. She'd eyed Lucinda suspiciously and demanded to know what she wanted.

'If you're after summat, yer'll get naught here,' she said. 'If yer want to service men, you'll do it elsewhere. I run a clean house here and don't harbour doxies.'

'I was looking for a child. She was adopted from the workhouse five years ago.'

'What do yer want her fer?'

'She is my daughter and I want her back.'

'Yer do, do yer?' The woman glared at her. 'I'll sell her fer five hundred guineas if yer like.'

'I have only a silver trinket box and a diamond brooch that was my godmother's,' Lucinda said. 'The child is my daughter. She was stolen from me at birth and I have just discovered that you have her. For pity's sake, let me take her. I will give you all I have.'

'Clear orf. The girl will fetch good money in a year or two. I've had offers for her already and they were more than you're offering. I know your sort. Yer think I'm green behind the ears. Men will pay a fortune for a wench like that—and I'll sell her to the highest bidder when the time comes.'

'No, you mustn't. Please, you can't,' Lucinda cried in distress. She could not allow such a wicked thing to happen. 'I'll get money for you. She's my daughter. I swear it on the Bible.'

'The price just went up to one thousand guineas,' the woman said, a gleam of avarice in her eyes. 'You've got a week to find the money or she goes to the highest bidder.'

'Let me see Susan, please.'

'Yer can see 'er—but no funny business. Try snatchin' 'er and I'll call me husband and yer'll be sorry.'

Lucinda promised she would not and waited while the woman went into what looked like a kitchen at the rear. Her nails curled into the palms of her hands as she reappeared, dragging a reluctant child into the taproom. Lucinda's heart plummeted as she saw how dirty and thin the little girl was. She wanted to weep for pity, but knew that she must show no emotion. Kneeling in front of the child, she tipped her chin with one finger and her heart turned over. She had seen those eyes before—a curious greenish-blue; she saw them every day when she looked at herself in a mirror. The child was hers. The warden had not lied to her.

Resisting the urge to snatch her in her arms and run, Lucinda smiled at the little girl, reached into her pocket and took out a small cake she'd brought with her. She offered it to the child, who looked suspicious.

'It is a cake for you,' she said. 'Listen to me, Susan. One day soon I am going to fetch you. I am going to take you to live with me.'

'Not unless I get me thousand guineas you ain't.' The woman shoved the little girl. 'Back to your work.'

'Please be kind to her,' she said as the child bit the cake, her eyes opening in wonder as she tasted its sweetness. 'I shall be back within the week.'

It had cost Lucinda so much pain to leave her daughter here. Her heart wrenched with pity as the child glanced back at her before disappearing into the kitchen.

'What work does she do?'

'Anyfin' I tell 'er,' the woman answered. 'Yer've got one week—and then she's gone.'

'I shall be back,' Lucinda said and left before she wept.

She'd known even then that her trinkets would not fetch one-tenth of the woman's demands for the child. Even had she sold the wedding gown she'd hidden, it would not have brought enough—though she believed it had cost many hundreds of guineas when Justin bought it for her.

Had she only brought her jewels with her she might have found the money easily enough. There was not enough time to return to Avonlea and fetch the jewels or even to ask Justin for a loan. Lucinda faced the facts. She could not raise such a huge sum and so she had only one choice. She must steal the child.

Susan had been stolen from her. She would steal her back.

First she had to make a plan. She had hired a cottage in the next village so that the innkeeper's wife would not become suspicious. She bought other clothes and a wig to cover the flame red of her hair and she wore a torn and dirty shawl, rubbing dirt into her cheeks. In this way she had managed to visit the inn yard without being noticed by the landlady on two occasions. She had discovered that the child was given the chore of carrying out the slops first thing in the mornings, after the guests had gone down to break their fast.

And so today was the day. She locked up the cottage and left for the inn to claim her daughter as her own. At a quarter to the hour of nine she was in the yard watching, sheltering behind a wagon that had come to deliver hay for the stables. When she saw the child carrying her heavy pail down to the midden, she ran towards her.

'Drop that and come with me,' she instructed her. 'I am going to take you away and look after you, my darling. That wicked woman will not punish you again.'

'Will yer give me a cake?' The child looked at her anxiously. 'Yes, my dearest child. I will give you a cake every day. Come with me now and I shall take care of you.'

The child stood the pail down, offered her hand and together they ran. They hadn't stopped running until they reached the crossroads and saw the mail coach heading towards them. Lucinda knew that it stopped briefly at the crossing and she ran to it as a gentleman got down, looking up at the coachman.

'Please take me to the next big town.'

'We do not stop again until we reach Watford, ma'am.'

'That will be perfect,' Lucinda said and placed the last of her money into his hands. 'The child will sit on my lap.'

'You've given me threepence too much,' he said and returned the coppers to her. 'Hop in and make sure the child behaves.'

'She will,' Lucinda said and put an arm about her daughter's thin shoulders. 'We shall both be as quiet as mice.'

Climbing into the coach, she pulled the child onto her lap, holding her close.

'It will be all right now,' she whispered. 'The nasty woman will not find us and I'll look after you. I'm your mother, you see? You were stolen from me when you were just a babe. I'd named you Angela and you are my daughter. No one will hurt you again. I promise.'

She had brought some food for the journey and took a small sugared bun from her bundle, giving it to the child. Angela's thin body felt warm against her as she ate contentedly and then fell asleep, her head resting against Lucinda's breast.

It was then that Lucinda realised she had only accomplished a part of her plan. The next phase would be more difficult. She had to find somewhere for them to live—there was no going back to that hovel of a cottage—and some way of earning her living.

Then she would go to Justin and tell him why she'd run away.

Tears trickled down her cheeks. She loved her husband so much and she feared he would hate her for what she'd done. Until this moment, all her thoughts had been centred on rescuing her child and it was only now that she had begun to realise the enormity of her cruelty towards the man she'd married. Afraid to tell him her secret, she had run away, leaving a simple note to say she had something she must do and would return when she could. He must have wondered why she had not confided her problem to him and he might not wish to see her.

For the first time Lucinda realised that in abandoning her husband so abruptly she might have lost her only chance of real happiness. She had been living in a nightmare, but now she had woken to the cold dawn of reality.

What was she going to do now?

'Where was this found?' Justin looked at the crumpled silk wedding gown, which was made of the finest materials available and had been a part of the many gifts he'd given his bride. 'And why was it not discovered before this?'

'It had been hidden behind some hay bales in a barn, your Grace,' the man said, looking uncomfortable. 'We looked in the barn for the young lady, sir. I swear we looked, but we did not think to move the hay because there was only the wall, or so we thought. The gown was found when the hay was used and someone saw a bit of silk sticking out.'

'Yes, I understand,' Justin said. 'Very well. Thank you for bringing it to me.' He took two guineas from his pocket, but the man shook his head.

'I need no reward for bringing it to you, my lord. We're all very sorry about what happened.'

'Yes, thank you.' Justin was short with the man, because he could not stand pity. His pride would not let him show his hurt to anyone. Lucinda had made a fool of him—and she'd done it deliberately. She must have hidden the gown, because if she'd been kidnapped it would not have been left behind. Besides, in all this time there had been no demand for a ransom.

After his tenant had gone, he paced the room. His nerves were at breaking point because of the hell he had suffered since his wife disappeared. Where on earth had Lucinda gone and why had she left him? Why run away on her wedding day?

There must be a clue somewhere.

His mouth firming into a grim line, he turned, left the room and walked upstairs to the apartments that should have been hers. He would search the rooms himself. Something must have been overlooked.

The rooms were empty and very neat when he entered. He began opening drawers and taking things out. Silk lingerie, stockings, gloves, scarves and handkerchiefs were tossed on to the floor. Costly gowns were pulled from the armoire and thrown carelessly onto the bed. Each chest was searched, but nothing was found. He looked at the jewel box on the dressing chest and opened it. All the jewels he'd given Lucinda were there, but he remembered that the case had a secret drawer. He pressed the button and saw that her favourite ruby brooch and also a diamond pin that her godmother had left her were gone. Giving a snarl of frustration, he knocked the case to the ground.

'Damn you, Lucinda. Damn you for leaving me to this hell on earth.'

Seeing the beautiful things scattered over the floor,

he felt some remorse for his temper and bent to retrieve a lovely pearl necklace from beneath the dressing table. Something white caught at the back took his eye. It was a piece of folded paper that had fallen behind the dressing table somehow and lodged halfway down.

He reached up to retrieve it and saw that it was a note addressed to him in Lucinda's hand. She *had* written to him! He began to read eagerly.

My dearest Avonlea,
Forgive me, but something has happened—something so shocking and disturbing that I must leave at once. I shall return to explain all to you as soon as I have solved this problem. I know that my absence will cause you unease and distress, but you may tell everyone that my mother is ill and say that I have gone to nurse her. It is not the truth, but I cannot explain now. I must hurry. I love you. Lucinda.

Why had he not had the room searched properly? If this letter had been found, it might have saved him hours of heart searching and distress. His throat caught with emotion. Lucinda did not hate him. She had not fled because she feared to be his wife. In fact, though they'd never spoken deeply about their feelings, it seemed his beautiful young wife loved him! All the nightmares that had haunted him since her disappearance had vanished, leaving just two questions.

Why had she gone so suddenly and what was so shocking that she could not tell him and ask for his help?

Chapter Two

Lucinda hesitated in the shrubbery. She could see Jane Lanchester working in her beloved garden. Kneeling on a cushion, Jane was planting a seedling, which would flower later in the year, and intent on her work. It was foolish to be nervous. Taking a deep breath, Lucinda lifted her head and walked towards her friend.

'Jane. Forgive me. I had to see you.'

Jane's head came up in surprise. For a moment she stared at her and then jumped to her feet and ran the short distance between them, her arms open in welcome.

'Lucinda! I have been in such torment, wondering if you were captive or dead. You naughty girl. Why did you not write to anyone?'

'It was difficult.' Lucinda looked at her awkwardly. 'Do you hate me for what I did?'

'Why should I?' Jane removed the gloves she wore for gardening. 'Come in and have some tea and tell me what has been happening. I am perfectly sure you had a good reason for what you did, as I told Avonlea. Does he know you are back?' Lucinda shook her head. 'He has been in great distress, you know. He couldn't understand your disappearance and thought you might have been abducted.'

'Surely not? I left a note promising to explain when I returned. It was on top of my jewel case.'

'I do not know what happened, but it was not found,' Jane told her. 'I think the poor man thought you were afraid of him—you weren't, I hope? I have wondered if I was wrong to advise you to marry him.'

'I love Justin very much.' A little sob left Lucinda's lips. 'I feel so awful for what I did that day, but I was in such a state I could not think. Afterwards, I wished I had waited and asked Avonlea's advice, but at the time all I could think about was—' She broke off, shaking her head.

'Come in and tell me all about it,' Jane said and then frowned as she saw a man striding towards them. 'Here is my brother. Do you remember Andrew? I think you met him once when he was in the army.'

'Perhaps I should go…the scandal…' Lucinda hesitated, but Jane grabbed her arm. 'Your brother might not wish to know me after what I did.'

'Nonsense. You will not run away now, Lucinda. You must at least talk to Avonlea. It is the right and proper thing to do.'

'Yes, I shall.'

Lucinda swallowed hard. Lord Lanchester was a tall, strong man with dark hair and eyes and at that moment he looked stern.

'Duchess,' he said without a hint of surprise in his voice, 'I told Avonlea that you would return. I hope you have been to see him to explain?'

'Lucinda wanted to talk to me first,' Jane said. 'I am about to send for tea. You may go away for half an hour, if you please, while we talk in private.'

'Please, it is not necessary,' Lucinda said. 'I shall tell you both that I left in such a hurry because I was being blackmailed. I know that I should have spoken to Avonlea and asked his advice, but I thought he might be angry—and if I am to be disgraced, he will be better off without me. It should be easy enough to annul the marriage.'

'Blackmail?' He frowned. 'Do you have the letter?'

'No…' Lucinda swallowed hard, because she did not wish to lie, but the blackmail note held too much information—information she did not wish to share with Jane's brother. Had he not arrived, she might have told Jane that she had stolen her daughter back, but it was too difficult to tell this stern stranger. 'I think I shall not stay for refreshments, Jane. Do you know if Avonlea is at home, sir?'

'I have come from him this moment. Do you know we have agents out looking for you, young lady? Your husband has been scouring the countryside for you, searching everywhere himself, day after day and even at night. He is at his wit's end.'

Lucinda's eyes filled with tears and she gave a little sob. 'He will be so angry with me. I should have written to him. He will not wish to see me.'

'You've upset her,' Jane said and put an arm about her shoulders. 'Andrew, you are a bully and I am quite cross with you.'

'Forgive me.' Andrew was suddenly contrite. 'I dare say you had your reasons, Duchess. I think you may find that Avonlea is more concerned than angry.'

'I do not think I can face him…'

'Of course you can.' Andrew produced a large white kerchief and handed it to her. 'If you will permit me, I shall take you to him and I will protect you. If he is angry, I shall bring you back to Jane—there, will that make it easier for you?'

'Yes, you must certainly return to us if Avonlea is unkind, but I do not think that the case. He cares for you dearly, Lucinda, and I know he is waiting anxiously for news,' said Jane and her brother took up the persuasion.

'He asked me to call because he had just found your letter. It had fallen down behind the dressing table and become lodged there. Avonlea discovered it by chance just yesterday and sent word to me because I'd been helping in the search for you.'

'Where did you go?' Jane asked, as Lucinda hesitated. 'I know Avonlea sent a messenger to your mama, but she said she had not seen you.'

'It took me a long time to reach her home…' Lucinda

faltered. 'I walked much of the way. I dare say Avonlea's messenger reached her before I did.'

'Why did she not write later?' Jane looked puzzled.

'Mama was upset with me. We parted in anger.'

'So you have not been staying with her all this time?'

Lucinda shook her head. 'Only for a few days. It is a long story, Jane. Perhaps another time. I think I should go to Avonlea now. I owe my husband an explanation.'

'Promise me you will come to me if you need help?' Jane said and reached for her hand. 'I am your friend and remain so always. If you are in difficulty, I shall do my best to help you.'

'I could bring shame on you,' Lucinda said. 'If you knew all…' She saw the question in her friend's eyes. 'No, at least not for the moment, Jane. I must speak with Avonlea first. I should have gone there immediately.'

She had wanted reassurance from her friend, but it was impossible to tell Jane her secret with Lord Lanchester standing there waiting for her.

'There is no need for you to accompany me, sir,' she said to him. 'I can quite well walk to the estate from here.'

'You will do no such thing. I shall drive you in my chaise. Jane, I shall come back immediately. Please have your refreshments and then we'll talk. I have to leave for London after nuncheon.'

'You will visit me soon, Lucinda?'

'Yes.' Lucinda gave her a wan smile. 'I shall come soon—perhaps sooner than you think.'

Jane squeezed her arm. 'Chin up, my dear friend. I am sure Avonlea will be kinder than you imagine.'

Following Lord Lanchester to the stables, Lucinda thought that it was all very well for Jane to say that Avonlea cared for her, but she did not yet know the whole story.

Her husband might forgive her reckless flight. He might even forgive her for not telling him that she had borne a child, but she was certain that he would not allow her to keep her newly discovered daughter. If it became known that she had an illegitimate child, people would gossip. Many would cut her and her shame would reflect on Avonlea and on her friends.

Jane had offered her a place to stay, but she would not wish to take in Lucinda's daughter. Even if she were willing to accept the child, her brother would forbid her. Jane was the kindest and wisest friend anyone could have. When they were at school together, she had confided to Lucinda that she did not want to marry.

'I dare say I shall be an old maid and help care for my brother's children when he marries,' she'd said and laughed. 'Or I may go and live in Harrogate and hold lots of card parties and poetry readings.'

Jane might dare to know her despite her brother's censure for she was possessed of her own fortune, but Lucinda would not wish to disoblige her. She had already made up her mind that she must make her own living and the impulse to visit Jane had come from a moment of weakness.

* * *

'I wish you will forgive me if I was harsh to you,'
Lord Lanchester said as he handed her into the chaise a
few minutes later. 'I do not know your story or why you
were being blackmailed, though I think Jane does—but
if you are in trouble and wish to confide in me I will
help you if I can.'

'You are kind, sir. I do not think anyone can help me,
for it would bring shame on your family if this became
open knowledge.'

He smiled at her. 'I scarcely think you have done
anything so very terrible, Duchess. It may be that a
problem shared would be halved, as they say.'

'I thank you for your kindness, but I do not wish to
trouble you, sir.'

Lucinda sat primly in the chaise, hands curled in her
lap as she was driven through the narrow leafy lanes
of Sussex that led to Avonlea's estate. As they crossed
onto the duke's land, her heart began to race. She knew
that some of his people had seen her and saw their heads
turn as they watched the chaise drive by. She felt hot
all over, knowing that she had already caused so much
trouble and scandal. If her secret were known, it would
be terrible for everyone she cared about.

'Believe me, nothing you could do or say would be
a trouble to me, Duchess.'

'Please…call me Lucinda,' she whispered, her cheeks
hot. 'I think Avonlea may wish to annul the marriage
very soon and I shall be Miss Seymour again.'

'I doubt he would be such a fool,' Lord Lanchester said and smiled at her. 'If I am to call you Lucinda, then you must call me Andrew, as my sister and close friends do.'

Lucinda blushed and gave a little shake of her head. 'You are so kind, sir, but I assure you, I do not deserve such consideration.'

He was bringing his horses to a halt and did not immediately reply, but as he assisted her down, his smile was warm.

'I wish to be your friend, Lucinda. Jane loves you dearly and she is not normally wrong in her choice of friends. When you are ready to talk I shall be there for you. I am certain Avonlea will not turn you away, but if he did I would open my doors to you.'

Lucinda thanked him shyly. 'I think I shall go in al—' She could not finish the sentence for her husband was coming towards them. Her heart caught with pain as she saw the distress in his face and realised that he had been under a great strain. There were dark shadows beneath his eyes and she thought he had lost weight. Had she done that to him? Her heart caught with remorse. She turned to meet him. 'Avonlea, forgive me…'

'Lucinda, my dearest. You are safe. Thank God! I thought you lost or dead.' Avonlea turned to Lord Lanchester. 'You found her and brought her back to me. How can I ever thank you, my best of friend?'

'You owe me no thanks, sir. Your duchess visited my

sister and I brought her to you. She was a little anxious, but I assured her you would not scold her too much. I believe she has something important to tell you.'

'Of course I shall not be unkind,' Justin said and looked at Lucinda. 'Come inside, my love. You look tired and pale. I would hear what you have to say. Lanchester, you have my thanks. I shall speak to you later.'

'When it suits you,' Andrew replied with a slight smile. 'My heartfelt thanks for your safe return, Duchess. Your friends are glad of it. Please call on Jane whenever you wish.'

'You are very kind, sir.'

Lucinda could not look at him or her husband. She walked towards the house, Justin at her side. Several servants had gathered in the hall and were looking at her curiously. The housekeeper bobbed a curtsy and asked if she could do anything.

'You may bring some tea when we ring,' Justin said. 'My wife has had a long journey and she is tired. We shall have nuncheon in an hour.'

Lucinda allowed him to make the arrangements. She was thirsty and hungry, and she knew that someone she trusted was caring for her daughter. Angela would be safe until she could return to her.

'Mama will be gone for a while,' she'd told Angela and kissed her before she left. 'I have to find somewhere nice for us to live, but then I shall come and fetch you.'

'You won't leave me?' Angela had clung to her. 'You won't let them take me back?'

'Never,' Lucinda vowed and held her tight. 'Mama loves you and she wants to look after you, but she cannot be with you all the time. She has to work and earn money to buy our food.'

Inside the small parlour at the back of the house, Justin shut the door firmly and then turned to look at her. His hands worked at his sides and she thought that she had never seen him display such emotion. Always when he courted her he had been the polite gentleman, teasing, flirting gently, courteous and considerate. If he had a temper, she'd not seen or felt it; even his kiss when she'd at last accepted his offer had been sweet, but passionless—which was perhaps why she had dared to say yes. Avonlea had seemed kind, but capable of expressing only warm affection; this stranger with his tight mouth and tortured eyes was someone she did not recognise.

'What was so terrible that you could not tell me, Lucinda? I took a vow to become your husband. Whatever trouble you were in I would have helped you.'

'Yes, I know,' she said and gave him a little smile. 'Afterwards, I wished I'd had the courage to tell you. I panicked, Justin. Please let me explain if I may. When I returned to my rooms after the church I discovered a letter. It was a blackmail letter and the sender demanded ten thousand pounds. He—or perhaps she—threatened to expose my secret and shame your good name. I ran away rather than allow it to happen. My first thought was for you—because I had wronged you.'

'A blackmail letter here in your room?' Justin looked shocked. 'I have considered all manner of reasons why you should leave, but I must admit that was not high on my list. May I enquire as to the reason for the blackmail?'

Lucinda drew a shuddering breath. 'I fear you will be angry and hate me.'

'I could never hate you.'

He had not denied that he might be angry, but she must find the courage to continue. Her words came out in a rush, tumbling over each other.

'It…happened one Christmas Eve. I was home from school and my father had friends staying. I was asleep when Father's friend fell on me and, though I woke instantly, I could not fight him off. He had been drinking and the stench of his breath sickened me. I tried to scream, but he covered my mouth with his hand. Beneath his weight I was helpless. He was my father's best friend, but he…he raped me and then told me that he would ruin Papa if I told anyone what he'd done.'

'Raped you? My God!' Justin looked as if someone had punched him hard. He recoiled and seemed stunned, turning away from her and then sitting down heavily in one of the comfortable wing chairs placed in pairs about the salon. 'Forgive me, this is a shock. It must have been a terrible experience for you, Lucinda.'

Lucinda went to him and knelt on the floor by his

side. 'I think even that was not the worst of it, Justin. I was distressed, but could tell no one—and then, at Easter, my mother discovered that I was with child.'

Justin looked down into her face, concern in his eyes. The thought of her suffering wrenched at his heart. She was so innocent and sweet—how could any man treat her so vilely? Anger raged through him, but for the monster that had violated her. He did not doubt her word for an instant. He reached down and touched her cheek as she gazed earnestly up at him.

'Your father covered the scandal, of course. Most fathers would do the same. What happened next?'

'I was sent to live with Grandmama. She was very unkind to me and caned my hands whenever it pleased her. When my child was born I was told it had died… but still my father would not allow me to go home or to enter society. Only after his death was I allowed the visit to Harrogate with my aunt.'

'Was that why you kept your distance from me at first?'

'My father told me I was dirty, a thing of shame, and that no decent man would want me. Both he and my mother said I should never marry. I defied her to wed you—and I meant to tell you the truth that night and beg you to forgive me, but then the note arrived and—'

'You were frightened and ran away.'

Justin stood up. He reached down, drawing her to her feet so that they looked into each other's eyes.

'Do you have the letter?'

Lucinda hesitated. She hated to lie to him, but if she told him the whole truth he would want to know if she had found her daughter and he would force her to give her up, because to do anything else would cause a scandal.

'No…I am sorry, Justin. I destroyed it. I should never have married you. I know you must hate me now. I shall go away and you may have the marriage annulled. All I ask is a small sum of money so that I may live quietly until I can find some respectable work.'

She would not have asked so much if it were not for her child. Until she could find a home of her own and a nursemaid to live in, Lucinda must pay for lodgings and the care of her daughter. Surely he would allow her something?

For a moment he studied her in silence, then, 'No, I shall not have the marriage annulled,' Justin said, his tone suddenly harsh and cold. The sound of it sent shivers down her spine and she looked at him, startled by his change of mood. 'I've had enough of gossip and of being laughed at behind my back, Lucinda. You are my wife and you will accept your duties as a wife.'

'Justin…' She faltered, her throat tight with emotion. Tears gathered in her eyes, but she held them back. 'I know how angry you must feel…'

'Do you, my dear?' His bitter tone flayed her like a whiplash. 'Had you trusted me enough to confide in me from the start, none of this need have happened.'

'Forgive me. I was so anxious.' Her voice was low,

scarcely more than a whisper. 'I did not think how it would look. Besides, if you had told everyone I had gone to my sick mother, it would not have seemed so bad.'

'Had I found your letter at the start, I might have done so.' He turned from her abruptly, walking to the window to gaze out. 'If you cared for me you might have trusted me, Lucinda. I would have given you a fair hearing. Do you not think it was your duty to tell me before you accepted my proposal?'

'Yes. I think now that I should have told you. I—I was afraid you would not wish to marry me if you knew that I had such a terrible secret.'

Justin turned to look at her, his face proud, eyebrows raised. 'You wished to be the Duchess of Avonlea, I suppose?'

'No…' Lucinda hesitated, then, in a voice caught with tears, 'I loved you, Justin. I loved you from the start. I suppose I hoped that if we were married you might forgive me.'

'You thought I would accept you rather than face the scandal of divorce?' His top lip curled scornfully. 'Well, you were right in that, my dear. I have no intention of either annulling the marriage or divorcing you. I hope in time that we may begin again, have a sensible arrangement. I need heirs after all and you are my wife. I dare say we may brush over the scandal now that you have returned. I shall say that you were called to the bedside of a relative and your letter was misplaced—which is in part the truth.'

'Justin…' She took a step towards him, her hand outstretched. It fell to her side as she saw the anger in his handsome face. 'Will you not believe that I care for you? Will you not try to forgive me?'

'I shall certainly endeavour to forgive you,' he said, but his eyes were cold, his mouth thinned with anger. 'But you will forgive me if I do not fall at your feet and tell you that everything is as it was. You will remain my wife and I hope in time we may find a way to be comfortable together—but as for the feelings…the affection I bore you, for the moment I must be honest and tell you that I feel nothing but disappointment.'

'Please…' She gave a cry of distress. 'I beg you not to hate me, Justin. I know that I have hurt you, but I was in some distress myself.'

'I fail to understand why.' His eyes held neither compassion nor warmth. 'You had the advantage of me for you knew your situation. Why the letter should occasion such shock I do not know—unless you meant to conceal the truth from me forever?'

How could she explain? Justin might have understood had she been able to put her feelings into words—but the shock, the numbness, incredulity and fear she'd felt on learning of her child's existence were too difficult to express.

'I was asked to pay ten thousand pounds for the writer's silence.'

'Had you given the letter to me, I should either have

paid or discovered the man's identity and threatened him with imprisonment.'

'You would still have hated me.'

'I do not hate you,' Justin said, a flicker of regret in his eyes. 'I feel hurt, betrayed by your lack of trust, Lucinda. Had you confided in me at the beginning, I think I might have learned to accept the fact that you were raped. You were not to blame for that—or for bearing a child—but your deceit, your thoughtlessness in running away and your lack of faith in me, have given me some disquiet. I must say honestly that you are not the woman I thought you.'

His quiet words, his dignity and the hurt in his eyes struck into her heart. She was overcome with guilt, realising just how deeply her thoughtless behaviour had hurt him. Justin was angry with her now. Lucinda was not sure why she had not told him the whole truth. It would have been better to have the whole thing out, but she had hesitated and now it was too late. He would undoubtedly either return the child to the woman who had so mistreated her or have her adopted by a worthy couple.

No, she would not give her daughter up! Although it was only two weeks since she'd rescued her, Lucinda knew that she loved her too much to think of letting her be adopted, even by a kind and gentle woman.

She loved Justin, too, but he no longer cared for her. A part of her wanted to walk away, to tell him that she would not continue with a loveless marriage, but her lips were frozen and she could not speak.

'You should go to your room and change. That gown is hardly suitable for my duchess,' Justin said. 'I am relieved that you are alive and unharmed, Lucinda. It will take a little time for me to come to terms with your revelation, but I hope in time that we may find a kind of contentment together.'

'Yes, Justin. I am sorry to have caused you so much distress.'

'I shall tell them to serve luncheon in an hour. Please do not keep us waiting.'

'I shall not,' Lucinda replied. Her pride was reasserting itself and with it a kind of anger. He was showing dignity and dealing with the situation in a civilised way, but she would almost rather he'd raged at her. 'I am truly sorry for hurting you.'

He made no reply, merely inclining his head as she made him a slight curtsy and then left the room.

Lucinda knew that the servants must be agog to know where she'd been, but she carried herself with pride and dignity as she walked up to her own apartments. Alice was there and appeared to be busy tidying the place as she entered. She curtsied, looking slightly flustered.

'Forgive me, my lady. Your room—his Grace searched it and then forbade me to touch it. I have been trying to make it respectable, but some of your things will need washing and ironing for they lay on the floor for a few days.'

'You may help me change into a fresh gown, if there are any decent enough to wear?'

'Yes, my lady. There is a morning gown here that is not creased.'

'Take your time with the others,' Lucinda said. 'I shall not scold you if things are not just as they should be; it is not your fault.'

'I fear the duke lost his temper, my lady.'

'Yes, I fear he did and that was my fault. Was he very angry with you, Alice?'

'For a time,' the girl admitted. 'I did not mind so very much, my lady. I am glad to see you returned.'

'If I were to ask you to help me—to keep my request private—would you do so?'

Alice did not hesitate as she said, 'Yes, my lady. I would do anything for you.'

'I am not certain yet,' Lucinda said and smiled at her. 'Do not look so anxious, Alice. It is nothing very terrible—but I might need you to take a message for me later.'

'Yes, my lady. You can trust me. I swear it on my life.'

Lucinda hid a smile. Her maid probably thought she had a lover. If she decided to trust her, she would soon learn the truth, but for the moment she must be cautious.

Lucinda was determined not to give her daughter up. She thought that rather than accept that Angela should be adopted, she would leave Justin and find a way to live independently. However, what little money she had was almost gone and she was not certain how she could earn her living.

No respectable lady would take her either as a governess or as a companion. Even if she did find work in a respectable household, the discovery that she had an illegitimate daughter would lead to instant dismissal without a reference. All that left was work as a seamstress or hard manual labour in a mill or on the land; even work as a servant would be denied her in most respectable houses.

Justin did not wish for more scandal and for that reason he had decided they would stay together and try to find a way to live comfortably. She supposed that when his anger or disappointment had eased a little, he might still find her attractive.

The thought of what she had done was almost unbearable. Justin had looked at her with such admiration and gentle warmth when he courted her, showing such patience and kindness to a shy young woman—and now his eyes were cold and unforgiving. She did not know how to bear his coldness, but the thought of never seeing him again was equally as painful.

She held back the foolish tears. What had she expected? She ought to have known that her husband would not accept her wayward behaviour as if it meant nothing. He'd believed her modest and innocent and must think her a cheat for having hidden her shameful past.

At least she had a roof over her head and the generous allowance Avonlea had given her in the marriage contract would be hers to use as she wished. She could use some of it to pay for Angela to be properly cared for nearby. It was not what she wanted, but what was her alternative? She knew she would find it difficult, if not impossible, to bring up her daughter in the way she wished alone. Perhaps it was best this way—and yet at the back of her mind she feared Justin's disgust and anger when he discovered her deceit.

She had hurt her husband too much already and she did love him deeply, whatever he might believe. If she left him again, it would convince him that she had never loved him and he would surely divorce her. Perhaps if she stayed he might learn to forgive her—and if he did, one day, she would tell him the rest of her story. It might make him angry again, but perhaps he would understand that the pain of discovering that her child had been stolen from her had made her forget everything else for a time.

Oh, it was all such a coil! Lucinda wished that she could return to the day Avonlea had asked her to wed him. Had she told him then he might have withdrawn his offer, but he might have accepted the truth and forgiven her—yet even had he done so, he would never have accepted her child.

She had no choice but to keep the child's existence a secret from him.

Justin went for a long hard ride after luncheon. Lucinda had looked so serene and beautiful when she came down to the dining room. He had felt a rush of desire at seeing her in one of the beautiful gowns he had purchased for her use. She was his wife, the woman he had chosen, and her revelations had left him feeling bruised and bewildered.

She was not the shy innocent girl he had thought her. Justin had believed her reticence in Harrogate had sprung from modesty and a natural desire to know him better. Now he wondered if he had been deceived in her character. Could he believe her story of rape? She had not told him before the wedding that she'd born an illegitimate child, nor had she given him any reason to believe that she was not the pure untouched woman he thought her. For a brief moment he doubted, but then dismissed the thought as unworthy. Lucinda had not been honest with him at the start, but he would not think less of her for what that evil man had done to her. The hurt in her eyes as she told her story was proof of her innocence, though she ought to have told him before they were wed.

Yet she ought never to have been faced with such a dilemma. No young girl should be subjected to such wickedness.

He thought that if he knew the man's identity he would break the rogue's neck. Fierce emotions raged through him as he considered taking revenge for the hurt inflicted on a vulnerable girl of sixteen. Justin would thrash the devil to within an inch of his life. Indeed, he would gladly see the man dead.

He wished that she'd kept the blackmail letter. He

might have been able to get to the bottom of this business, but, as things stood, it would be like looking for a needle in a haystack. Who had sent such a letter on their wedding day? How had that person discovered the secret that Lucinda's father had so carefully hushed up?

Of course these things were never a complete secret. Someone knew the child had been born. There must surely have been a doctor or a midwife at the birth—or perhaps a servant in Lucinda's grandmother's house. It would be there he should begin his search if he intended to make enquiries.

Did he wish to discover more? Justin frowned. It was after all his wife's secret, but if she were being blackmailed, he had a duty to protect her—and not just for the sake of his good name. Even if she paid the fellow—or woman—to keep quiet, they would come back for more. It was the nature of such creatures.

There was only one way to deal with blackmail and that was to meet threat with threat. He would make whomever had done this thing shiver in their boots and, if they continued with their evil purpose, he would see them punished.

The agents who had searched for Lucinda were discreet. He was certain he could trust them to discover the whereabouts of Lucinda's grandmother—or, if she were no longer living, her servants. No need to disclose his wife's secret. He would question the servants and then, if they answered openly, any doctor or midwife who had presided over the birth of Lucinda's child.

She had told him the child had died—but was that certain? Justin frowned as he thought about the probable scenario. Mr Seymour would not have permitted his daughter to keep the child. It was possible that he might have ordered that she be told the babe was dead while in truth he'd had it adopted.

The net widened, for anyone involved in the handling of that secret adoption might have decided to use blackmail when they heard of Lucinda's wedding plans. It was clear that it was her marriage to a wealthy man that had brought the toad crawling out from under its stone. Someone had seen an opportunity because she was to be the wife of an important man.

Justin felt angry that his wife had been subjected to such a foul blackmail on her wedding day. It had been meant to be a joyous occasion and had ended in distress for them both.

He felt a pang of regret when he recalled his own harshness towards her. He had felt such jealousy, such disappointment and pain when he learned that she was not the shy virgin he'd thought her that he'd lashed out. He'd promised he would not be unkind to her and he'd broken his word. He was uncertain why he had acted in such an uncharacteristic manner. At the start he had believed he could accept what she'd told him; after all, it had happened before they met—but then emotions he had not recognised welled up in him and his anger erupted. Why? Yes, she had deceived him, but he felt it was more her uncertainty that made her hold back rather than deliberate malice. At one time he'd briefly considered marrying a widow and the loss of the lady's maidenhead to her first husband had not disturbed him one whit—why then should he feel such rage because Lucinda was not a virgin?

Why should he be jealous? It had not been meant to be a love match. He'd chosen her because she did not throw herself at him every time he so much as looked at her, as almost every other lady he'd met did constantly. It was her smile, her quiet charm and her sweetness that had made him notice her. She had not changed. It was Justin who felt differently, though at this moment he could not explain the conflicting emotions that raged within him or their cause.

Justin knew that he was in the wrong, but for the moment he could not quite forgive her for not confiding in him sooner. The look in her eyes had wrenched at his heart. She'd seemed to beg for something—something he had not been able to give. His own lack disturbed him, adding to his feeling of rage and he'd lashed out without thinking. In time his hurt would ease and he hoped that they might still have enough respect for each other to make a go of their marriage, but for the moment he needed to be alone.

He would tell Lucinda that evening. There was some business in London that needed his attention. It meant that he would be away for perhaps ten days. When he returned he hoped that he would have come to terms with his disappointment and they might begin again. It must be better for both of them to go on with the marriage than suffer a painful divorce. He would recover from the scandal, but she would be ruined. He could not do that to her. It would be cruel and unfair.

Relieved to have settled the matter in his mind, he returned home. The servants must not suspect anything, for there had been enough scandal. He would take tea with Lucinda in the small salon just as if nothing had ever come between them. If he suspected that he had not been quite truthful with himself in his motives for his decision, he was not yet ready to face the possibility that he might care more deeply for his lovely wife than he'd thought possible.

Romantic love was a myth. To give one's heart without reserve was to invite pain. Affection was sufficient and once he had recovered from this absurd attack of jealous rage, he would resort to being the considerate husband he'd always intended to be.

That night, Lucinda sat in front of her dressing mirror brushing her hair when Justin knocked and asked if he might enter. She gave permission and he came in, looking at her oddly as she stood and turned to face him. Something in his expression spoke of hunger and a need to take her in his arms and for a moment she hoped that he intended to make up their quarrel, but his next words chilled her.

'Forgive me, I did not intend to disturb you, Lucinda. I said nothing downstairs for I would not have the servants hear me. I must go to London tomorrow on business. You will give me your word to remain here and do nothing to cause more scandal.'

His harsh words hurt her. 'Why should I cause more scandal? Can you not accept that I am sorry for harming you?'

'Perhaps. I was merely making myself clear. I need a little space to come to terms with what you told me earlier. I should be no longer than ten days—perhaps less. When I return we shall take time to know each other properly. I think perhaps we wed in haste. We know very little about one another's lives.'

'I told you that when you asked me to wed you, Justin.'

'I believed I knew you,' he said and a tiny nerve flicked at his temple. 'Now I know that I was wrong. I think we must both work at this, Lucinda. I did not mean to be so harsh earlier. Had I not cared for you, it would not have been such a shock to learn that you were not what I thought you.'

'Yes, I understand you must feel disgust and anger,' she said, but kept her head high. 'I have apologised for not telling you—but I am as I was. I did nothing to encourage that man's attack, I promise you.'

'You will give me his name?'

'What do you intend to do?' She was startled, her eyes on his face.

'He may well be your blackmailer—had you not thought of him?'

'No,' Lucinda whispered, putting a hand to her throat. 'I have not thought about who wrote the note.'

'You have not wondered?' Justin looked puzzled. 'Surely you must realise that whomever it was will most likely try again. Next time I insist that you bring the letter to me.'

'Yes,' she said, not daring to meet his eyes. 'But it was not signed.'

'No, it would not be—but sometimes there is a clue. Was it well written or badly formed?'

'Oh, I had not thought…well written, I think. Yes, the letters were clear and there were no spelling or grammar mistakes.'

'Then it makes it more likely that it was either your father's friend himself—or perhaps the doctor who assisted at the birth. Who else would know your secret, Lucinda?'

'Grandmama, my parents and the doctor—also my grandmother's servants. They knew what had happened, I am sure.'

'Yes, they must, but most servants could not write a letter of that quality. I think it narrows the options a little.'

'Unless…Grandmama had friends. She may have told someone in confidence.' Lucinda raised her eyes to his. 'Why is it important?'

'Because I must be ready in case whomever it is tries again. You will not pay, Lucinda. You will have nothing to do with this person, whomever it may be. I shall deal with the problem, do you hear me?'

'Yes, of course.'

'Very well. We shall not speak of this again unless we must.' He moved towards her. For a moment she thought he meant to touch her or kiss her, but instead he picked up a perfume bottle from the dressing table and held it to his nose. 'This is such a haunting scent. I kept smelling it when you were away and it brought you closer. I am glad to have you back, Lucinda.'

She swallowed hard. 'Thank you for accepting me.'

'You are my wife. What else should I do?'

The expression in his eyes caused Lucinda's heart to race. For a moment she thought he would take her into his arms and kiss her. Had he done so she would have clung to him, returned his kisses and then confessed her secret, but the look faded. He inclined his head to her, then turned and walked away without touching her or speaking further.

Lucinda stared at the door for some moments after he closed it behind him. She almost wished that he had raged at her. His quiet, controlled anger was hard to bear. She could not blame him, because she'd brought it on herself, but it still hurt. Justin had been so courteous towards her, so careful and caring of her feelings and her comfort. Where had that charming, gentle, teasing gentleman gone? Would she ever see him again—or had her thoughtless deceit destroyed him?

Sitting on the edge of the bed, she discovered that

she could no longer hold back her tears. They trickled unheeded down her cheeks for some minutes, then she wiped them away. She would not waste time feeling sorry for herself.

She must think about the future. If she was to keep her daughter and hide the secret from Justin, it would mean taking Alice into her confidence. Her maid was honest and would help her by taking messages to her daughter and making excuses for her absence when she went to visit the child.

It was not an ideal arrangement keeping Angela in the old cottage at the edge of the estate, but it was all she could do for the moment. She had been so lucky to find that Nanny was still alive and living a precarious existence since her dismissal from Mrs Seymour's employ.

'She is a little love, but too thin,' Nanny said as Lucinda explained the circumstances. 'Yes, of course I will look after your daughter for you, my love. I never agreed with the way your father treated you—and to tell you she was dead, that was wicked. Had I been in a position to help you before this I should have done so, but I was dismissed instantly for having a bad influence on you.'

'That was unfair.'

'Well, it is past and the child is the important one now.' Nanny smiled and touched her head, but Angela sniffled and looked apprehensive, as though she feared she would be smacked or bullied.

'She has been ill-treated, so you must not scold her

too much. I know her speech is bad, but correct her kindly, Nanny. She will learn by example.'

'Yes, of course she will. I never smacked you, Lucinda, and I shall not smack this little darling—but she must start to learn her manners for she is your daughter.'

'For the moment I cannot acknowledge her. My husband would not allow it.'

Nanny looked at her sadly. 'You should tell your husband the truth, Lucinda. He couldn't let you acknowledge her, of course, but if he is a good man he will allow you to see her—and he'll find a decent place for us to live.'

'I hope in time to confide in him, but for now it must be our secret.'

'Very well.'

Nanny had agreed reluctantly. Lucinda knew she would care for the child as if she were her own, but she did not approve.

Alice might not approve, either—but for the moment Lucinda had no choice.

Perhaps after Justin's return, if they became friends again, she could tell him. He might not let her have the child with her, but he might allow her to have Angela near her and visit sometimes.

Retiring to her bed, Lucinda lay restless, her mind in turmoil. If Justin discovered that she had lied to him again, he would hate her.

Justin lay sleepless. He had brought the decanter of brandy to his room, hoping that a glass or two of his favourite tipple would dull the edge of his need, but at the moment it did not seem to have worked. The desire to touch and kiss his wife was burning through him, making him groan. Had he been less proud, more sure of his own feelings and hers, he would have gone to her, taken her in his arms and begged her to forgive him. Being close to her that evening had made him aware just how lovely she was—and how much he burned to make her his wife in truth. He was a fool to let himself be hurt. Why not simply make this quarrel up with her and forget everything in her arms—bury himself in her perfumed flesh?

No, that was foolish. His father would have called him a weakling for considering such an action. Justin had been strictly reared to understand the position he held as head of one of the leading families in England. Indeed, the first duke was rumoured to be one of Charles I's by-blows, borne of a titled lady who had kept her secret even from the king until later in life when she made a request for her son and was granted the title on his behalf. His father's words ran through his mind.

'Remember what you owe yourself and the family, Justin. Feeling must always be denied for, if once set free, it will ruin any man. You are of noble blood and must never forget your duty. Our family has upheld the true virtues of honour and decency for centuries. Do not be the one to break that slender thread.'

His father would say it was his duty to annul the

marriage at once, to send Lucinda away in disgrace and marry a girl of impeccable reputation.

No, he could not do that. Justin was angry and hurt, but beneath the pain and the rage he knew that he still wanted his beautiful wife. He still cared what became of her. To abandon her to the gossips would be cruel and senseless. Deep within him the need to protect her from hurt had asserted itself. He must not let what had happened ruin both their lives.

Somehow he must come to terms with the situation and the only way to do that was to put a little distance between them for a while. If he stayed here, he would not be able to keep from her bed.

Chapter Three

Lucinda set out early the next morning, just after she'd seen Justin drive away in his curricle. It was cool and she was wearing a warm cloak to cover her gown, which was one of her plainer ones. She had saved some of the sweet biscuits and a soft white roll that had been sent up for her breakfast. Her daughter enjoyed sweet trifles, perhaps the more so because she had never tasted a cake until recently. Nanny said she ought not to have too many, but Lucinda felt a deep hurtful guilt because of the way her daughter had been mistreated and she wanted to spoil her.

She wished with all her heart that she might have the child living with her at the house and acknowledge her openly, if not as her own child, as a child of a relative sadly deceased. However, she knew that it was impossible. The fact that she must deceive Justin added to her grief, but for the moment there was no other way.

Perhaps in time he might learn to trust her and then she might confess her secret, but even an indulgent husband would not allow her to have the child with her permanently. The likeness between them was marked and someone might guess her secret.

As she approached the small cottage she had rented for her child and Nanny, Angela saw her from the window and came out, running to meet her. Lucinda opened her arms, sweeping her up and hugging her tightly as she burst into tears.

'I thought yer would never come back,' Angela said and looked at her with reproach. 'You promised to take care of me.'

'And I shall,' Lucinda promised and kissed her cheek. She smelled of soap and her skin shone. Wearing the pretty dress Lucinda had purchased for her before they came here, she looked beautiful, her stick-thin body beginning to show signs of the good food she was now eating every day. 'I promise you that no one will hurt you again, my darling. Nanny is good to you, isn't she?'

'Yes…but I want to be with yer…you,' Angela corrected herself and then sucked her thumb, her eyes wide and expectant.

Lucinda pulled the thumb from her mouth and smiled. 'You will spoil your pretty hands if you do that, dearest. Mama has to work to provide a home for you and Nanny. I shall come to you whenever I can, my darling, but you must be good for me and do as Nanny tells you.'

'She is no trouble at all,' Nanny said as Lucinda looked at her enquiringly. 'Did you notice that her speech is improving already?'

'Yes, with a few slips,' Lucinda said and kissed her child before setting her down. Angela went off to play with some brightly coloured bricks that Nanny had given her, a relic from her mother's childhood. 'She will learn by our example, Nanny. I am sorry I could not return last night, but I was afraid to leave the house too late in case it was noticed.'

'You have not told him about the child.' Nanny shook her head in disapproval. 'I fear you're laying up trouble for yourself, Lucinda. When he knows you've deceived him he will be angry.'

'I do not wish to hurt my husband,' Lucinda said. 'He was angry with me when I told him why I left that day, though he insists that our marriage must continue.'

'What do you want?'

'I…love him,' Lucinda confessed, her voice breaking. 'At least, I love the man he was when we married. He seems so harsh now, but I know that is my fault for hurting him. Nanny, it is so hard, so very hard. I love them both. How can I choose one or the other?'

'Perhaps it would not be necessary if you told him the truth?'

'He would not accept her—how could I expect it?' Lucinda asked, blinking back the tears that threatened. 'It would break my heart to leave him and yet I must see her every day—I must!'

'Well, there is nothing to prevent you while I am able to care for her—but that may not be forever. I am nearly sixty and she will need a home until she is old enough to care for herself.'

'In time I shall try to make other arrangements, but for now I must leave her in your care.'

'And you may do so safely,' Nanny promised. 'I love her as if she were my own, just as I loved you.'

'Yes, I know, that is why I came to you.'

'Where is your husband now?'

'He went to London on business. I think he hopes that a little time apart will be healing for us both. The revelation I made was a terrible shock for him.'

'How much worse might it be if he learned that you had a child—that you had lied to him? You must be careful when you come here,' Nanny said and looked doubtful. 'But we shall say no more. Play with the child while you have the chance. In time she will get used to your coming and going.'

'Yes, of course. She must. Even if she lived with me I should only be able to see her a few times a day.'

'Children belong in the nursery until they are older. It is the way of things amongst your class, Lucinda. It is just that at the moment she is fearful that she will be taken back to that dreadful woman,' Nanny said. 'That will not happen while I have breath in my body. If I had my way, that woman would be thrown into prison and left there to rot—and others like her who exploit children.'

'How fierce you are, dearest Nanny,' Lucinda said and laughed softly. 'I see that I do not need to worry for Angela while she has you.'

Lucinda was conscious of the housekeeper's curious looks as she returned to the house later that day. Clearly the woman thought it strange that she had been gone for such a long time.

'I should like some tea,' she said. 'It was such a lovely day that I walked farther than I knew. I will take tea in the small parlour at the back of the house, please.'

'Yes, your Grace.'

'Please, Mrs Mann, I would rather you called me "ma'am" or "my lady." I am not used to such a grand title.'

'As you wish, ma'am. I shall bring your tea at once.' The housekeeper started to walk away, then stopped and looked back. 'Miss Lanchester called earlier. I told her you had gone for a walk.'

'Oh, how unfortunate,' Lucinda said. 'I should have liked to see her.'

'Miss Lanchester asked if you would take tea with her this afternoon?'

'Yes, I think I shall. I shall change my gown and you may have the carriage sent round. Please do not bother with the tea. I shall wait and take a dish with my friend.'

'But you must be famished, ma'am. You've had nothing since breakfast.'

'Oh…I took one of my breakfast rolls with me. I like to go for long walks and seldom need much in the middle of the day. You may tell Cook to give me an extra roll and biscuits in the morning—or a croissant or two. Also fruit, if we have apples or soft fruits that I may carry with me to nibble as I walk.'

'Yes, my lady. If it is your wish.'

Clearly Mrs Mann thought it a very odd request. Ladies in Lucinda's position did not spend hours walking about the countryside alone and they certainly did not eat in public.

Amused by the housekeeper's ill-hidden disapproval, Lucinda went up to change for the afternoon. Angela had cried and clung to her when she left her and that had made Lucinda reluctant to leave, but Nanny told her the tears would stop as soon as she had gone.

'Children often cry when their mothers leave them, but they soon get used to it. Angela will settle to a routine. I shall begin easy lessons soon and, as she begins to want to learn, she will not miss you so much.'

Lucinda accepted her word. Nanny had had a great deal of experience of such things. Besides, Lucinda could not spend all her time with her daughter.

Nanny had brought some books and toys with her, but she would need more as Angela grew. There must be a nursery here at Avonlea House, but as yet Lucinda had not visited it. She made up her mind that she would ask Mrs Mann about it that evening and then she would see what she could find that might be useful. All nurseries had old books and toys pushed away into cupboards;

they would not be missed and she could take them to her daughter.

Feeling much better about her situation, Lucinda hurried to change into a fresh gown. She did not think she would disclose her secret to Jane just yet, though she might have done so the previous day if Jane's brother had not arrived at the wrong moment.

Her thoughts turned to Justin and she wondered what the business was that had taken him to London. Was it important—or simply an excuse to put some distance between them?

The meeting with his lawyer took longer than expected. It was late in the afternoon when Justin left his office and began to walk towards his club. He was feeling thoughtful, reflecting on the scene with Lucinda the night before he left her. She'd looked so beautiful when he went into her bedchamber and the scent of her had made him weak with longing. He'd known a fierce desire to sweep her into his arms and make love to her. It was merely his foolish pride that had kept him from making up their quarrel instantly.

A quarrel of his making! Lucinda had not quarrelled at all. It was he that had driven a rift between them with his foolish pride. Now that he'd had leisure to reflect, he knew that she'd been placed in an intolerable position and he was angry, not with her, but himself for not being more understanding, and with all the people who had hurt her.

He understood her father's anger when her condition

became known, but if she had been raped Mr Seymour's anger ought to have been directed at the man who had taken such foul advantage of her.

The past three days had given Justin time to come to terms with the shock and to reason things out in his mind. Lucinda had not set her cap at Justin. Indeed, she had given him no encouragement at the start, as if she felt herself unworthy or unfit for marriage. His persistence had brought her to a change of heart. While she ought to have told him the truth, he could understand her fear—especially if her heart was touched.

If she loved him, as she professed, she would have feared his rejection. Yet she ought to have known that he cared for her and would listen to her story with sympathy.

It was not her secret that had hurt him so much as her lack of trust, Justin thought. However, she had told him the truth now and he must respect her for that because… he did not wish to lose her. He was not certain why he disliked the idea of an annulment; it was not fear of scandal, though he would be loath to sully his family's good name. No, it was more—an odd feeling that his life would become an empty wasteland if Lucinda were no longer in it. During the time she was missing he'd never allowed himself to consider his own feelings, but he'd never given up hope that she would be found.

To throw away all the good that could come from his marriage because his wife had been the victim of an evil man would be ridiculous.

He had a few more people he must speak to in town and then he would return to Avonlea. Justin could only hope that his show of temper had not alienated Lucinda altogether. He would try to save their marriage, because he did not wish for a final parting. Meanwhile, he would buy her a pretty trinket to show her that he was sorry for his show of temper.

Lucinda looked around the nursery. It was a large pleasant room that had a sunny aspect and would be warm even in winter. She thought how pleasant it would be if Nanny and Angela could live here. The cottage was well enough for the moment, but as her daughter grew she would begin to wonder why she was forced to live in a cottage while her mother lived in the big house through the woods.

Sighing, Lucinda opened the cupboard door. She had discovered a hoard of treasure in the form of books and small toys. So far she had taken a doll with a wax head, which might have been used by a dressmaker to show off her latest designs, a carved wooden horse and two picture books.

She was reaching for an abacus when a noise behind her made her aware that someone was there. She turned with a little start, feeling absurdly guilty.

'You startled me, Mrs Mann. Did you wish to speak with me?'

'Will you be out this morning, ma'am? Cook wondered what to do about luncheon.'

'Oh, yes, I shall,' Lucinda said. 'I was just admiring

the nursery. I think my husband and his siblings were fortunate children to have such a pleasant room.'

'Yes, it is nice,' Mrs Mann said. 'Were you thinking of having it refurbished? I know the last lady of the house thought that Nanny's room needed some attention.'

'Yes, perhaps I shall,' Lucinda said. 'I shall speak to his Grace about it. Thank you, you may go now.'

'I was wondering about some of the rooms in the west wing, my lady. When you have time you might wish to take a look—especially at the attics. In the old days the servants had rooms there, but they were moved to the east wing because the rooms needed repairs. His Grace's father spoke of having them improved, but it did not happen. Some of the maids are sharing and it would be better if we could use those rooms again.'

'Yes, I understand,' Lucinda said. 'I shall look at the rooms this afternoon when I return—if that suits you?'

'Yes, ma'am, whenever you wish.'

Lucinda waited until the housekeeper left and then reached back into the cupboard. She took out the abacus. It would help Nanny teach Angela her numbers and was only wasted here. No one used these apartments and would not until... The thought of having Justin's child brought a smile to her face. If that were to happen, she would be very happy—yet deep inside her there was pain because Angela would be shut out of this family. Even if Lucinda made time to visit her once a day—and when Justin returned that might be more difficult—she would always be on the outside, never taking her proper place in her mother's life.

Tears stung Lucinda's eyes as she hid the abacus under her cloak and went downstairs. Giving her daughter sweetmeats and toys was a poor substitute for a proper home and the security she truly needed. It was useless to repine! The child would be waiting. She must hurry or Angela might have a tantrum. She did have a temper; though Nanny did her best to calm her, she was not as young as she'd once been and the child played her up at times.

'I thought she was just being naughty at first,' Nanny said as they stood by the child's bed and looked at her flushed face. 'She cried for you most of last night and this morning she threw her milk at me—but then she became hot and I realised she was not feeling well.'

'Do you think she has a tummy upset?'

'Perhaps. She ate her supper last night, but this morning did not touch her boiled egg. I thought perhaps we should have the doctor—what do you think?'

Lucinda laid a hand on the child's brow. 'I think she has a fever. I shall walk into the village and ask the doctor to call. I shall tell him the child belongs to my cousin and that she died. You are her nanny—that much at least is true.'

'More lies, Lucinda?'

'What else can I do?' Lucinda asked. 'I brought some things for her—but she is too ill to want them now. I shall go and fetch the doctor straight away.'

* * *

Leaving the cottage, Lucinda walked very fast down the narrow lane that led to the village. The doctor's house was at the edge of the green. She went up the path and knocked loudly. A smiling apple-cheeked house-keeper answered the door within a few seconds.

'What is your business, mistress…your Grace?' The woman looked startled and dipped a hasty curtsy. 'Forgive me. I did not realise… Please come in, my lady.'

'Is your master at home?'

'Yes, my lady.'

'I would see him at once.'

'Had you sent for him, he would have attended you, my lady.'

'No matter, I am here and my business is urgent. Please take me to your master now.'

'Yes, of course. Please come this way, my lady.'

Lucinda followed, her heart thudding. She must be very careful in her deportment. Concern for the child of a cousin was acceptable, but she must do nothing to make him suspect that she was Angela's mother and not merely her second cousin.

Lucinda was late returning to Avonlea that afternoon. The doctor had taken his time examining Angela and then questioned her severely about the child's nutrition. She had explained that her cousin had fallen on hard times and that she had known nothing of their poverty until her cousin became ill and subsequently died.

'I was called away unexpectedly to her deathbed,'

she lied. 'I had some trouble in sorting out her affairs after the funeral and in finding a good woman to look after her child, who still cries for her mother.'

As Angela had woken and clung to her, weeping and crying, the doctor had seemed to accept her story. He said that her sickness was merely a tummy upset and suggested that perhaps her diet was too rich.

'If she has not eaten well for a long time, too much food may have upset her digestion. You should give her plainer fare and introduce meat and puddings slowly.'

'It may be my fault for giving her sweet biscuits and cakes. I wanted to spoil her,' Lucinda said. 'We shall follow your advice, Doctor.'

'She does have a little chill, which may have made her feverish,' the doctor said. 'I shall give you a mixture for her—if you can spare the time to return with me to fetch it?'

'Yes, of course.'

Lucinda knew that another journey would make her late for her appointment with Mrs Mann, but she had no choice. The look the housekeeper gave her was one of reproach, but she apologised, saying that she had forgot the time.

'Well, I'm sure your Grace may do as you please. However, the matter of the rooms in the west wing is something that you ought to attend, ma'am. It is more usually for the mistress of the house to make a decision on the servants' welfare.'

'Yes, of course. It may seem to you that I have neglected my duties.'

'It is not for me to tell you what to do, my lady.'

'No, but perhaps I should have consulted with you on menus and things? I prefer to wait until the duke returns so that I may be certain of his preferences.'

'Yes, of course, ma'am. Do you know when his Grace intends to return?'

'In a few days,' Lucinda said airily. 'He has business and will be back when he is ready.'

'Yes, ma'am, as you say.'

'Very well, please take me to these attic rooms—and anywhere else that concerns you.'

'His lordship has had much of the house done, my lady, but the attics seem to have escaped his notice.'

'I dare say he was not aware that the maids are over-crowded in the east wing.'

Lucinda followed the housekeeper up a narrow staircase, which was conveniently hidden behind a door, concealing it from the casual eye. As the west wing was kept for guests they would not notice the door leading to the attics, but it was usual for the servants to come and go by way of a back staircase. It made it easier for them to service the guests' rooms and reach their own without intruding.

Looking round the various attic rooms, Lucinda saw what Mrs Mann meant about their needing refurbishment. In some places the ceilings had crumbled and it looked as if the plaster might fall, though two of the rooms needed only some decoration.

'I think it may be necessary to have a repair to the roof here,' Lucinda said, gazing up at the source of the problem, which was a patch of damp. 'Clearly that is what caused the leak in three rooms.'

'The roof was repaired last year,' Mrs Mann told her. 'It is just the ceilings—and a coat of whitewash, and then some rugs on the floor.'

'Yes, I see. Well, I shall speak to my husband when he returns. I am not certain that it is within my power to order repairs of that nature, Mrs Mann. Be patient for a while and I shall see what may be done.'

'Yes, ma'am. If you are satisfied with things as they are.'

A little sniff accompanied her words. Lucinda knew that the housekeeper was less than satisfied with her response to the problem, but an idea had occurred to her—an idea that was daring and outrageous, but which could make her life much easier.

'I shall attend to the matter,' she said. 'Surely the maids can manage for a little longer?'

'Yes, ma'am, if they have to—but in the summer these rooms can be very hot, especially if there are too many sharing.'

Lucinda felt a little guilty as she returned to her own room and began to change for the evening. Jane and Andrew Lanchester were coming for dinner that evening and they were bringing some guests, people with whom Lucinda was slightly acquainted, which should make it a pleasant evening for all.

She would visit her daughter again in the morning and see how she was faring, but in the meantime she would consider her plan to bring both Nanny and Angela into the house.

Justin had decided to leave town that afternoon. He would be home sooner than he'd planned, but he had set his business in hand and found himself restless, unable to settle. His anger had cooled somewhat, but the hurt was as sharp as ever. Yet he wanted to see Lucinda, to see her smile and hear her voice. Most of all he wanted to lie with her in the beautiful bedchamber he had lavished so much time and money on in preparation for their wedding.

He frowned as he wondered how best to proceed with repairing the rift between them. While he was eager for their marriage to be a true one, he was uncertain of Lucinda's feelings. She had consented to be married after some initial reluctance—was her reluctance merely because she'd feared to tell him her secret or might she have another deeper reason for her hesitation? Did she fear her husband's attentions in the bedroom? She had never shown any reluctance when he kissed her—but there was more than kissing to being a true wife.

Clearly, she had been ready to accept her duties as a wife or she would not have wed him, but Justin did not wish for a complacent wife. He had expected that his bride would be innocent and had planned to be gentle and patient on their wedding night—but the knowledge that she had been raped put a new light on the situation. Much as he desired her, he might have to put his own desires to one side for the time being. He would need to be very gentle with Lucinda if he wanted her to respond. Indeed, he might have to wait some time before he took her to bed.

Before he made love to his wife he must regain her trust. Otherwise, he might destroy her and his hopes of a good marriage.

Having made up his mind to leave for Avonlea that very afternoon, he summoned his valet, intending to ask that his bags be packed in readiness. However, when the man came in answer to the bell he was bearing a letter from Justin's lawyer. Breaking the seal, he frowned. It was a matter of business that had arisen from his fresh instructions concerning his will and he was requested to attend the lawyer's office at his earliest convenience, which meant that his departure might have to be delayed by at least one more day.

The delay was annoying, but the business could not wait. Sighing, Justin took up his hat and silver-topped walking stick and left the house. The sooner this business was finished the sooner he could go home to Lucinda.

'The doctor's mixture did her the world of good,' Nanny said when Lucinda visited soon after breakfast the next morning. 'She had honey and rolls and she's nearly back to normal. It was just a little chill after all.'

'Is she still in bed?'

'I left her sitting with her books, but I heard something just before you came in and she may have decided to get up and play.'

Lucinda went upstairs. Her daughter had dressed herself, her gown only half-buttoned at the back, and her tangled curls evidence that Angela had not considered it necessary to use the brush. When she saw her mother her eyes welled with tears, which spilled over and ran down her cheeks.

'My poor love, come here to me,' Lucinda said and sat down on the bed, drawing her on to her lap. She kissed and cuddled her, then buttoned her bodice properly and took up a hairbrush. Angela's hair soon looked respectable and shone. Lucinda noticed that her arms were much better now and her legs had stopped looking like sticks. She was beginning to recover from years of ill treatment, but of course the mental scars were still there. 'Shall we go for a little walk in the woods?'

Angela shook her head. 'Will you read to me from my books?'

'Yes, if you wish it. Come downstairs and we shall sit in the big chair by the fire and read a story.'

Angela scrambled to her feet, seized the book she wanted and proceeded down the stairs. Lucinda smiled inwardly, because it was clear to her that her daughter was feeling much better.

The next hour or so was very happy for them both, but the tears started once more when Lucinda told her that she must leave. Angela screamed and clung to her. She calmed a little when Nanny pulled her away and told her she must be good, but the sight of her child's reproachful face pulled at Lucinda's heartstrings as she left the cottage and began to walk back to the house.

The tears trickled down her cheeks as she thought of her daughter's distress. In the future she might not always be able to visit her every day and the child would not understand that her mother had another life—a life she could not share with her.

Lucinda was starting to shake with sobs as she saw the fallen tree lying just ahead of her in a small clearing. She sat down, her head bowed as the tears fell thick and fast.

A part of her longed for Justin's return from town. She wanted desperately to see him, to be a true wife to him with no secrets between them—but she could not give up her beloved child. There was no way out of her predicament. If she confessed to her husband, he would be angry again—and he would force her to give Angela up.

'Duchess—Lucinda?'

The man's deep voice startled her. She raised her head, and saw Andrew standing just a few feet from where she sat. Feeling guilty, she rose to her feet and brushed a hand over her face.

'Lord Lanchester…I did not hear you come.'

'Are you unwell?' He moved closer, looking at her

with concern. 'You have been crying. Is there something I may do to help you?'

'No, it is nothing. Nothing at all,' Lucinda said and lifted her head proudly. 'It was a silly tantrum, that is all.'

'I do not think you are the kind of woman who has tantrums,' he said and handed her a large white kerchief. 'You may be pleased to know that he has returned this very morning.'

'My husband has returned?' Lucinda's heart missed a beat. She caught her breath. 'You have seen him?'

'I saw him driving his curricle on his way here.' He hesitated. 'You are in some trouble, I think. For the moment you may prefer to keep your own counsel—but should you need a friend, I am here.'

The warmth and sincerity in his voice brought a flush to her cheeks. She gave him a small shy smile—the smile that unbeknown to her had won more than one man's heart.

'You are very kind, my lord.'

'Tell me, are you in some difficulty?'

'If I am in some trouble, I fear there is nothing you can help me with. My problem is one I must solve alone.'

'There are very few problems that will not be made easier by sharing them,' he said and smiled. 'I shall not push my friendship on you, Lucinda—but please know that if you need either my sister or myself we are always there for you.'

'Thank you. I know you are sincere, sir.' She raised her head. 'I must go home. My husband will wonder where I am.'

'You like to walk, I believe?'

'Yes, I walk most mornings if it is fine.'

'I shall not keep you.'

Lucinda watched as he walked away from her, farther into the woods that formed a boundary between the two estates. She had thought of them as being Avonlea property, but in actual fact they were right on the edge of her husband's estate and it was natural that Lord Lanchester might choose to walk this way home if he had been to the village.

Had he seen her walking here before? Had he perhaps seen her enter the cottage? She was not sure who owned the cottage for she had rented it through an agent. It might even belong to Lord Lanchester.

Supposing Lord Lanchester learned that the woman who had rented the cottage for her nanny and child was the bride of his close friend the Duke of Avonlea?

Would he feel it his duty to tell Justin? A trickle of fear ran down her spine. She did not know what to do. Perhaps it might be best to confess her secret to her husband at once?

Her stomach was fluttering with nerves as she went into the house a short time later. Her dress was crumpled from playing with the child and she'd hoped that she might escape to her room to change before seeing her husband, but even as she started to ascend the stairs, Justin came out into the hall and called to her.

'Lucinda—will you do me the courtesy of sparing me a few minutes of your time, please?'

'Yes, of course,' she said and turned, walking to meet him. 'I am glad to see you back. I hope you had a good journey?'

'You do not seem surprised to see me.'

'I met Lord Lanchester as I was walking in the wood,' Lucinda said. 'He mentioned that he had seen you driving your curricle through the village.'

Justin frowned. 'Mrs Mann told me that you spend most of your day walking. I was not aware that you enjoyed rambling to that extent?'

'Yes, it is a favourite pastime with me,' Lucinda said, feeling very conscious of the lies she must tell him. 'Did your business go well?'

'I dare say my lawyers will see to it,' he replied. 'As you know, I went mainly because I needed a little time to think. I have decided that I shall put the past behind us, Lucinda. There is still some gossip, but I have told people that you were called to a sick relative; though some may still whisper behind your back, I think the gossip and speculation will blow over. The best thing is to give the impression that we are perfectly happy in our marriage. To that end I have decided that I shall give a ball here at Avonlea.'

'A ball?' Lucinda's heart fluttered. 'Does this mean that you have forgiven me?'

'It means that I am trying to put the past behind us, Lucinda. For the moment we shall continue as we were. Outwardly, we have the perfect marriage. As yet I do not believe I wish for more. We shall get to know each other again and perhaps come to an understanding. What happened is in part my fault. I rushed you into marriage. We must get to know one another before we can be man and wife in all senses of the word.'

Lucinda's hopes had soared when he spoke of a ball, but now she felt a coldness form about her heart. He looked so grave and she missed the gentle smiles that had made her knees go weak when he had courted her. He did not seem much like the charming man who had spoiled and flirted with her. It was that man she adored and longed for.

When she'd been considering her answer, Lucinda had wondered if she could bear any man to touch her after what had happened that fatal night. However, Justin's gentleness and the tenderness of his kiss had made her feel such sweet longings she had felt she could overcome her bad memories and accept Justin's loving.

'Then I shall do my best to be the wife you want, Avonlea,' she said and raised her head proudly. 'I shall give Mrs Mann instructions to prepare for guests. How many do you wish to invite?'

'I think we must invite everyone who attended our wedding. It is only fair to give them the reception they were cheated of then—do you not think so?'

'Yes, perhaps.'

Lucinda held back the emotion that was building inside her. She still had the guest list she had used for their wedding. Most of those invited were Avonlea's friends, some of whom she'd never met. It would be embarrassing to face them all at such a glittering occasion, but it must be done. She owed her husband this and more besides.

If he had taken her into his arms and kissed her, she could have borne it all so much easier. Indeed, she might have shed tears and confessed her secret had he been the gentle considerate man she'd fallen in love with, but he was a stranger, a man she did not recognise.

'I shall do whatever you wish, Avonlea.'

'I'm glad to hear that, Lucinda. Now, please go and change your gown. You look like a hoyden. Remember that you are a duchess now and try to behave in an appropriate manner.'

How his words stung her! Was he being deliberately cruel or did he not understand that she would have found it difficult enough to carry off her new social standing even if he had been loving and kind? As it was she felt alone and isolated.

Escaping to her rooms, she shut the door and stood with her back against it, fighting the tears. The burden of her secret was hard enough to bear, but Avonlea's remote manner made it so much worse.

She brushed the tears from her eyes, refusing to break down as she had in the woods earlier. Her hus-

band had told her to behave like a duchess and she
would find the strength to do it somehow.

Justin looked at his reflection in the dressing mirror
and swore. He was such a fool. Why must he be angry
again? Why could he not have given Lucinda the gift
he'd purchased for her, kissed her and told her he cared
deeply for her—that he wanted to make her happy? It
was what he'd planned, but the sight of her with her hair
tussled and her gown creased had alerted his suspicions.
She looked as if she might just have come from the arms
of a lover.

Her mention of Lord Lanchester had made him so
angry—and jealous. Jealousy was an ugly emotion and
one he did not like in himself. He had not realised that
he could experience the emotion so sharply and his
reaction to it was primeval and savage, not at all the
behaviour of the gentleman he prided himself on being.

A gentleman was reasonable at all times, courteous
to those around him and most of all, honourable. It was
not honourable to feel as if he would like to murder his
best friend.

Shaking his head, he felt his mouth curve in a wry
smile. He must learn to curb his temper or he might not
be answerable for his actions.

Chapter Four

'That is a pretty gown, Lucinda. It becomes you very well.'

'Thank you, Avonlea.' Lucinda inclined her head but did not smile. For the past two days they had managed to behave with civility towards one another. Her husband paid her compliments and appeared satisfied with the arrangements she was making for the ball, but he was still distant, a little cool in his manner, though at times she saw an expression in his eyes that puzzled her. 'Do you have plans for this morning?'

'I was thinking of riding into Thaxted to visit someone. Did you wish for the carriage? If you are going visiting, I could accompany you tomorrow.'

'I know very few of your friends,' Lucinda said. 'I have not felt able to visit, though I believe one or two of your neighbours have called. I was unfortunately out at the time—but perhaps tomorrow we could go visiting together?'

'Yes, we shall do so. I was unaware that you had not troubled to make yourself at home to our friends.'

'It…was remiss of me. I must settle on a day when I am always here,' Lucinda replied, refusing to meet his eyes. 'I have visited Jane Lanchester and she has been here on three occasions.'

'That is all very well, but you must be aware of your position, Lucinda. As my duchess you are expected to keep a certain standard. You should be at home on at least one day a week and visit friends on another—and you must concern yourself with what is going on in the district. We hold various functions for the villagers during the year and my mother enjoyed opening the church fête. I believe the vicar used to call once a month to tell her what was needed for the poor of the locality.'

'Forgive me. I did not know what was expected. You did not mention my duties, Avonlea.'

He looked at her for a moment in silence, then his expression softened. 'No, I have not discussed these things as I ought and that was remiss of me. I have neglected my duty towards you, Lucinda. I beg your pardon. My visit this morning has been arranged for a while, but tomorrow I shall take you visiting—and this evening we shall discuss some of the things that are expected from the duchess. I shall give you my mother's diaries. They will help you, I dare say.'

'Yes, thank you,' Lucinda replied. 'I shall not keep you, Avonlea. I have things to do.'

He was standing very close to her, his eyes curiously intent as he looked down at her. His hand reached out and he touched her cheek, stroking his fingers down to her mouth, smoothing his thumb over the softness of her bottom lip. She trembled inwardly, thinking he might kiss her and wanting it, longing for the smile that would tell her the man she loved was back, but it did not happen.

'You are very beautiful, Lucinda.'

'Thank you. I'm sorry if I've disappointed you, Justin.'

'Nonsense. I am at fault. I am thoughtless and too demanding. There is plenty of time for you to learn your duties.'

He nodded to her and strode away. As soon as she was certain he had left, Lucinda ran upstairs and fetched her cloak. She had not been able to visit her daughter since her husband's return. Angela would be upset and she must make the most of what time she had.

It was mid-afternoon when Lucinda left the cottage and began to walk home as fast as she could. Her daughter had wept when she saw her, clinging to her all day. Leaving her was very hard and Lucinda had delayed until the last moment, knowing that she would not have time to visit the next day.

'Stay with me,' Angela begged her. 'Do not leave me, Mama. I promise to be good if you take me with you.'

'I cannot take you yet,' Lucinda said and kissed her, putting her into her nurse's arms. 'Be a good girl and I shall come as often as I can.'

'Angela is always good,' Nanny said. 'She is learning her numbers and her letters—and to speak as she ought. She will do well enough when you have gone, Lucinda.'

Lucinda knew that her friend spoke wisely. Children always clung to their mothers. Had she been able to have her at Avonlea she could not have spent more than an hour or so with her each day, for she had many duties. The child must learn to be a young lady and with that came discipline. It was because she had to leave her in the cottage that she felt so guilty, she supposed, but there was nothing more she could do for the moment. She was finding it hard enough to do all the things that Justin seemed to expect of her.

Justin ought to have known when he asked her to marry him that she would not be accustomed to so many servants or the way things should be run in such a large house. If he wanted her to behave as his mother had, he should have married someone who had been taught these things—or at least shown her what to do and given her time to learn.

'We meet again, Duchess.'

'Lord Lanchester…' Lucinda laughed as she jumped. 'You startled me. I was lost in thought and did not see you there. I was in a hurry to get home for tea.'

'If you do not mind, I shall walk with you,' he said. 'I was hoping to catch Avonlea for a few minutes.'

'You must take tea with us,' Lucinda said. 'You and Jane will come to the ball, I hope?'

'I should not miss it for the world,' he said and smiled at her. 'You will save the first waltz for me, Duchess?'

'Yes, of course. I should like it if you would call me Lucinda, sir.'

'I am honoured to be your friend,' he replied and was rewarded by her shy smile. 'Jane is helping with the village fête next month. Your ball will be over by then and she thought you might like to open the occasion for them. I did it last year and your husband the year previously.'

'Oh, yes, that would be pleasant. Perhaps Jane will tell me what I should say?'

'You need only say how happy you are to be there and that you wish everyone a good afternoon,' he said. 'You might make a little presentation of some small gifts for the children—sweets or tin whistles, something of the sort.'

'Yes, I believe Mama did something of the kind when we had a fête for the church in our gardens,' Lucinda said and laughed. 'I remember how good it was to be given such treats when I was a child.'

'You are still young and innocent yourself,' her companion said. 'You deserve all the treats I am sure Avonlea gives you.'

'Yes, perhaps,' she said, but turned away and did

not meet his look. They had left the wood behind and were walking on Avonlea land now. Hearing hoofbeats behind them, she glanced round and saw that her husband was riding towards them, having come from the direction of the park. 'Here he is now…'

'Ah, yes, just in time for tea as you expected,' Andrew said and stopped walking as Justin pulled his horse to a halt and looked down at them. 'Justin, I was on my way to see you when I met your enchanting duchess, who has kindly invited me to tea.'

'Yes, of course, good to see you,' Justin said and dismounted, leading his horse as he walked beside them. 'Lucinda, my love, you look beautiful. Walking in the fresh air suits you. I must try it myself.'

'Thank you.' Lucinda glanced at him. His eyes were intent, not angry but thoughtful and certainly not remote. 'We were speaking of the fête next month, after the ball has taken place. Jane wondered if I might open it and I have said I will. I trust that pleases you, Avonlea?'

'Jane thought everyone would like to get a better look at your duchess,' Andrew said and grinned. 'You've kept her pretty close, Justin—and the locals want their share of her. I've told her all she needs to do is smile and look pretty—and perhaps bribe the children with some sweets.'

'Oh…' Lucinda laughed softly. 'That is not quite what you said, sir. I believe I can find something appropriate to say that may please.'

'I am certain of it, Lucinda.'

His smile was so warm that she blushed.

'I dare say Lucinda will grow accustomed to these things in time. I shall give her some pointers once she decides to take up her duties.'

'Oh, no one expects too much just yet, old fellow,' Andrew said. 'You are hardly wed and with Lucinda being called to the bedside of a cousin as she lay dying, well, you are still on your honeymoon. I am surprised that you did not whisk her away to Paris as soon as she returned.'

'Her cousin…is that what people are saying?' Justin's gaze narrowed. 'Yes, it was unfortunate, of course, but we have plenty of time for visiting Paris. I thought Lucinda should get to know everyone and that is why I arranged the ball.'

'Everyone always loves your balls. What is the theme this time?'

'I've left that to Lucinda,' Justin replied. 'We have had several themes in the past: eastern palaces, knights and dragons. What had you in mind, Lucinda?'

He had not mentioned that the ball needed a theme! Lucinda felt a spurt of anger, but controlled it. How was she supposed to know that there was always a theme for the ball? Yet her fertile mind soon supplied an answer.

'I thought we might have witches, elves and trolls,' she said and smiled. 'Unless that has already been used?'

'Witches and wizards,' Andrew said before Justin could reply. 'I don't think I recall that one—sounds like great fun to me. You must remember to put it on the invitation, Lucinda, give everyone a chance to prepare a costume.'

'I dare say we could provide a tall hat for everyone and a mask,' she said, warming to her theme. 'A dark flowing gown for the ladies and a domino for the men and there you have your disguise—of course, anyone brave enough to come as an elf or a troll would need something more daring.'

'Are you putting us on our mettle, Duchess?' Andrew looked much amused. 'I reserve the right to prepare my own costume and so will Jane. I think we shall surprise you.'

Lucinda's eyes lit up with mischief. 'Oh, yes, that sounds so much fun. I think we shall all enjoy seeing each other's costumes—do you not think so, Justin?'

She turned to look at him and saw that his expression had changed again, not distant but distinctly colder.

'If it pleases you both, who am I to cavil?' he asked. 'I also shall endeavour to come up with my own costume and surprise you.'

'I had no idea a ball could be so amusing,' Lucinda said. 'It was good of you to suggest it, Justin. I shall enjoy it so much.'

'It is my mission in life to make you happy, my dear Duchess,' he replied gallantly, but she caught an inflection in his voice that told her he was controlling himself with some difficulty.

After tea, Lucinda left the men to talk and went up to her rooms on the pretext of a rest before changing for

the evening. In fact, she had a sentence to add to the pile
of invitations she had already completed. She could only
be thankful that she had not put them out for posting
that morning. Had Lord Lanchester not mentioned the
theme, she would have disappointed those who were
expecting the ball to have its own theme.

It was neglectful of Justin not to tell her. There was
so much she needed to know if she was to follow in the
footsteps of those who had come before her at Avonlea.
She had already disappointed Justin in the matter of her
innocence; she must try very hard to be a good hostess
for his friends.

That evening at dinner Justin was polite, but distant
once more. After they had dined he did not linger over
his port, but accompanied her to the small parlour that
he preferred in the evenings when they had no guests.

'How did you happen to meet Lanchester this afternoon?' he enquired as he stood by the fireplace and
sipped the glass of port he had carried with him.

'I had been for a walk and we met by chance. As
he wished to see you, we walked back to the house
together.'

'Have you consulted with Mrs Mann about the food
for the ball?'

'Yes, Justin. I asked her to show me some menus
that might be suitable for supper and approved the one
I thought best. Did you wish to approve it yourself?'

'No, I trust you to have made the proper decision

with Mrs Mann's help. She has been here many years and my mother said she was a treasure.'

'Yes, I am certain she is very capable.' Lucinda hesitated, wondering whether she ought to ask about the attic rooms, then decided to leave it for the moment. 'I should be grateful for your mother's diaries if you would give them to me, Avonlea. I had no idea that a theme was needed for the ball until Andrew mentioned it.'

'You are on first-name terms with Lanchester?'

'Oh, yes. Jane and I are such good friends. I do not use his name often, but since you and he are such close friends and neighbours it would seem foolish to stand on ceremony.'

'Neighbours, yes. We were not always friends. We fought a duel over a woman once, but we both fired in the air and made it up afterwards. In truth, she wasn't worth wasting the shot.'

'That is rather unkind, Avonlea.'

'She was an opera singer—which is a polite name for her true trade, if you must know.'

'I see…I suppose she was your mistress.'

'Andrew's actually until I cut him out.'

'Then you were at fault.'

'It was for a bet. Some of the fellows wagered that I could not do it—so of course I had to prove them wrong. I'm not sure he has forgiven me.'

'Would you have forgiven him, had it been the other way round?'

'Lord, yes, he hardly cared for her.'

'I think Lord Lanchester would not have fought over a woman he did not care for.'

'He is no white knight, Lucinda. I should be careful of walking in woods alone with him.'

'Avonlea! You are not suggesting that he—or I—would think of...' She gave him a reproachful look. 'I am not a lightskirt, whatever you may think of me.'

'No, of course. Forgive me.' He looked conscious. 'I did not mean it that way, Lucinda. Andrew is a normal man and he likes you. Alone in the woods he might be tempted to take advantage.'

'He is my friend, but he is also yours. Excuse me, I think I shall go to bed.'

He was on his feet and caught her arm as she got up to leave. 'No, Lucinda, forgive me. I did not mean to offend you. It was a careless remark, nothing more.'

'What happened—the rape—I did nothing to encourage him. I give you my word.'

'I believe you. I am a fool,' Justin apologised. 'I do not mean to quarrel with you, Lucinda. It is just my pride. Of course I do not think you of easy virtue.'

She sighed, her throat tight with emotion. 'I think I have killed your affection for me. I fear this marriage will not work.'

'We shall not let it fail.' The pressure of his fingers was almost painful as he looked down at her. For a moment passion blazed in his eyes and then he bent his head, brushing his mouth softly over hers. Her lips parted on a sigh and his tongue entered her mouth as he deepened the kiss. Lucinda's fingers moved at his nape as she relished his caress, a little shiver running through her. Her body had begun to heat and she wanted to cling to him, but held back for fear of displeasing him. His eyes darkened and he frowned as he withdrew. 'Go to bed, Lucinda. I shall not disturb you.'

Her disappointment was sharp. For a moment she'd thought he had forgiven her, but then she'd sensed his withdrawal. What had she done wrong?

'Very well, good night, Justin.'

Walking away from him, she felt the sting of tears, but fought against them. She must learn not to be hurt by his moods and his harsh words. If this was to be her life, she had to learn to cope with her secret grief and show a smiling face to the world.

Lucinda walked swiftly, wanting to be home before Justin came to look for her. Their quarrel of the previous evening was still sharp in her mind and she had no wish to cause a breach between them.

It was as she was walking across the smooth lawns that she saw her husband coming towards her and knew that she had been discovered.

'You are up early, Lucinda?'

'You know that I enjoy a walk early in the morning,' she said with a smile that covered her trepidation. 'Do you not recall the morning that you took me to see the swans?'

'The swans…?' Justin was puzzled, then he smiled. 'Yes, of course. You were staying with Jane Lanchester and expressed a wish to see the new cygnets on the lake. I came for you early and we had breakfast here.'

Lucinda nodded. 'It was that day you proposed to me, Justin. We had such a lovely time. We went for a long walk and you arranged a picnic by the lake. I fed croissants to the swans and you said they would do much better on the special pellets you keep for them—but you did not scold me.'

'It is not my wish to scold you, Lucinda.' Justin looked rueful as he offered her his arm. 'I shall try to do better, my love—if you will forgive me for my shocking temper.'

'Of course I forgive you. You are my husband.'

'Perhaps you would like to go for a drive later?'

'Yes, thank you. I should enjoy that very much.'

'Then it will be my pleasure to take you.'

Lucinda's hand trembled slightly on his arm. His manner was charming and he was once more the man she had married—but his mood would turn to anger again if he guessed where she had been that morning.

How much longer could she keep her guilty secret?

For the next ten days Lucinda had coped by getting up very early. She was at the cottage by seven each morning and returned by nine-thirty, giving her maid instructions that she would breakfast alone in her room at a quarter to ten. Since most ladies did not leave their rooms much before noon, she was able to see her beloved daughter and attend to her duties in the house without occasioning notice.

On the day of the ball she returned at nine-thirty as usual to discover Justin sitting in a chair in her boudoir. He rose as she entered, his eyes taking note of the plainness of her gown and her hair hanging loose about her face.

'Is it your habit to rise so early on the day of an important ball? I should have thought you would take the opportunity to rest, Lucinda.'

'You know I like to walk,' she replied with quiet dignity. 'Since it is necessary for me to fulfil my duties here, I have found it convenient to walk before breakfast. The business of the day is done before nuncheon and I am free to spend my afternoon with you should you wish for company—or to receive friends.'

'I like to ride before breaking my fast,' he said. 'It would be pleasant if you could accompany me sometimes.'

'Yes, of course if you wish it—if you let me know in time.'

'Very well. In future I shall mention my preference before we part for the evening. I did not think I should need to make an appointment with my own wife, but since you are so busy I must make it a rule.'

It seemed that nothing she did was right for her husband and her eyes stung with the tears she would not shed. These past few days had been pleasant enough on the surface; for a moment as he'd kissed her, she'd believed the old Justin was back—but his resentment was still there, eating at him. At times she saw passion in his eyes and believed he was close to making love to her, but each time he drew back, retreating behind that cool reserve.

'If you wish, I can change into a suitable gown now.'

'I think not,' he said and moved towards the door, glancing back at her. 'Did you happen to meet anyone on your walk this morning?'

'I glimpsed one of your keepers in the wood, but other than that saw no one. Should I have seen someone or something?'

'It was merely an idle question,' he said. For a moment his eyes dwelled on her, as if questioning or searching for answers he could not find. 'Everything is ready for this evening. You should rest while you can, Lucinda. You will not wish to be tired this evening.'

'I shall not tire myself, Justin. However, I wish to see for myself that everything is as it ought to be. This is our first ball and I want everything to be perfect for your friends.'

'I hope they will be your friends too, Lucinda,' he said, frowning as he went out.

She sat down at her dressing table, her heart racing. Why had Justin been waiting for her to return? Could he have discovered her secret?

She might have to tell him soon, but not yet. If they quarrelled again before the ball, it would create an atmosphere. She must wait until after this evening and then perhaps she would confess her secret. If Justin understood why she went for a walk every day, he might not be so suspicious.

* * *

Guests began arriving soon after eleven that morning. Justin had advised Lucinda to rest, but since he had gone riding alone and not returned, she was left with the duty of greeting his friends and arranging for them to be shown to their rooms.

'Some of his Grace's relatives have special rooms that are kept for their use,' Mrs Mann had told her a few days previously. 'And other friends like to be put at the rear of the house rather than the front, but I have a list of accommodation for you to approve.'

Lucinda glanced at the list. 'I have no fault to find, but I would like to see the rooms once they are ready, just in case anything else is needed.'

At the start the housekeeper had been disapproving, but she was gradually warming towards Lucinda. When she had suggested that there should be flowers in all the guestrooms, brandy for the gentlemen, wine and sweetmeats for the ladies, her housekeeper had smiled and agreed.

'They are the kind of things that guests like to find in their rooms, because it saves them asking for extras to be brought. Some people ring their bell for service all the time, but others do not like to seem too demanding.'

'I think it is nice to have something at hand in that time between going up to your room and dressing for the evening—and before bed. So if all the rooms are supplied earlier in the afternoon, it will save the maids having to run upstairs a dozen times before dinner.'

'That is thoughtful of you, my lady. I suppose you have not had the time to consider what should be done for the attic rooms?'

'I need a little more time to consider.'

Lucinda had put the matter to the back of her mind, because the ball was more pressing and Angela had seemed fairly settled at the cottage. She still cried when her mother left her, but she was becoming less clinging, growing used to the idea that her mother came and went each day.

What would she do if Justin decided to take her to Paris or perhaps London? It was bound to happen in time. Lucinda could only hope that by the time he was ready for such a visit her daughter would be happier, content to stay with Nanny.

With the arrival of her guests, Lucinda had no time to give her daughter more than a passing thought. She was constantly greeting people, many of whom she had never seen before. It was a relief when Justin returned at noon and apologised for leaving her to cope alone.

'I managed well enough. However, I am sure your guests will be pleased to see you.'

'Our guests, Lucinda,' he reminded her. 'You are the hostess here, my dear.'

'Yes, of course.'

Jane and Andrew Lanchester did not arrive until the early evening, when everyone was gathering for the ball. The guests who were staying had been served high tea and given sandwiches, lemon barley, brandy and wine in their rooms. A lavish supper would be served at about ten and the dancing began at seven.

Everyone was excited when they took off their cloaks, exclaiming over each other's costumes. Jane was wearing a flowing green gown, because she said it was the true colour for witches. She wore her long dark hair loose about her face and a pendent of lapis lazuli about her neck

'The lapis has magic powers,' she said with a smile. 'I am, of course, a white witch and use my magic only for good—some of your other guests look more sinister.'

Their guests had various ideas of what a witch or wizard should look like. Most of the men had chosen black and taken what could only be described as a medieval theme, wearing tight hose and tunics that fitted to the waist or fell in loose folds to mid-thigh, depending on their age and stature. The ladies were less adventurous, though several had dressed in flowing medieval style gowns similar to Jane's. One lady had very long nails, which she had dyed with a green colour that looked very effective; some wore a velvet mask, and others had a pointed hat, which they soon discarded.

Andrew Lanchester had come dressed as a medieval knight. He grinned at Lucinda as he saw that she was wearing a green-and-white gown with fronds, which fluttered like leaves of silk, hanging from an embroidered band beneath her breasts. On her head she wore a tiny skullcap of gold threads.

'I think you must be the Queen of the elves,' he said.

'I am Sir Lancelot and I've come prepared to rescue any ladies in danger of being enchanted by these wicked wizards.'

Lucinda laughed. 'I am not sure that any ladies are in danger at the moment,' she said. She glanced at her husband, who was wearing a green-velvet tunic that fitted into his waist and then flared out in little pleats, his tight-fitting hose in a matching shade. He had a little fringed cape of black silk and beads that fell in a point over one shoulder. Again it was the medieval style, but had something of an elfish look. 'I am quite disappointed that no one dressed up as a troll to frighten us all.'

'I doubt that anyone was certain of what a troll should look like,' Andrew said. 'I do not believe I have ever met one—what does a troll do, do you imagine?'

'He or she lives under a bridge, eats rotten fruit, has exceedingly bad manners and is very aggressive,' Lucinda replied laughingly.

'Indeed?' Andrew raised his right eyebrow. 'I believe I have met one or two after all, but they do not appear to be here this evening. Clearly, you had the good sense not to invite them.'

'Trolls need no invitation,' Lucinda said. 'Perhaps it is as well that they have decided to stay away.'

The servants were circulating with trays and people helped themselves to glasses of champagne. To give the ball an atmosphere, Lucinda had asked the servants to hang banners of green-and-black silk, from which dangled little spiders, toads and black cats, which she had made herself from paper, ribbon and scraps of velvet. Justin had discovered a beautiful crystal ball, which had been set in the middle of a display of prickly holly, some white lilies and little dishes of biscuits in the shapes of witches, wizards, toads and black cats.

Outside the ballroom there were lanterns hung in the trees and Lucinda had painted silhouettes of witches, wizards and black cats on the glass so that when it got dark they would throw shadows onto the lawns. There was to be a firework display at the end of the evening, which the gardeners had been busy setting up all day, and the guests would watch from the safety of the veranda.

Lucinda and Justin opened the ball together. Everyone smiled and applauded them as they performed alone for a few minutes, then gradually other couples joined in and soon everyone was dancing. As soon as Justin released her, Lucinda was besieged by gentlemen wishing to dance with her.

'This is a jolly fine evening, duchess,' one rather portly gentleman told her. 'These clothes are a deal more comfortable than the tight breeches they make us wear these days.'

'You make an excellent wizard, Sir John,' she said and smiled at her husband's cousin. 'I am so glad you are enjoying yourself.'

'I can't recall when I've enjoyed an evening more.

Your decorations are enchanting—naïve and different. Justin tells me you did it all yourself?'

'Yes, I thought it would be amusing. I copied the silhouettes from a children's book I found in the nursery.'

'Well, I like it better than some of these fancy affairs they hold in London where everything is so formal and professional—there is a bit of fun about what you've done, m'dear. Not enough of it about if you ask me. Justin is a lucky dog.'

'How kind of you to say so, sir.'

Since his remarks were more or less what everyone was saying, Lucinda felt relieved. She had not had time to send to London for professionally made decorations, but had enjoyed making them herself.

'You were always good at drawing,' Jane said when they spoke later. 'I was thinking we might employ a designer for our Christmas ball this year, but I think I shall not bother. Perhaps you will help me decide on something pretty to decorate our ballroom?'

'I shall be delighted to,' Lucinda said and smiled as Andrew came towards them. 'I was a little anxious— I did not know I was expected to have a theme until your brother mentioned it, but everything has turned out well.'

'I believe this is our dance, Duchess?'

'Yes, I believe it is,' Lucinda said and offered her hand.

It was their second dance that evening. Andrew had marked her card twice at the beginning and their first had been a waltz. This was a more lively country dance and she was soon laughing up at him as they threw themselves into the fun of it.

She was enjoying herself and it was not until the end of their dance, when she left Andrew to circulate and make sure that all her guests were having a good time, that she noticed Justin staring at her.

She inclined her head and smiled at him. His look was neither hostile nor angry, but rather puzzled, a little whimsical, as if he were trying to make up his mind about something.

She wondered what he was thinking. He had opened the dancing with her and she'd seen him dance with Jane Lanchester and one or two of his relatives, including Sir John's wife, but mostly he seemed content to move about the room, engaging his friends in conversation.

He approached her at supper and asked if she were having a pleasant evening.

'Yes, Justin,' she said and smiled without restraint. 'I think it has all gone well, do you not agree?'

'Everyone is congratulating me on my choice of a wife. They like your manner, Lucinda, and the refreshing change you have brought to Avonlea.'

'Oh…' Her cheeks burned. 'I am just being myself. I might have sent to London for the decorations had I thought there was time, but I was not sure who to use—and I enjoyed making the decorations myself.'

'As a first attempt it was well done,' he said, a note of qualified approval in his voice. 'I dare say people are prepared to be generous to a young and lovely bride holding her first ball.'

'Thank you, Justin. I shall, of course, consult your mother's diaries in the future now that I understand you prefer a more professional approach.'

Keeping her head high and refusing to let herself be hurt, Lucinda walked away from him to join her guests. Was everyone just being kind because it was her first ball? She had thought they genuinely liked what she'd done, but it seemed that Justin thought her efforts were amateur and not up to the standard he was accustomed to. If they were just humouring her, it was too lowering.

'Your Grace.' A lady she had met only briefly earlier that evening came sailing up to her. She was wearing a purple gown, but had sewn black beads to the hem and now Lucinda noticed that she had stars, a moon and a black cat repeated around the gown. 'May I congratulate you on your theme this evening? I love the way you have done these little murals and the hangings are so effective—as are the lanterns now that the light has gone outside.'

'How kind of you, Lady Morgan. I fear it is all a little amateurish, but I was not sure who to consult in the matter of decoration.'

'Not at all, I am all for using your own talent, Lucinda—may I call you Lucinda? I am giving a house party next month and I should like your advice about a theme I have in mind. Perhaps we could talk in the morning?'

Lucinda felt a rush of emotion. 'I should be delighted. I am grateful for your approval, Lady Morgan.'

'Do call me Veronica, my dear. I have every hope that we shall become good friends.'

'Yes, I hope so, too.' Lucinda swallowed hard. The lady's approval, coming as it did after Justin's remarks, had made her emotional. 'I have few real friends in society as yet.'

'But everyone likes you,' Lady Morgan said. 'You will be the toast of the town when you go to London in the spring.'

'You are so kind.' Lucinda smiled, the cloud lifting. She was by nature a happy person and she determined that she would gain friends and make her life as pleasant as possible. 'I shall look forward to our talk tomorrow—at about eleven, if that suits you?'

'Perfectly.' Lady Morgan smiled. 'I hope you did not mind my bringing my nephew with me? Simon was staying and asked if he might accompany me.'

'You mean Mr Royston?' Lucinda glanced at the young man standing a few feet away. He was, she noticed, staring at her oddly, but smiled and inclined his head as he saw her interest. 'No, of course not. Had I known he was your guest I should have added his name to the invitation.'

'I was sure that would be your answer. I believe him to be a great admirer of yours, Duchess—but, of course, everyone will be at your feet after this evening,' the lady said before sailing majestically away to talk with her nephew.

Lucinda glanced at the young man once more. Something in his look at that moment made her feel uncertain, for his expression was calculating and cold rather than admiring. Briefly, she wondered why he'd told his aunt that he was an admirer. She did not recall having met the gentleman before that night, though there was something about him that disturbed her. Her thoughts were interrupted as someone spoke behind her.

'Shall we dance?'

Lucinda turned in surprise to find Justin behind her. Her heart raced madly, because the expression in his eyes made her remember the first night they had met. She consulted her dance card and discovered she had a space; inclining her head, she accepted his outstretched hand.

'Why not?' she said. 'We have danced only once this evening. In Harrogate we danced three times that first evening and my aunt forbade me to dance with you again for it looked so particular.'

'I thought you the most perfect woman I had ever seen,' Justin replied as he swept her into a waltz.

Lucinda tingled with pleasure. To be close to him like this was both a delight and a torture. She wanted to melt into him and let herself drift away on a cloud of enchantment, but kept a little distance between them. She must remember that she was a duchess.

Her throat was tight with emotion. If only her terrible secret had not come between them, how happy she might have been. She wondered what their guests would think if they knew she had a secret child hidden in a cottage in the woods. Ladies who smiled on her this evening would no doubt turn from her in disgust if they guessed her shame.

'What are you thinking?'

Justin's voice scattered her thoughts, bringing a warm flush to her cheeks. 'Nothing in particular.'

'You looked sad—and that is my fault.' Justin's voice was suddenly deep, husky. 'I do not mean to hurt you, Lucinda. I am sorry if I offended you earlier. Your decorations are delightful. I did not mean to be critical. Mama's designers could not have done better.'

'I am a mere amateur.'

'Yes, but you have style and clever fingers. Your dress is charming. I hope you are satisfied with your ball?'

'Yes, of course. I think the costumes are more medieval than like witches or wizards, but some people have gone to more trouble. Did you see the beading on Lady Morgan's gown? She has motifs of witches, stars and cats.'

'I had not noticed. Your gown looks like fairy gossamer.'

'I am the Queen of the elves,' Lucinda said and gave him the shy smile that had been missing for a while. 'I think you must be an elf or a pixie.'

'That was my theme. You wondered if anyone would

have the courage to come as an elf, so I thought I would oblige you, but I could not quite manage the ears. I tried to make some pointed ears, but they flopped and looked more like a rabbit.'

Lucinda's laughter rang out, causing one or two heads to turn indulgently their way. 'You needed something to stiffen them. I would have helped you had you asked me.'

'I wanted to surprise you.'

'You make a fine elf king even without the ears,' Lucinda said. 'I think Jane looks lovely this evening. Green suits her, do you not agree?'

'Miss Lanchester is always elegant, but her looks pale beside yours, Lucinda. Indeed, you outshine most ladies of my acquaintance.'

'Only most?' She tipped her head to one side, teasing him. 'Your cousin Alfred was far more flattering. He said I was the most beautiful woman in England.'

'Alfred was probably in his cups,' Justin said and then looked struck. 'No, I did not mean that—you are, but he has a reckless tongue when he drinks too much wine.' He pulled a wry face and laughed, his eyes sparkling. 'I am not making it better, am I?'

'No, but I understand you.' Lucinda smiled forgivingly. This was the man she had fallen in love with. He had come back to her, at least for a little while. 'Your cousin is a pleasant gentleman, but over-fond of his wine and a little expansive in his compliments.'

'You are very forgiving,' Justin said and there was

an odd reflective expression in his eyes. 'I should try to follow your lead.'

'The case is rather different. I had little to forgive,' Lucinda said and then wished she had not as the smile faded from his lips.

'We shall not speak of it again,' Justin said and his lips tightened. 'I have made up my mind. We shall be husband and wife in truth and forget the past.'

'As you wish, Justin. I have never wished for anything else.'

Lucinda smiled serenely, but her heart was thumping so hard that she could scarcely breathe and she felt a spasm that was half-nerves, half-delight curl through her stomach.

Then, feeling that she was being watched, she turned her head and saw that Mr Royston was staring at her again. There was such a strange expression in his eyes—a look almost of gloating. A shiver of ice trickled down her spine. Why would a man she hardly knew look at her so knowingly?

Simon Royston's eyes followed the beautiful duchess as she moved gracefully through the dance. She was undoubtedly a great success. Her first ball had hit the right note and everyone was talking of her wit and talent. She was thought to be a great asset to the duke.

A sly rather unpleasant smile touched Royston's mouth as he wondered what some of these proud ladies would think, if they knew as much as he did. His gaze narrowed as the young duchess glanced at him. She turned away, a faint flush in her cheeks, as though she found his interest in her disturbing. Laughter rose inside him as he savoured his secret. The time was coming when he would put his knowledge to good use.

His misfortune was that he had expensive tastes. For the past two years or more he had been living beyond his means, his lifestyle supported by a run of luck at the tables. Of late his luck had deserted him. Royston was deeply in debt. His aunt had given him a thousand guineas, warning him it was the last time that she would pay his debts. He'd gambled on doubling his stake and lost. On the verge of fleeing abroad for a year or two, he'd stumbled across something that could make his fortune.

All he had to do was choose his moment.

Chapter Five

The ball was over and the guests who had but a short journey to their homes were taking their leave, while those who had come some distance were saying goodnight and going up to their rooms.

'It was a lovely evening,' Jane Lanchester said as she kissed Lucinda's cheek. 'I enjoyed myself so much. You must dine with us soon, Lucinda.'

'I shall look forward to it. I believe we have two engagements for next week, but nothing the following week.'

'Then keep the Tuesday night free,' Jane said. 'Andrew will ride over with the formal invitation in a day or so.'

'Yes, I shall put it in my journal,' Lucinda said. She offered her hand to Andrew, who took it and kissed it. 'I hope you enjoyed yourself, Lord Lanchester?'

'Indeed, I did, Duchess,' he said and grinned at her.

'Alack, there were no damsels in distress, but perhaps another time.'

'He is incorrigible,' Jane said and gave him a push towards the door. 'I pity his poor wife when he marries.'

'Why should I need a wife when I have a sister to nag me?' he asked, but his eyes were merry and there was affection for her in his voice.

'Is that the last?' Justin came up to her as she went back into the hall. 'A few of the gentlemen wish to play cards. You must be tired, Lucinda. I shall not come to you tonight—or should I say this morning? We shall begin our new life this new day, my love.'

'Good night, Justin.' Lucinda wasn't certain whether she felt sorry or relieved that he did not intend to visit her that night. When she was in his arms she longed for more than the sweet kisses that turned her flesh to melting need, but how would she respond when he wanted more of her?

For a moment a memory flashed into her mind, causing her to shudder. Resolutely, she dismissed it. She had faced and conquered her fears before promising to wed Justin. That evil man would not ruin her chance of happiness! She refused to let what he'd done to her overshadow her life.

Justin was a gentleman, courteous and caring. She had believed she was ready to overcome her memories and become his proper wife. However, their estrangement had left her feeling a little uncertain of her husband's true feelings. For a moment as he'd looked at her earlier, she'd felt he truly cared for and wanted her and she wanted nothing more than to be that man's wife—but she would hate it if he came to her in anger or with indifference.

She wanted Justin to love her, deeply, passionately, as she loved him, but she was very afraid that he never would now. He wanted a wife to give him heirs, a woman he could be proud to call his duchess. Lucinda must strive to become that woman.

Going upstairs to her room, she found Alice sitting up for her.

'You should have gone to bed, Alice. I could have managed.'

'It is my job to sit up for you and my privilege,' Alice replied. 'You know I would do much more if you asked it of me.'

'I have not asked yet, but I may do so quite soon,' Lucinda said. 'If I told you a very private secret, you would not repeat it to a soul?'

'Cross my heart and hope to die.'

'Then perhaps I shall soon now,' Lucinda said. 'But for now you may retire.'

Lucinda was thoughtful as she sat down to brush her hair. Justin disliked her going for long walks. If she furnished the two attic rooms with Alice's help, she might bring her daughter and Nanny to the house.

She ought to ask Justin, of course, but if he was almost ready to forgive her she did not want to spoil things between them again. The empty rooms were above the guestrooms. Except when they had house parties that wing of the house was usually empty. No one would notice if a child cried sometimes.

She was sleepy as she slid into bed and pulled the covers up around her. It was outrageous to think of hiding her daughter in the attics of her husband's house, but Angela had been coughing recently and Nanny said she thought the cottage might be damp.

'It had not been used for a while and I think the roof leaks when it rains,' she'd said. 'It will do during the summer, Lucinda, but repairs will need to be done before the winter if we are to stay here.'

She must think of something to tell the servants and Mrs Mann. Alice would be privy to the truth, but they could not hope to keep the child's presence a secret for long.

She had told the doctor that Angela was her dead cousin's child. It might be best to continue with the same tale. Perhaps if she told Justin she wanted to help her cousin's child…

As soon as he saw Angela he would guess the truth. No, she could not lie to him, so she must try to keep her secret a little longer. Perhaps she could find another cottage for Nanny and her daughter, though if they were farther away it would make it difficult for her to visit.

Lucinda knew that she had been deliberately shutting out the thoughts uppermost in her mind. Justin had allowed her one more night to sleep alone, but after that he intended to claim his rights as her husband.

Her heart was racing as she settled down to sleep. She was apprehensive, because she was not sure how to receive him. He could be charming and gentle, but he could also be cold and forbidding—which man would come to her bed?

Justin yawned as he sought his bed after the last of the gentlemen had retired for the night. As host he had no choice but to keep his guests company until the end, but he had never felt less like playing cards.

Why did Lucinda have to be so very beautiful? Watching her laughing and dancing with their guests, he had felt a hot surging desire—a need so strong that it had taken all his willpower to keep from sweeping her up into his arms and running off with her somewhere private where he could make love to her.

He was not sure when his feelings had become more intense. At the beginning he'd believed he felt affection and liking for the shy sweet girl he'd asked to be his bride, but of late he had been aware of a change. Perhaps it was merely the frustration of knowing she lay such a short distance from his bed. A few strides and he could be with her—he could take her into his arms and…but he must be patient. He had quarrelled with his bride over something that was not her fault and could not expect her to fall into his embrace with cries of love.

He did want her to love him. Justin wrinkled his brow. He had not thought love important when he proposed, imagining that mutual respect and liking would suffice—but now he knew it would not. Something had

changed. He was not sure what or why, but it had suddenly become important that Lucinda should want him
in her bed.

'She has the snuffles again,' Nanny said when Lucinda asked where her daughter was the next morning. 'She
was hot and miserable and so I left her in bed.'

'This cottage is not suitable,' Lucinda said. 'I must
make different arrangements for her.'

'The child is strong and will be better soon,' Nanny
said. 'But the bedrooms are cold and damp. I think I
might bring our mattresses down here to the kitchens
when it rains.'

'It is not fit for either of you to be here,' Lucinda said.
'Leave it to me, Nanny. I shall find somewhere for you
very soon—and now I must sit with Angela for half an
hour. I do not wish to be away too long this morning,
because we have guests.'

Lucinda found her daughter flushed and hot. She
complained of a headache and a tummy ache, but after
a while went back to sleep.

She must find somewhere for the child that was
warm and dry, Lucinda thought as she walked back to
the house that morning. Two of the attic rooms should
be sufficient for their needs. Some of the rooms needed
attention, but the two rooms she had thought in good
condition would house Nanny and Angela—at least
until she could find a better cottage close by.

Making up her mind to confide her secret to her
maid, Lucinda quickened her step. Alice could carry up

bedding and one of the footmen could take up clean dry mattresses. There was a bedstead in each of the rooms, also a chest in one and a table and chair in the other.

It was not ideal, but it would have to do for the moment.

When she had eaten breakfast, Lucinda kept her appointment with Lady Morgan. They had spent a pleasant hour talking together before some of the gentlemen joined them for refreshments.

After nuncheon, the gentlemen had played a game of cricket on the lawns while the ladies had sat in basket chairs and applauded. Justin had scored the most runs for his team and, flushed with success, he had come to perch on a cushion at Lucinda's feet when tea was brought.

At a quarter to six the ladies went up to change for dinner, the gentlemen following a few minutes later. As Lucinda was changing, the door to the dressing room opened and Justin came through. He was clad only in breeches and shirt, his feet bare. Lucinda's heart caught, her breath coming faster because he looked so handsome and there was something very sensual about bare feet and his tight breeches. She felt her stomach tighten, a spasm of what she dimly recognised as desire shooting through her. In that moment she longed to be alone with him, to be held in his arms and kissed, feeling disappointed as he addressed the maid, 'No, you need not go,' he said as Alice curtsied and prepared to leave them together. 'I came only to bring my wife a trinket.'

He laid a box on the dressing table. 'You did very well today, dearest. I think we shall have permanent guests if you continue to make them so comfortable.'

'Most are leaving tomorrow, Justin.'

'Yes, I know, but my cousins will stay another day or so—and some of my friends have already invited themselves for the shooting next month.'

Lucinda opened the box he'd given her, gasping with pleasure as she saw the beautiful baroque pearl on a slender gold chain.

'This is lovely, Justin. Thank you.'

'I think you deserve it for all your hard work.' He bent to kiss her cheek. 'I shall come to you tonight,' he murmured against her ear.

Lucinda nodded, but said nothing. She glanced at Alice as her husband went back through the dressing room to his own bedchamber.

'Is everything prepared?'

'Yes, my lady. I asked Jenkins to help me. He is very friendly towards me and he likes you. I told him you were bringing the child of a deceased relative here and needed somewhere quiet since the child has been ill.'

'Did he think it strange that I should choose the attics rather than the nursery?'

'He did not say so, my lady.'

'Do not think I like to deceive my husband, Alice. I dare not tell him for fear that he would be angry and send her away.'

'It isn't right that you should have to hide the child,'

Alice said. 'I had a cousin who bore a child out of wedlock and she was treated worse than a thief. You were not to blame for what happened, my lady. Why can others not accept the child and allow you to be happy?'

'It is the way of society. An illegitimate child is a badge of shame, Alice. I could not expect my husband to allow me to keep her as my own—but if I could keep her openly as my cousin's child it would content us both.'

'Why do you not ask him? The duke is not an unkind man—though he has a fearful temper. I thought he might kill me when you disappeared after the wedding.'

'Poor Alice. It was not your fault. Had my letter not fallen down behind the chest, he might not have been so angry.'

'I think it must have been a gust of wind that blew it there. The window was open and the curtains had tangled when I returned. I closed the window, but never saw your note.'

'I should have put it on the bed, but I was in too much distress to think clearly.' Lucinda stood up to go downstairs. 'I shall bring the child and Nanny here early in the morning. You must be ready for us and take them up the back stairs.'

'Yes, of course, my lady. You know you can rely on me.'

Alice agreed readily, but looked a little doubtful, and Lucinda knew that her maid thought she ought to tell her husband the truth. It would be the proper thing to do, but she was afraid of making him angry again.

Perhaps after they had become man and wife in truth it might be easier. If Justin were pleased with her, he would be more likely to accept her child into his house.

He was coming to her tonight. Her heart was racing as she left her room to go downstairs for dinner.

Would she please him? Was he truly ready to forgive her and to forget?

They had fewer guests that evening, but those that remained were either Justin's relatives or his close friends and the atmosphere was relaxed. Lucinda laughed quite a lot, because his cousins flattered and teased her. Because she was enjoying herself the time soon passed and she found herself saying good-night to everyone. Justin said nothing, but his eyes told her that he was eager to visit her that night.

As soon as Alice had unfastened her gown and taken it away, Lucinda sent her to bed. She put on one of her prettiest wrapping gowns and sat brushing her hair before the dressing mirror. She had just applied a little perfume to her wrists and a spot behind her ears when the door of the dressing room opened and Justin came through.

He was wearing a long satin-striped dressing robe and his feet were bare. Lucinda guessed that he was not wearing anything beneath the robe and her pulses raced. She stood up anxiously, trying to still her nerves as she waited for him to come to her.

'You look lovely as always,' he said, his eyes dark with passion. 'I have been thinking of this moment all day, Lucinda. I think we must put all the unpleasantness of the past weeks behind us and become husband and wife in the proper sense. I have been foolish to let my disappointment stand in the way of our marriage.'

'You know that I am truly sorry for any pain I caused you?'

'I believe you did not mean to hurt me. Perhaps you did not realise the agony I should feel not knowing whether you were in trouble—or even if you were alive.'

'Had you found my note you might have understood at least a part,' she said and, gathering her courage, moved towards him. 'I do wish to be a good wife to you, Justin.'

'You will be, just as I shall be a good husband,' he said and smiled. 'Come here, Lucinda. What happens now is meant to be a pleasure to both of us. I know you must have been deeply distressed and scarred by your experiences, but I shall not hurt you. I shall be gentle with you, though I hope in time you may learn to enjoy and anticipate our loving.'

'I do not fear you,' Lucinda said, looking at him earnestly. 'It was a part of the reason I hesitated to accept your offer, Justin. I wondered if I might not be able to respond, but when you kissed me I discovered that it made me want to be in your arms. If you are patient with me, I shall try to respond as you would wish.'

'You need do nothing but be yourself,' he said softly

and bent his head to caress her mouth with his own. His kiss was sweet and tender, drawing an instant response from her. She put her arms about his neck, her fingers moving at his nape, her lips parted on a breath of pleasure. 'You are so sweet. You taste like honey and wine and you smell divine.'

'I want to please you,' Lucinda said and touched his cheek. 'Show me how to be all the things you want, Justin—in bed and in the life we lead. Help me to make you proud of me, teach me what your duchess should know.'

He gave a little groan. 'I was a beast to say those things to you, Lucinda. Please forgive me. I was hurt and struck out, but I do care for you. I want you and—I am proud of you. You managed everything faultlessly this weekend, with little help from me.'

'Hush, forget it and love me,' she murmured. 'I want so much for us to be as we were before...'

Justin moaned softly and bent to lift her in his arms. He carried her to the bed and laid her down, untying the strings of her robe and letting it fall open so that his eyes could feast on her beauty. Her skin was creamy and soft, unblemished despite the child she'd borne, her nipples dark, her breasts full and firm. Watching her at the ball as she laughed and danced with the bevy of admirers she had gained so swiftly, he had felt jealous and envious of the way she smiled at her friends—especially Andrew Lanchester.

She seemed so at ease with him, laughter lighting

her eyes as she looked up at him. It had pained Justin to see the laughter fade as she met his own gaze. He had realised then that he had demanded too much, crushed her spirit, hurting her by his harshness when all he wanted was to hold her and kiss her, to lie with her as his wife.

'It is all I want,' Justin said and discarded his robe. He kneeled on the bed beside her, lifting her to help her out of the satin robe so that she lay naked amongst the sheets. Then he bent his head and began to kiss her breasts, caressing them with the tip of his tongue so that her nipples peaked and hardened. Lying beside her, he stroked the smooth arch of her back as he pulled her towards him. His hand moved down her thigh as he caressed and fondled her, his lips seeking hers in a long hungry kiss.

Lucinda did not flinch from him, though she did not reach out to caress him in return. Justin longed for her to touch and stroke him as he stroked her, but she lay quiescent, trembling a little in his arms as he loved her, though once or twice her lips parted on a sigh.

When his hand moved between her thighs she stilled, her eyes opening. He saw the fear she was trying to hide and he kissed her, moving his fingers slowly, gently, giving her time to discover that a man's intimate touch could be pleasant rather than a humiliating punishment. Gradually, she relaxed again, a little sighing moan leaving her lips.

Lucinda would not deny him if he took her now, but

despite his hunger and the burning need in his loins, Justin knew that if he took their loving all the way that night he might lose something precious. He wanted her to be eager for his touch and he suspected that she was nervous, steeling herself for what was to come, though determined not to refuse him. In his haste to make love to her he had neglected to consider her feelings sufficiently. Because of what had happened to Lucinda when she was sixteen he must take great care not to hurt her.

'I believe we shall need a little longer to know each other,' he said. 'Tonight I shall pleasure you, but I shall not enter you, Lucinda. You must learn to trust me and welcome my touch before we become truly one.'

'I do trust you,' she said and pressed her face against his chest. 'I'm sorry if I am a disappointment to you, Justin.'

'Hush, my sweet. Do not weep. Let me show you that there is pleasure in loving and many ways to please the one you love.'

Lucinda lay looking up at him with wide eyes as he bent his head and began to kiss and caress her with tongue and lips and the sensitive tips of his fingers. As Justin kissed her breasts, her navel, licking delicately at the tender flesh between her thighs, and then the most secret centre of her femininity, she quivered and trembled, giving a little moaning cry. Yet still her hands lay unmoving by her sides and she did not touch him.

As she lay trembling in his arms, he saw tears on her cheeks.

'Forgive me if I have distressed you. I wanted only to show you that it is not usually the way it was for you that night. I wanted to teach you how to find pleasure in the marriage bed.'

'I wish I could be the shy virgin bride you wanted,' she said in a muffled voice, her face against his shoulder. 'I must be such a disappointment to you.'

'No, my love, you are not,' he said and drew her close to him, stroking her back. 'Hush, Lucinda, do not weep. I am sorry. I should have waited until you were ready.'

'I shall forget,' she vowed, her words distorted because she had buried into his side like a little kitten seeking comfort. 'I shall make you proud of me. I shall learn to be the wife you need.'

'Go to sleep,' he said and kissed her hair. 'We shall do much better when you are used to me.'

Lucinda lay still beside him and after a while realised that he was sleeping. He had one arm over her, holding her to him, and she found that comforting, but she was afraid she had let him down yet again. Justin had been kind, but he needed more from her. Something she had not known how to give.

His kisses and his touch had made her feel that she wanted him to love her, but then she'd lain like a block of wood not knowing how to respond. Her father had called her a shameless hussy and her grandmother had ridiculed and beaten her for showing any emotion other than contrition.

Justin had been gentle and patient with her that night,

but she knew he'd wanted something more from her. His touch had made her cry out, giving her an exquisite pleasure, but she had given him little in return. She sincerely wished to be a good wife and please him in all ways, but something inside her had held back, perhaps because she feared to be hurt, not so much physically but in other ways.

She loved Justin, wanted him to love her, but she knew she could not measure up to his high standards. He expected so much of her and she had failed him in every way.

If he discovered that she had lied to him about her daughter, if he knew that she had been visiting her daughter in the woods or guessed what she meant to do now, he would be so angry.

Lucinda lay sleepless as the first rays of dawn penetrated the crack in the curtains. It might be better if she took Angela and ran away again. Surely Justin would be relieved to be rid of a wife who could never be what he wanted? He might be angry or hurt for a time, but then he would be glad she'd gone; he would divorce her and marry again.

A little voice inside her urged her to leave before it was too late and her husband discovered what a wretch she was, yet she could not bear to leave him. She bent over him as he slept, her fingers itching to stroke his body as he had stroked hers. She had longed to touch him, to kiss him and tangle her legs about him as he gave her pleasure, but she was afraid that he might think her wanton. If she showed desire and need, Justin might think she was shameless, as her father had called her.

It might have been better had they never met. Tears trickled down her cheeks. She loved the man she had married and, as he kissed and caressed her so tenderly, giving so much and taking nothing, she had felt that he was once more that man. Her guilt at deceiving him was sharp. Justin did not deserve to be cheated and lied to—and that was what she was doing by bringing her bastard into his house.

If he discovered the truth, he would never forgive her.

Lucinda crept from the bed and went into the dressing room, where she put on a simple gown that fastened in front and needed no assistance from her maid. She looked back at Justin, who was still sleeping as she left the room, closing the door carefully behind her.

Trying not to feel guilty, Lucinda put her regrets from her mind. She must fetch Angela and Nanny before most of the servants were up and about. Once they were installed in the attics Alice could tell people that the child was Lucinda's cousin's. In time Justin might discover what she'd done, but perhaps he would believe the story.

'She seemed a little better last night,' Nanny said. 'It was warmer, of course. I think once she is in a dry place she will soon begin to thrive. She has already begun to fill out, Lucinda—it is just her chest. The damp of this cottage does not suit her.'

'The attic rooms I have found for you are warm and dry. When the nights are cold, perhaps I can move you into the nursery where you can have a fire.'

Nanny frowned at her. 'You have not told your husband. Do you not think he will be angry when he discovers what you've hidden from him?'

'Yes, I fear he may. It may be that we shall have to leave Avonlea and find somewhere else to live, but then we shall look for a small town and I shall take up the trade of seamstress. Justin has given me a generous allowance each month since our marriage, which is paid into a bank and I have hardly touched. I dare say he would not ask me to return it if we separated.'

Nanny shook her head doubtfully. 'This is not like you, Lucinda. You have always been honest and candid in your dealings with others. I know you care for this man. It might break your heart to leave him.'

'Would you have me abandon my child to others?' Lucinda's eyes pricked with tears. 'I thought she had died at birth and I mourned her, though I had accepted it. When I first saw her—so pale and thin and ill treated, I could not bear it, Nanny. She was born of a cruel rape, but she was not to blame. Yes, it would break my heart to leave Justin, but he does not need me as Angela does.'

'I cannot deny the child needs you. When she is well she plays happily enough for hours, but when she is feeling unwell she cries for you. I try to comfort her, but it is you she wants.'

'We must go quickly,' Lucinda said. 'If we are swift,

no one will know you are in the house for a while and perhaps I may persuade Justin to let me have my cousin's child stay with us.'

'You should ask him sooner rather than later,' Nanny warned. 'If he truly cares for you, I do not think he would tell you to abandon the child—but a decent house with servants and warm dry accommodation might be provided somewhere.'

'Somewhere I would not be able to visit very often,' Lucinda said and her head lifted, an expression of determination in her eyes. 'If Justin cares for me, he should accept my child. I would have told him if he had been more reasonable at the start.'

'Well, you know your heart best,' Nanny said, but shook her head.

'Bring your bundles and I shall carry Angela,' Lucinda said and went up the cottage stairs to lift the sleeping child from her bed. Angela stirred and murmured something, but did not wake as she was carried down the stairs and out of the house.

Justin woke and slid his hand across the bed. Lucinda was not there and the sheets were cold. She must have risen some time earlier. Her perfume lingered and haunted him, but he wanted to find her warm soft body lying close to him, to make love to her again in that first luxuriously sleepy moment after waking. He knew that she was still nervous of the act of love, which was understandable after what had happened to her, but she had responded to his touch. Little did she know what it had cost him to refrain from taking his own pleasure of her. He was not sure how long he could control his need to bury himself in her sweet warmth, but perhaps she might be ready to accept him next time?

Rising, he went into the dressing room. She was not there, but he thought that a cloak she had left lying over a chair had gone. Where was she? It was not yet eight o'clock.

Had she gone for one of her long walks? He was thoughtful, edgy and frustrated as he went through his own dressing room into his bedchamber, his mind beginning to search for answers to so many questions. What did Lucinda do on her walks? She had mentioned meeting Andrew Lanchester on more than one occasion, but did she go to meet him or someone else? Did she have a lover? Was that why she had lain unresponsive, not rejecting his touch, seeming to welcome him and yet giving little of her inner self?

Justin had been patient with her. He did not wish to hurt her after the torment she must have endured the night she was raped. He had refrained from the final act because he wanted her to welcome him with no reserves. It would be wrong to force her when she was clearly not ready.

Perhaps he should have waited longer before attempting to make it a true marriage? Watching her at the ball had made him realise how much he wanted her, but he had expected too much. Women had always been eager and responsive to his touch, but Lucinda had suffered in a way that most could not contemplate.

He was a clumsy fool. If he wanted the shy trusting girl he had wed to return to him, he must be gentle with her. He must take his time, court her and make her love him again. He must curb his impatience and think of her needs, not his own, because he cared for her more than he'd realised. He'd been angry and harsh because he was disappointed in her lack of trust when she ran away. Now he must curb his temper and show his wife that he admired and cared for her; he must teach her to love him, but slowly and with infinite care.

Dressing in riding clothes, Justin went downstairs to the hall just as his wife entered the front door, which was held for her by one of the footmen. She gave the man one of her delightful smiles, which made Justin irrationally jealous. His good intentions fled. Once, those smiles had been reserved for him, but now it seemed she smiled at everyone except her husband.

He spoke more sharply than he intended, 'Where have you been? I woke and you were gone.'

'Forgive me. You were sleeping and I thought if I went for my walk early, I should return in time for us to breakfast together. If you wish, I could change into my riding habit and we could go out together.'

'Perhaps another day,' he said and frowned. 'Why could you not sleep? Were you unhappy?'

'Why should I be?' she asked, her cheeks pink. She could not look at him as she said, 'You did not disappoint me, Justin—though I fear I am sadly lacking in the things you desire of your wife.'

'Not at all,' he said and moved towards her. 'Forgive me, I am a grouch at times. I shall return in an hour or so and we shall have refreshments together in the small parlour, if that will suit you?'

'Yes, of course. Enjoy your ride, Justin.'

'We have made a start, Lucinda. We must try to do well by one another. I wronged you and I am determined to make it up to you.'

'Thank you,' she said, but turned her face away.

Justin thought she was on the verge of tears. Clearly, she was not happy as things were. His harsh manners had made him appear a monster and she was a gentle girl.

He had a temper and his pride made him quick to fire up. As he left the house and walked down to the stables, Justin made up his mind that he would not force his attentions on Lucinda again. Instead, he would court her as if they were not married, letting her come to know him all over again. Perhaps then she would be able to show some feeling when he eventually made love to her in the future. He would not let himself imagine a future that left them estranged forever.

Unaware of her husband's thoughts, Lucinda hurried up to the attic rooms that Alice had prepared for Nanny and Angela. She discovered that her maid had exceeded her orders, bringing toys, a comfortable rocking chair and cushions and other comforts from the nursery.

'She is a little darling,' Alice said, looking up as Lucinda entered the room. The child was on her lap and eating a sweet biscuit that Alice had brought for her. 'She will do so much better now that she is here with us, my lady.'

'It feels warm in here,' Lucinda said and placed her hand on a chimney breast that served a room on the lower floor. 'The heat from the rooms downstairs filters up here. I shall make sure that a fire is kept going in the room below this one—I think it must be the library.'

Did Justin often sit in his library when they were not entertaining guests? Lucinda was not sure. She recalled that there had always been a fire lit in the evenings even when there were no guests.

How far did sound travel? Angela laughed and ran about when she was well and happy. She was already looking more at home in this room, which was probably the kind of room she'd had at the inn, where the best chambers were kept for guests.

If Angela shrieked or cried—would Justin hear and wonder where the child was in the house?

She would not be the only child at Avonlea. Lucinda had seen children in the kitchen garden sometimes: a boy of perhaps nine and a girl only a little older than her daughter. She believed that they belonged to one of the gardeners and came to the kitchens to bring fruit and vegetables in their baskets. Cook always gave them one of her sweet shortbread biscuits or a rock cake. Lucinda had seen them sitting on a bench in the walled garden, munching the treat before taking their empty baskets back to the greenhouses, where their father worked.

If Justin heard a child laugh or cry he might think it was the gardener's children—or perhaps just wind in the eaves.

Lucinda tried to forget her guilt. She was not sure how long she could keep her secret from her husband, but she must try for as long as possible. What alternative did she have? Her father had made it plain that no decent man would wish to know her because of her shame. How could she ask Justin to accept her child? He would naturally refuse and then Lucinda would be forced to choose between them—and she couldn't. She could not bear to lose either of them. Justin was her husband and she loved him, but she loved her daughter, too. She wanted to make the child happy, to see her running and playing in the sunshine like normal children, though she would need to be careful Justin did not see her. At least she need not be away from the house for such long periods. Instead of spending two or three hours with Angela, she could pop up for half an hour two or three times a day.

Seeing how Alice had taken to petting the little girl, playing with her and holding her on her lap, Lucinda felt a warm content spread through her. Angela would not feel lonely and miserable with only an old lady for company. Alice would visit her often and perhaps some of the other servants might venture here when they became accustomed to the idea.

Smothering her unease at deceiving her husband, Lucinda stayed to read her daughter a story, then kissed her and left the little group together. Alice's duties were light for she was asked to do little in this house, which had an abundance of servants, other than help her mistress dress and take care of Lucinda's clothes. It was clear that she would spend most of her spare time in the attics, and Lucinda felt as if a burden had lifted from her shoulders. Now that she need not worry about her daughter, she could give all her attention to her husband.

She would try to please him in every way she could and then perhaps—when he had truly forgiven her—she might be able to tell him about her daughter.

Chapter Six

Justin visited his library most mornings and, before his marriage, had spent most of his evenings there reading or drinking wine with friends. However, since Lucinda's return he had scarcely spent more than a moment there selecting a book to read until he settled to sleep. Knowing that Lucinda was lying in the next room had kept him wakeful for many a night since his return from London. He had hoped that he would be sharing her bed more often, and he'd found it easy enough to sleep by her side, but finding her gone that morning had made him realise that perhaps he'd hoped for too much.

She had clearly not been able to rest or she would not have risen to go walking at such an early hour. He had ridden hard before joining his wife for breakfast in the parlour and come to a decision. He would not intrude on Lucinda's privacy again until he was sure that she wished him to lie with her.

That meant he would need a good book and a stiff drink to help him quell the need and hunger that he knew he would feel when he thought of her lying only a short distance from him. Had he wished for a marriage of convenience he could have assuaged his physical needs with a mistress, but he had given his last light o'love a generous gift and parted on amicable terms before he wed. He had felt such a burning desire for his bride-to-be that he had not envisaged returning to the married lady who had obliged him—or taking a new mistress.

Had Lucinda's terrible experience made her incapable of feeling passion in the marital bed? Justin considered the idea. No, he was sure she was not frigid. She had not shrunk from him and her body made its own response to the pleasure his touch had given her, making her cry out. He wanted her to be as eager for their lovemaking as he was, but the first indication that she wished for his attentions must come from her. He was not an insensitive brute and would not demand more than she wished to give.

She was so beautiful and the scent of her aroused his senses to a white-hot hunger—but he wanted her to love him, to want him as much as he desired her. Perhaps in time she would be able to forget that terrible night. He must be patient and give her that time.

Smiling ruefully as he looked along his bookshelf that evening, Justin intended ON picking out a much-used and loved volume of Shakespeare's plays, but his hand hovered as he heard a sound. It was a cry…a wailing cry that a child in distress might make. Where did it come from? He looked about him. The long room was in shadow because only one branch of candles had been lit and the light it shed did not reach into all the corners. Yet he did not think the sound had come from within the room; it sounded distant, faint and from somewhere above.

He had thought the attic rooms were empty. Mrs Mann had spoken of refurbishing them, but he'd put off the decision because he thought it was an outdated way of housing the servants. In summer the attics could become overwarm and in winter might not be warm enough. He had been toying with the idea of adding a farther building where the servants might have proper accommodation and perhaps set up a little school for the estate children. His hesitation had been because he was not certain whether to add the extension to the house or set it at a distance. Some of the servants would still need to live in, but if there were some separate accommodation it would make it possible for couples to marry and remain in service.

The notion would shock some of his friends. Marriage between the maids and footmen was not encouraged and in some houses the girls were forbidden followers. Justin had seen the gardener's children about the gardens, though they were careful not to intrude into the formal areas where his guests might walk. The gardeners had their own small cottages and it seemed logical that his house servants might wish for something similar. Over the years, Mrs Mann had complained of some of her best girls leaving because they wanted to marry. If some way of keeping them could be found, it would be more convenient for everyone.

The sound had not come again. Perhaps he had imagined it, but it was possible that one of the maids might have a child she wished to keep hidden in the house. It would not be the first time it had happened. These huge old houses had so many rooms, half of them used only for storage or shut off and empty because they needed refurbishment.

He could not be bothered with the problem now, though he might speak to his agent in the morning and ask his advice about where the new extension might be built.

Taking his book from the shelf, he turned and left the library and so did not hear the next sobbing cry that reverberated round the room.

'Hush, my darling,' Lucinda said and rocked her child in her arms. 'Mummy is here now. You are safe, Angela. Nothing can harm you here.'

'I had a bad dream,' Angela said and sucked her thumb. 'I woke and it was dark and I thought you had gone and I was back with her.'

'No, she will not find you here,' Lucinda promised and kissed her wet cheeks. 'Go to sleep, my love. I am not far from you now. I shall come in the morning and we shall see each other every day.'

The child settled and eased back into the thick blankets that Alice had brought to wrap her. Lucinda sat by her side, stroking her head until she was certain she was asleep, then she rose and walked softly from the room.

'Did you hear her cry?' Nanny asked as she emerged from her own room.

'No, I just came up to say good-night,' Lucinda said. 'It is strange for her again. She has been very unsettled, but I think she will be better here. She is not coughing now.'

'Your Alice brought her a tisane that helped her throat. It had honey in it and she drank it all. She will be much better here and Alice is helping me with her clothes and food. I had wondered how long I should be able to manage alone, but we shall do well here.'

'Alice loves her. She will be a good mother one day— far better than I can be.'

'You have done all you could. You should go back now, my lady, or your husband will wonder where you are.'

'Yes, you are right,' Lucinda said and looked at her in concern. 'You look tired, Nanny. I hope she lets you sleep tonight.'

'I am sure she will now that she has seen you.'

Lucinda nodded and left the room. As she walked down the stairs and made her way back to her own wing, Lucinda wondered if anyone else had heard the crying.

She was certain the servants would know what was

going on, but they still had one or two guests—and she thought the sound might carry to the library.

Entering her bedchamber, Lucinda saw that someone had been in and placed a rosebud on her pillow. She picked the small red bud and held it to her nose. It smelled heavenly. Who had been here in her absence? She thought it might have been Justin and the thought sent a flicker of nerves spiralling in her stomach. He would wonder where she'd been. What could she tell him?

Gathering her courage, she went through the connecting dressing room and knocked at the door of his bedchamber. There was a moment's pause and then Justin opened the door. He was wearing a blue silk robe and his feet were bare. His eyes narrowed as he looked at her.

'Is something wrong? You are not ill? I came to your room and you were not there.'

'Alice wanted me to help her with something. She had a bird in her room and she is frightened of them.'

'Could she not have asked one of the other maids?'

'It was no trouble for me.' Lucinda could not look at him as she lied. 'I wanted to thank you for your gift, Justin.'

'I saw the rose flowering and, knowing how sweet it smells, thought of you,' he said and smiled at her. Moving closer, he looked down at her for a moment and then bent to kiss her cheek. Lucinda trembled, her heart racing with anticipation. She breathed deeply, wondering if he would take her to his bed and make love to her, as he had before. She longed for his kisses and his touch and yet she was still nervous.

'You are as beautiful as the rarest flower, my love. You may rest easy this night. I shall not disturb you. I merely came to say good-night and give you the rose.'

'I see…' Lucinda's throat felt tight with disappointment. Despite her nerves, she wanted him to love her, to teach her all she needed to know to please him as he had pleased her, but he did not want to sleep with her because she was not what he wished for in a wife. He was considerate, a perfect gentleman, but he did not love her. Somehow, she had failed him once again. 'Good night, Justin. I wish you sweet dreams.'

For a moment she hesitated, wishing that she dared to go to him and tell him of her feelings, but he would despise her, think her wanton and turn from her in disgust.

She turned and went back through the dressing rooms, feeling tears burning behind her eyes. He had tired of her so quickly! She had hoped that if they lay together most nights they would become friends; the barriers would crumble and they would begin to love and to trust one another.

Once in her room she threw off her wrapping robe and crawled into bed, feeling miserable. Justin did not want her. She had killed his love when she told him her terrible secret and now, after last night, he did not even wish to lie with her.

The tears could not be stopped once she was in bed. They trickled down her cheeks, seemingly of their own accord. She did not sob, but lay quietly, rigid and shivering.

Her father had been right. She was a shameful thing and no decent man would love or want her.

Justin smothered an oath as the door closed behind her. Her perfume was in his nostrils, haunting him as it always did when she was not with him. He felt the grinding ache in his loins and knew that he would lay thinking of her, burning with the need to make love to her.

Why had he not swept her up in his arms and taken her to his bed?

The sight of her in that wrapping gown had tempted him sorely. Indeed, it had taken all his willpower to stop himself kissing her, but he'd known that if he took her in his arms his resistance would crumble. He could have lost himself in her moist warmth, but she would've lain there like a statue, trembling, afraid. No, he would not force his attentions on her and distress her no matter what it cost him. Only when he saw desire and wanting in her eyes would he make love to her again.

If he had accepted her story at the start with understanding instead of showing anger and jealousy, Lucinda might have come to him without fear. He had been at fault from the beginning. Believing a marriage of convenience based on mutual liking and respect sufficient, he had not taken the time to know his bride. Had he waited longer rather than rushing her into marriage, she might have confided in him. He could only hope that it was not too late to begin again. When Lucinda knew him better she might understand how good their lives could be.

Carrying the branch of candles to the chest beside his bed, Justin opened his book. He was an intelligent man, not a slave to his lust. He would conquer this need even if he had to go down to the kitchen yard and sluice himself under the pump.

Hell and damnation! Marriage was not supposed to be like this, he thought and groaned as he read the lines of romantic poetry. He could not think of anything less likely to dampen the fires burning inside him, but the trouble was his mind did not want to think of anything but his lovely wife.

Lucinda woke when Alice brought her a tray of tea the next morning. She pushed herself up against the pillows and smiled at her.

'This is so kind of you, Alice.'

'I wanted to ask, my lady…' Alice looked at her uncertainly. 'Do you think it would be all right if I brought the child down to the nursery wing sometimes? There are such wonderful things she could play with there and it seems a shame not to use them.'

'Perhaps—if my husband is out,' Lucinda was doubtful, but she, too, had felt it was a shame that all the treasures of the nursery were going to waste when Angela was such a lively intelligent child.

'I'll be very careful, my lady. I've told the others that I'm helping to look after a motherless child that you've taken in out of the goodness of your heart. Mrs Mann said she'd heard that you went to the deathbed of your sick cousin on your wedding day. She says you ought to have left your letter where it could be found, but concedes it was a charitable thing to do.'

'Does she believe my husband knows the child is there?' Lucinda felt a prick of conscience.

'Well, I might have let her think something of the sort, though I didn't actually lie to her.'

'I am getting in so deep, Alice.' Lucinda sighed. 'I should have told the truth in the first place, but I hesitated and it gets harder.'

'Well, my lady, I think it should be your right to have the child here if you want her. I shan't censure you—and if you ever needed help with her I should be ready to leave here and do whatever you wish.'

'I know you love her and I am so grateful. I must gather the courage to tell my husband and hope that he will listen and not become angry.'

Alice was about to say more when the door from the dressing room opened and Justin walked in. He was dressed in riding clothes and looked surprised, as if he had not expected to find Lucinda here.

'I thought you might have gone for a walk?'

'Not this morning,' Lucinda replied. 'You are about to go riding. If you will wait, I should like to come with you, Justin.'

'Twenty minutes?' His eyebrows arched. 'I shall walk down to the stables and arrange for your mare to be saddled. Can you be ready by the time I return?'

'Yes, I shall hurry. Alice will help me. I promise I shall be no more than twenty minutes.'

He smiled his disbelief, but made no further comment before leaving the room. Lucinda jumped out of bed. She washed hastily in the water left over in her jug from the previous evening and dressed in the elegant green-velvet riding habit Alice had hastily laid out for her. Catching her long hair in a net, she placed a hat at a jaunty angle and pinned it in place.

Smiling at Alice, she left the room and ran downstairs and out through the hall to the courtyard at the front of the house, just as Justin approached with a groom and two horses.

A smile of amusement touched his mouth as he saw her.

'Determined to prove me wrong, my love?'

Lucinda laughed joyously. When he looked at her that way her heart raced and she remembered why she'd fallen in love with him. It was not his fortune or his title that had persuaded her to marry him, but the teasing smile that turned her knees to water.

'No, of course not. I did not wish to keep you waiting longer than necessary, Justin.'

'I should have waited had it taken you longer,' he said, his eyes moving over her with approval. 'I do not think I have seen you wear that habit before, Lucinda. It suits you well.'

'It is the first time I've worn it. This is the first time we have ridden out since we were married.'

'Yes, it is,' he agreed. 'Let me give you a hand up, my love.'

Lucinda nodded, accepting his assistance. She was soon seated and ready for their outing, watching as he mounted without assistance from the groom. Justin gave a little nod and the groom stood back from Lucinda's horse. A lad had exercised the mare, but this was the first time her mistress had mounted her for weeks and she was a little skittish, shying and dancing as they moved down the drive. However, once they reached the first expanse of open grass, Lucinda gave her her head and they were soon racing through the parkland. Justin's horse sprinted ahead at first, but after letting it race for a short time, he brought it back to her and they rode side by side.

Lucinda glanced at her husband, laughing as she felt the breeze in her face and smelled the freshness of the early summer morning. They seemed to have entered a warmer phase of the season and it was uplifting to see the hedges bright with wild roses. Above their heads the sky was a cloudless blue and somewhere a meadowlark was trilling its sweet song.

For a while they let the horses run, then, as they came through the park to a stream beyond which lay the church and a few scattered cottages, they slowed to a walk.

'Shall we tether the horses and walk by the river for a few minutes?'

'Yes, that would be pleasant,' Lucinda said. 'The water looks so still and brown. I think they will soon be cutting the reeds.'

'Yes, I dare say they will,' Justin said. He had dismounted and now he came to assist her. He took the reins and tied them loosely to a bush, then offered his hand to Lucinda. She took it and they began to stroll along the bank in the direction of an old oak tree. 'In spring the year seems to stretch ahead with so much promise, but the summer goes too quickly. I think perhaps in the autumn we shall visit Paris, Lucinda.'

'Yes, of course, if you wish it.'

She wondered what she would do with Angela when the time came to visit Paris and perhaps London. Justin would expect her to visit friends and to enjoy a busy social life. Had Angela been their daughter she would probably have remained at the estate in the care of a nanny and various maids. As she grew up she would have had a governess and a music tutor and then, in time, perhaps been sent to a finishing school.

'I wish to please you, Lucinda. What would you like to do?'

'I am very happy here, but... Yes, I should like to visit Paris and perhaps London in the spring—or Bath.'

'Are you happy?' Justin turned to look at her, his

eyes searching her face. 'I know I was unkind to you for a while—but you have forgiven me?'

'Yes, of course. Have you forgiven me, Justin?'

'Yes, I think so,' he replied honestly. 'I was angry, hurt and it has taken a while to heal my foolish pride, but I think I have managed it. I truly wish to make you happy, my dearest Lucinda. I want us to have a good life together.'

'I am sure we shall. If we can begin again...'

His hand reached out to her, his fingers trailing the arch of her soft cheek to her mouth. He traced the fullness of her bottom lip with his forefinger, then bent and kissed her softly on the mouth.

'There is no reason why we should not begin again, is there?'

Lucinda felt her cheeks getting warm. When he looked at her like that she felt so guilty. He was being very generous to her and she had deceived him dreadfully. She would have to find the courage to tell him the truth about her daughter.

'Justin...' She hesitated as he looked at her intently, her heart racing. He was so handsome and she longed to throw herself into his arms and confess everything. If only she dared—if only he would understand and forgive her. For a moment the words hovered on her lips, but as his right eyebrow arched she lost her courage. He would feel disappointed in her again and the barriers had just begun to come down; a confession now would ruin everything and she so much wanted to see that look of teasing approval in his eyes. She wanted him to love her. 'I am hungry. Shall we return to the house and have our breakfast?'

He laughed and reached for her hand, lifting it to his lips to kiss the palm. 'For a moment I thought you wished to say something profound or important.'

'Being hungry is important,' she replied and smiled naughtily to cover her confusion. Sometimes, when she saw the man she loved, she was overcome with distress. She wished that she had told him the truth long ago. If she'd been honest with him before she accepted his proposal, none of this need have come between them. 'Do you not agree?'

'It depends on what you are hungry for,' he said and the look in his eyes made her knees feel weak. He looked at her as if he would devour her, as if he wanted her, desired her passionately—and yet he left her to sleep alone. Why? If he wanted her, why did he not claim her?

It was on the tip of her tongue to ask, but they had reached the horses. Justin helped her to mount, the touch of his hand sending shivers of anticipation down her spine. She gazed into his eyes, wishing that he would kiss her, but he did not, simply tossing her up into the saddle.

Perhaps he knew that she had deceived him. No, he could not or he would be angry. He did not love her, but he had decided to make the best of their marriage. She blinked hard. She had hoped that Justin would come to love her when she was truly his wife, but now she was not sure that it would ever happen.

Keeping her face averted as she urged her horse to a gentle canter, Lucinda held the tears at bay.

Why could Justin not take her in his arms and tell her that he loved her? He claimed he had forgiven her, but something was keeping them apart.

Justin followed his wife at a slower pace. He had been so tempted to make love to her by the river. For a moment as she looked at him, he had felt she wanted him to kiss and touch her, but then she'd spoken of wanting her breakfast. He'd felt the sting of disappointment once more. Lucinda seemed to encourage and invite, but if he carried her to his bed she would not respond.

What a coil it was! At times he would swear that there was fire beneath the surface, that Lucinda was a loving passionate woman—but she had lain passively while he loved her, showing little emotion, though her body had responded in the end. When they kissed she clung to him, moved her fingers in his hair and moaned with longing—but when he loved her she gave nothing.

Lucinda's beauty tantalised and drew him, her smiles set him on fire, but there was always a moment of reserve, a moment when she drew back. What could he do to erase the horror of rape from her mind?

It was in his mind to have it out with her when they reached the house, but then, as they rode into the court-yard, he saw a gentleman dismounting. Lord Lanchester had come calling at an early hour. Justin swore beneath his breath. At any other time he might have been delighted to see his friend and would undoubtedly have asked him to join them for breakfast, but it was deuced inconvenient that morning.

'Andrew,' he said as he dismounted and a groom led the horses away. 'How are you? I trust Jane is well?'

'Blooming as always,' Andrew replied. 'She asked me to ride over and invite you both to sup with us this evening. We have some delicious strawberries—and I think fresh salmon and venison are on the menu this evening. Knowing your passion for strawberries, Jane thought you might enjoy her strawberry shortbread, Lucinda.'

'Yes, I think we should love to come,' Lucinda said. 'Our guests have gone and we should otherwise have dined alone.'

'Then I shall give her the good news,' Andrew said and offered her his arm as they entered the house. He glanced back at Justin. 'There is a small matter of business—if you can spare me the time?'

'Yes, of course, after breakfast. You will join us, of course?'

'I ate earlier, but I will take some coffee with you.'

'Of course,' Justin said politely. He watched as his friend said something to Lucinda and heard her laughter ring out. She was comfortable with Lanchester, able to be herself—but with her husband she had that slight reserve, which placed a barrier between them. Jealousy curled through him like a viper's tongue, injecting poison where it touched.

Why was Lucinda so at ease with her friend? What had Justin done that made her wary of him?

His gaze narrowed as he watched them laughing and talking. It was odd that she had not planned to walk out this morning. Had she known that Andrew was coming here?

The thought was insidious and unworthy, but he could not quite dismiss the suspicion. Always the same question haunted him. Yet he knew even as the thoughts chased through his mind that he wronged her. Her sweet innocence could not be false and he would be a rogue to think ill of her.

Lucinda had turned her head to look at him, her eyes bright with laughter. 'Andrew says we should invite our friends here to pick strawberries next week, Justin. He says it is a custom with you to share your crop—is that so?'

'Some years we have far more than we need. If the crop is heavy, we sometimes have a picnic and let people pick the fruit. We use a different variety for jams and puddings, but the large berries for eating do not keep long and it is a shame to waste them.'

'Then we should do it this year. I asked the gardener yesterday and he said there is a fine crop, but most are not ready for another week. How did you get yours so early, Andrew?'

Her attention had returned to her companion. Justin

felt the anger build inside him, but he controlled it with an iron will. It was foolish to be jealous just because she had a friend. He would not have expected to feel such deep jealousy, but then, his marriage was not as he'd expected, either. What had once been warm affection and liking for Lucinda had become something more—a stronger emotion that he hardly recognised.

After breakfast Lucinda left the men to their business and went up to her room. Alice did not answer when she rang her bell, so she struggled out of her riding habit alone and dressed in one of her simpler gowns that fastened at the front.

She tidied her hair, checked her appearance in the mirror and then left her room. Before she went downstairs, she would spend a little time with Angela. She was about to make her way to the attics when she remembered what Alice had asked her earlier. She had not actually given her permission for the child to use the nursery, but she hadn't denied it, either. Deciding to look in at the nursery before trying the attic, she turned towards the staircase of the east wing. It was here that young members of the family were housed when they stayed and where the governess and tutors would live when Lucinda gave Justin children—if that ever happened.

Lucinda sighed, because unless Justin made love to her regularly, it was unlikely they would have the large family she craved. As an only child she had been lonely sometimes and promised herself that one day she would have at least four children. She had one of the four, but she could not look far into the future, because the cloud of her deceit was ever present. If Justin discovered that she had lied to him, he might send her away in disgrace.

She would hate to leave him now. For a little time that morning as they rode and walked together she had felt closer to him than since before her wedding.

As she approached the nursery she heard the sound of laughter. Alice had taken her reticence for approval and brought the child here to play. She opened the door and saw her daughter on the back of a beautiful wooden rocking horse. It was painted white with black spots and had a silky mane and tail and dark eyes. Angela was shrieking with delight as Alice rocked her harder.

Lucinda stood watching for a few minutes. She had not seen her daughter as relaxed and happy as she was at this moment and her heart wrenched with pity and love for the child. Angela had known pain and deprivation for the whole of her young life. It was hardly surprising that she had cried for her mother so much at the start, but now, here with Alice, she had become a different child.

This was as it should be, Lucinda thought. If Alice continued to make Angela so happy, it might be best if Lucinda found another maid to wait on her some of the time. She could take the other girl with her when she went to Paris or London and Alice could remain here to care for her daughter.

In a way that was unfair, because Alice had been

very good to her and to Angela, and she deserved the pleasure of a trip to Paris. However, she might prefer to take charge of the nursery and Lucinda would bring her presents to make up for any disappointment.

Angela had seen her. She waved to her mother, but instead of scrambling down and running to her as she had been used to do, she continued to ride the horse for a time.

Alice came to her, looking slightly anxious. 'I will take her back to the attic after she's had her nuncheon, my lady. You do not mind that I brought her here?'

'No. I can see that you understand her, Alice. I was wondering if I should select another girl to look after my clothes and help me dress when you are looking after her. Would you feel cheated or that I had demoted you?'

'I should be proud to look after the child,' Alice said. 'My sister Marie is just sixteen, my lady. She has been helping Ma for the past year, but we were looking for her to enter service. She is a good gentle girl. If you agreed, we could share the task of looking after the child and take it in turns to serve you.'

'Would that suit you, Alice?'

'Yes, my lady.'

'Very well, bring her to see me. I think it might work very well. If you take it in turns to dress me, no one will find it odd. You may say that your sister is learning from you, and when you are not with me you may be with the child—and Marie may do the same.'

'My mother taught us both to dress a lady's hair and to care for her clothes. She was in service before she left to marry. She would have liked to return to service when we were old enough to work, but the only work open to her is in the fields or scrubbing floors.'

'That is not right,' Lucinda said and frowned. 'Ask your mother to come with Marie. I might find some work she would enjoy doing—if she has some talent in sewing.'

'Oh, yes, she does fine work, much finer than mine, my lady.'

'Angela needs pretty clothes. Your mother can make her some dresses,' Lucinda said and smiled. 'Now, I shall spend a little time with my daughter—and then you must take her back to the attics.'

'I thought we might take her in the garden early in the morning? I've seen the gardener's children playing in the kitchen gardens, my lady. I dare say the duke would not notice the difference.'

'Perhaps not,' Lucinda said. 'She must have fresh air, of course. I may join you when I can—but there are many demands on my time and in future I may have less and less to spend with Angela.'

'You spend more time with her than most ladies in your position,' Alice said. 'Children become accustomed to a routine. Nanny is good and kind, but she is too old to give Angela all the attention she needs. When we have Marie to help, Angela will not need to be bored or lonely.'

Lucinda nodded. Angela had come down from the rocking horse now and was sitting with some brightly coloured soldiers. Placing a cushion on the floor beside her, Lucinda sat down and picked up one of the lead figures. She thought that these must have belonged to Justin; they looked as if they had been played with and loved.

Angela glanced at her, but went on playing with the toys. Only a few days ago she would have wept or clung to her mother, but now she simply accepted that she was there. Even when Lucinda placed a kiss on her head and then got up to leave, she hardly looked at her.

How much happier her daughter was here than in the cottage. Lucinda knew that she had Alice to thank for a large part of the change, but it was also the good food that was easily available here and the warm dry rooms that had brought about this little miracle.

Angela might miss her for a while when she went to Paris, but she would not fret as she had. In time she must learn her lessons and though Nanny was able to teach Angela her letters and numbers, she could not give her the accomplishments that a governess would.

Lucinda was thoughtful as she went downstairs. She wanted to consult Mrs Mann about various things and to arrange the fresh flowers that had been brought to the house that morning. It was not one of her at-home days so she did not expect visitors, but Justin might ask her to sit with him in the parlour and play the spinet for him.

Her anxiety over her daughter had eased now that Angela's health had improved; seeing her playing happily had relieved the pressure on Lucinda. If only she could tell Justin the truth. How would he respond? She'd seen his short temper and he had told her in no uncertain terms that he couldn't bear her deception. Would he fly into a rage and send them both away?

Lucinda knew that she would find it very hard to leave him now. It would break her heart.

Chapter Seven

Justin had gone out on business. Mrs Mann told her that he had left soon after Lord Lanchester and he was not expected back until that evening.

'I believe Mr Johnston had bad news about one of the tenants,' the housekeeper told her. 'He is his lordship's agent for such matters, my lady.'

'Yes, I think I have spoken to Mr Johnston,' Lucinda said. 'If he does not mean to return, I shall require only some tea and perhaps a scone in the little parlour for nuncheon. I ate well at breakfast and need little until tea.'

After leaving her housekeeper, Lucinda refreshed the flowers in the main rooms downstairs. She wrote a short letter to her mother, enquiring after her health and telling her that she was at Avonlea. Taking it through to the hall to leave it for franking with the others, she noticed that there was a letter waiting for her. Something about the writing made her hand tremble as she reached for it, and when she broke the seal she gave a little cry of distress.

Your husband will divorce you if he guesses that the child is yours and not your cousin's. You are a liar and a cheat and the price for my silence is fifteen thousand pounds. I shall give you one month to find the money and then tell you where to deliver it. Should you ignore my demand, your husband will learn what a shameful thing you are.

Lucinda screwed the letter into a ball. Keeping it tight in her hand, she went into the main parlour, where a fire was burning. She was about to toss it into the fire, but then hesitated. Justin had told her that if she received another blackmail letter she should give it to him and let him deal with it, but how could she? He would immediately want to know more about the child and then he would be furious with her. She had laid herself open to this wicked blackmail by keeping the child with her. Justin would have every right to be angry with her.

This deceit had gone on long enough. She must tell him the truth and then show him the letter. Smoothing the paper out, she tucked it inside her gown and went upstairs to change into a more suitable gown. Justin liked to see her looking pretty and elegant and she must not disappoint him.

In the event, Justin did not return home until six o'clock that evening. He sent her an apology and went straight to his room to change before they left to dine with the Lanchesters. The carriage was sent for and there was no time to discuss anything, because any delay would have made them very late.

'Forgive me for deserting you without warning,' Justin said as the carriage moved off. 'One of my tenants died today. His widow has five children under the age of ten and she was afraid that I should turn her from her cottage. Her eldest son should have the farm when he is older, but for the moment he cannot manage it, though he has helped his father for some time. I have been trying to work out a solution to the problem and it took longer than I expected.'

'Have you done so?'

'I discovered that the widow has a brother who was working as a labourer. He is to move in with them and run the farm until the boy is old enough to take over from him. I have promised that he shall have ten acres of his own land when the time comes if he treats his sister and her children fairly. These things do not always work as well as it might appear they should, but I think Jed Harper will do right by her.'

'What happens if she marries again?'

'If I like her husband, I may sort something out then.' Justin shook his head and smiled reassuringly. 'You need not bother your head over these problems, Lucinda. What have you been doing with yourself?'

'I spoke to Mrs Mann about the menus, arranged some flowers and then sat with a book for most of the afternoon.'

'You did not wish to go visiting?'

'I—I had my womanly courses and was in a little discomfort,' she said, looking away. 'I shall visit friends tomorrow in the morning, I think.'

'Yes, you must. I know it is difficult for you, Lucinda. You lived very quietly at home, but you need friends. When we go to London you will want to have some acquaintances to visit and invite to your parties.'

'Yes, of course.'

Lucinda twisted her hands in her lap. She was not sure that she would still be his wife by the time he visited London for the Season. The blackmail letter had made her realise that she could not keep her secret much longer. She would do her best to forget it this evening and tomorrow—as soon as she had the chance—she would tell Justin about her daughter being in the house. For now she must put her worries to the back of her mind and enjoy this special evening with their friends.

Justin was thoughtful as he dressed the next morning. Lucinda was clearly feeling a little under the weather. She had claimed it was simply her womanly courses, but he suspected that there was something on her mind— something that troubled her. Perhaps she would confide in him later if he asked what it was? He would not question her unless she wanted to unburden herself, but he believed that things were a little easier between them and if she could tell him about her problems it might drawer them closer.

He must ride out alone this morning. He had noticed

that some of the cottages at the far side of his estate looked to be in need of repair. It was his agent's job to see that these things were attended to, but he knew that some estate owners refused to spend a penny more than they needed to. He preferred to attack a problem before it became impossible to rectify and he wished to investigate for himself.

When he returned, he would sit in the parlour with his wife and perhaps they could talk…

Lucinda interviewed Alice's sister and mother. It was agreed that Marie should bring her things to the house and begin work the following day. Mrs Brown was pleased with the task she had been given and would visit twice a week and work on her sewing at home.

Feeling satisfied that things were progressing as they ought, Lucinda walked up to the nursery wing. She had arranged that both Alice and Marie should have rooms together here. It would be pleasant for the sisters and they would be able to take better care of the child that way. Angela would still sleep in the attics with Nanny, but spend a part of her day in the nursery and she would have a walk in the gardens in the mornings. It was the best Lucinda could do and might only be for a short time since she'd decided to confess everything to Justin that afternoon.

As she entered the nursery, she discovered that Marie and Alice were together and playing a game of blind man's buff with Angela. Marie flushed as she saw her new mistress, explaining that she had wanted to tell Alice her news and get to know the child.

'I am pleased to see that you are eager to begin,' Lucinda said and laughed as Marie was caught and made to don the blindfold. 'I should like to join you all, if I may?'

'Yes, Mama, play,' Angela said and caught her hand, drawing her into the game. She giggled and pushed her towards Marie so that Lucinda was caught and obliged to wear the blindfold.

Lucinda laughed and began to feel her way about the room, trying to capture someone, but they all managed to avoid her, causing Angela to shriek with laughter.

'You wait, little miss,' Lucinda threatened. 'I shall find you in a moment.'

'No, you won't. Can't catch me,' the child chanted. 'Can't catch me…'

Lucinda heard the sound of her voice, but deliberately moved another way, making the child laugh out loud again. To hear her was such a delight and, for a while, Lucinda forgot the threat of blackmail and exposure hanging over her.

'Have you seen my lady wife?' Justin asked of Mrs Mann as he handed her his gloves and hat in the hall. 'I should like a word before nuncheon. Perhaps you could hold it back for half an hour?'

'Yes, of course. I'm not sure where the duchess is, sir. I believe she might be in the east wing—the nursery floor.'

'The nursery floor?' Justin arched his brows. What was Lucinda doing there? Since they had not lain together it was unlikely she was making plans for the nursery. It was more usual to leave such things until a birth was certain. He himself had decided against doing anything until Lucinda told him she was expecting their first child, which was unlikely to happen until their present situation was resolved. The reason he had made no preparations was because his mother had miscarried so many times.

He knew that he had once had a younger brother, but the boy had died of a fever when he was but three years old. Several miscarriages had occurred after the tragedy and then it seemed his parents had accepted that Justin would be their only child. He wondered if his mother's seeming indifference towards him had stemmed from her losses—had she feared to love too much lest an accident befell her only surviving child, and was he too much like her for his own good?

He was thoughtful as he went into the east wing and walked up to the first floor, which housed the nursery. Younger family members used these guest rooms and their governesses and tutors, of which there were none at the moment. His cousins had not yet married and all his uncles and aunts were too old to have young children. Justin had often regretted that he was an only child and that there were no children in his family.

Hearing a sound, which was unmistakably a child's laughter, he paused at the top of the stairs. He could not have imagined the laughter. It reminded him of the noise he'd heard in the library the other day. How could a child be here?

Frowning, he walked along the passage and stopped outside the nursery door. Had it not been left open just a crack he might not have heard anything, because the door was stout and meant to stop sound travelling, but now he could hear the sounds of laughing voices. One was certainly a child but the others…that one was Lucinda. He could not mistake *her* voice.

Pushing the door open, he saw that a game was taking place. There were three adults and a child. One of the women was Lucinda's maid, the second a girl he did not recall having seen before—and the third, his wife. Lucinda was wearing the blindfold, and as he watched, she caught the child. She reached up to remove the blindfold and laughed down at the girl, then something made her look up at him and all the colour drained from her face.

Justin was struck first by the utter despair and guilt in her face, and then, as he looked from her to the child, he understood. The likeness between them was unmistakable. He might have been unsure had she not told him her secret, but the look in her eyes left him in no doubt of her distress at having been caught.

For a moment rage coursed through him, but years of breeding gave him the strength to incline his head and walk away without a word.

His hands balled at his sides and for a moment he

felt as if he could scarcely breathe. His mind was reeling from the shock. Lucinda had lied to him. Again. He remembered distinctly that she'd told him the child had died, though he had speculated that perhaps she had been deceived on that score by her parents. Now it seemed she might have known her child had survived all along. How could she lie about something like that? And to bring the child—her bastard—into his house without so much as a word! What on earth did she imagine she was doing? Anyone who happened to see her with the child would wonder and the more astute would piece the puzzle together very easily.

Had she no care for her reputation or his good name? To bring the child she had born out of wedlock into his house without asking or consulting him was a flagrant breach of his trust. Reaching his study, he slammed the door behind him. His feelings were pent up and needed release. Noticing a brass inkwell that he had suddenly taken an unaccountable dislike to, he snatched it up and threw it into the fireplace, where the glass inset smashed and spilled its contents onto the surroundings.

Justin's mind whirled. The house could not hold him in this mood. If he did not get out and away, he might explode.

Leaving by the French windows, he walked through his favourite garden without seeing a thing, heading for the stables and the release he needed. A hard ride might help to dissipate the rage inside him, but the problem would not go away. What was he to do with a wife who had no thought for her husband's good name or her own—and where did he place a child that could ruin any chance Lucinda had of becoming a woman who was both welcomed and admired in society?

Lucinda felt as if she had been turned to stone. The look in Justin's eyes before he turned and walked away had been like a sword thrust to her heart. He was so angry—and he had every right to his anger.

She felt shame and despair wash over her in equal measures. She had behaved in a reckless manner, thinking only of herself—what she wanted, what she thought best for her child. Suddenly, the enormity of what she had done hit her and she realised how this must seem to Justin. He had been angry before, but now he would despise her.

'Do you think his Grace guessed?' Alice said, looking at her in shock. 'It is my fault. I should not have brought her here, but she needed something more than those attic rooms.'

'Yes, she needs a proper home,' Lucinda admitted. She felt numb, unable to think or decide what she must do for the best. 'I must apologise to my husband. Please, take Angela back to her room—and do not look so devastated, Alice. It was I who brought her to the house, not you.'

Lucinda went to her own room first. She washed her face in cool water, tidied her hair and her gown, glancing in the mirror to make sure that she looked respectable. She must have looked like a hoyden when she was playing with the child, not at all the duchess Justin wanted or needed. He had requested her to remember her position and must be disgusted with her behaviour.

He had reprimanded her once before for her appearance. She'd known what he expected of his wife, yet she had not heeded his wishes and she had brought her daughter into the house without his knowledge and permission.

As she walked downstairs, her heart was racing like the wind. She was afraid to face Justin in his white-hot anger and it was a brief reprieve when she was told that he had gone riding.

She felt as if she was suffocating. Leaving the house, she walked through the formal gardens and headed for the woods. It was a warm sunny morning, the birds singing their hearts out from the trees about her. She could smell the dry sweet smell of bracken and the undergrowth, which had turned brown in the dry spell. Entering a clearing, she saw a fallen tree and sat down on the trunk. What a foolish selfish girl she had been! She should have told Justin the truth long ago. He might have helped her. Now he must hate and despise her. She could not tell him of the blackmail letter and she could not hope to pay the money demanded of her.

Tears began to trickle down her cheeks. She bent her head, putting her hands to her face, her shoulders shaking as the sobs poured out of her. It was all such a mess. She had behaved so badly and she could not expect Justin to love her or care for her again.

'Lucinda! What has happened to make you so unhappy?'

Looking up, she saw the tall comforting figure of Lord Lanchester and stood up, wiping her face with the back of her hand. He produced a large white kerchief and gently mopped the tears from her cheeks.

'Thank you,' she said and gulped. 'I am so very foolish and you must not think Justin is to blame, for he is not. It is all my doing—my grievous fault.'

'I do not think you can have done anything so very bad, Lucinda.'

'I fear you do not know. I have done such a dreadful thing. Justin will never forgive me.'

'Can you tell me?'

She shook her head. 'I wish that I could tell you, sir. I am in such distress—but I think this is something I must mend for myself.' She handed him his kerchief and attempted to smile. 'You must think me a watering pot, my lord.'

'No such thing. I think you beautiful and brave. It is clear to me that you are deeply troubled. Do you wish me to speak to Justin on your behalf? I know that he has a hot head. Maybe I can make things easier for you.'

'Please say nothing of me,' she begged. 'We have quarrelled—at least, there is a quarrel brewing. I must return and wait for him to come to me.'

'I shall walk with you. If he offers you harm, tell him he will answer to me, Lucinda.'

The fierce note in his voice made her look at him sharply. 'Justin has every right to his anger. If you knew what I had done, you might not wish to know me.'

He stopped, turned her and then reached for her hand, holding it between his large ones. 'Nothing you could do would make me think less of you, Lucinda. I know that your heart is good and whatever you have done was because you thought it right.'

'Yes, it was right for me—and for someone else,' she said. 'But Justin is my husband and he deserves better than I have served him. If he disowns me—may I come to Jane, just until I am settled?'

'Is it so serious?'

She inclined her head. 'I have not been unfaithful, yet I believe he has the right to send me away if he chooses.'

His hand held hers as she would have removed it from his clasp. 'If Avonlea is so blind that he does not know what treasure he has in you, Lucinda, I shall welcome you to my home and do all I can to help you.'

Her eyes stung once more. 'I would not ask for so much, perhaps a bed for a night—just until I can find accommodation for myself and...' She hesitated, then, 'Forgive me, it is too much to ask even of a friend like Jane.'

Before he could say more she broke into a run, leaving him staring after her.

Justin returned to the house just before tea. He had ridden off the worst of his mood, but his thoughts were no clearer than when he'd left the house earlier. Lucinda had betrayed his trust by bringing her child into the house and she'd lied to him once more. It was that which hurt him so much. Her lack of trust in him again; it was hurtful and thoughtless. He could find no excuse for her behaviour. His mother would have found her actions outrageous, nay, scandalous, and his father would probably have disowned him for bringing such a woman to his house and thereby dishonouring the family name.

Justin was, he had discovered, more hurt than shocked. He had accepted her story of being raped and would have, had she told him at the time, done his best to see that her child was properly cared for. He knew that he should properly insist that she gave up the child completely, but it must cause any woman distress to be irrevocably parted from her child. As a concession he would allow her to visit the girl sometimes in secret.

Yet was it not too late to cover up the shocking scandal she had created? His servants must all be aware of the child in the house. He was not sure what excuse Lucinda had given for bringing her here—but he hoped she had been sensible. If they were careful, the whole matter might be swept under the carpet and forgotten.

He was glad that he had not flown into a rage. It would be best if the servants believed that he had sanctioned the child's visit—for that was all it could be, of course. Justin had not yet decided what to do with Lucinda's daughter, and until then it might be better to allow things to remain as they were. To march into the nursery and have the child dragged away screaming would only make matters worse. No, he must discuss this in a civilised manner and make Lucinda understand that she could not keep her daughter here.

He would speak to her in private once the servants had brought in their tea. Surely, her own common sense must tell her that she could not continue in this way?

Lucinda knew that Justin had returned and gone straight up to his room. She debated whether to go after him and try to apologise, but decided that it would be best to wait until he was ready to speak to her.

She went to the parlour where they normally had tea when there were no guests and sat down, waiting for Justin to come. Her nerves were jangling and when the door opened she rose to her feet, feeling almost sick. Was she about to be cast out by an outraged husband?

'Lady Mariah Fanshawe,' the housekeeper announced as she entered the parlour. 'Her ladyship has just arrived, your Grace. Shall I give her the green room as usual?'

For a moment Lucinda was speechless as the very elegant and beautiful woman swept into the room and moved towards her in a cloud of expensive and slightly overpowering perfume.

'My dear Duchess,' the woman gushed. 'Forgive me for arriving uninvited and unannounced like this, but I was dying to meet you. I have but recently returned from Italy and I did not know of Avonlea's marriage.'

'Yes, of course.' Lucinda nodded to the housekeeper.

'The green room if Lady...Fanshawe normally has it when she visits. And serve the tea now, please.'

The woman looked at her and burst into laughter, a low seductive laughter that seemed to imply so many things.

'You do not know who I am, of course. How naughty of Justin not to tell you about me, Lucinda! I may call you that, I hope? We grew up almost as sister and brother after my parents died—and I was desperately in love with him until I grew up and married my darling Winston.'

'Is Winston with you?' Lucinda said, beginning to recover from the shock.

'Always, though not in the flesh. I have been a widow for the past fifteen months—which was why I decided to travel. One must wear black for such a long time and it simply does not suit me. I cannot weep and pretend that I am heartbroken. Winston was more like a father to me. He spoiled me shamelessly and gave me my own way—which was something Justin would not and the reason I turned him down and broke his heart by marrying a man twice my age.'

'Please, won't you sit down?' Lucinda was both bewildered and fascinated by the whirlwind that had invaded her sitting room. 'I was expecting Justin for tea. He does not know you are coming?'

'I lived here for years when I was in the schoolroom.' Lady Fanshawe tapped her fingers on the wooden arm of her elbow chair. She had taken the one Justin normally used and seemed quite at home as she looked about the pretty room. 'I am so pleased you have not changed this, Lucinda. I was afraid everything would be different—and I think of this as home, you know.'

'I had no idea,' Lucinda said. She glanced up as the door opened and Justin walked in, rising nervously to her feet. 'Justin—we have a visitor. Mrs Mann will bring tea in a few moments.'

'Mariah!' Justin's tone registered shock, as did his face. She had risen to her feet and moved towards him, opening her arms for his embrace. 'I had no idea you had returned from Italy. You might have written to let us know you were coming.'

'You always told me this is my home,' she said in a scolding tone and placed a kiss on his mouth, her arms going about him, her fingers playing in his hair as she ruffled it. 'Please do not tell me that things have changed. I am sure poor darling Lucinda will be glad of my company if you are always such a bear.'

'Mariah, behave yourself,' Justin said, but he was smiling at her with the ease of friendship. 'Lucinda, I apologise for this mad scamp. She has no notions of propriety at all and never did.'

'You see.' Mariah turned to Lucinda in a haze of perfume and smiling charm. With her dark blond hair and greenish eyes, she was a sultry beauty, irresistible, because she refused to be resisted. 'That is why I turned him down and married my darling Winston. He never scolded me once in the whole of our marriage.'

'You bewitched the poor fellow,' Justin accused and took a chair by the window where he could sit and look at them. 'He hardly knew where he was before you had him marched to the altar.'

'But he adored me and he was blissfully happy until the last hour of his life,' Mariah said and smiled. 'He would not wish me to mourn him, Justin. He was forever telling me that he did not know what he had done to deserve me.'

'No, I dare say he did not. Poor fellow.'

Mariah pouted at him. 'You are such a grouchy bear, Justin. I pity poor darling Lucinda. What a time she must have with you.'

'Oh, I think my wife need not be pitied,' Justin said and his gaze centred on Lucinda.

She blushed, but was saved from replying by the arrival of their tea. The next half an hour flew by as they ate tiny cakes and tarts and sipped a fine China tea. Mariah's chatter filled any silences and Lucinda found her an easy guest. Indeed, she was so at ease that it might have been her home and Lucinda the guest.

'Well, I shall go up and rest before dinner,' Mariah said at the end of some thirty-odd minutes. 'You can abuse me all you wish in my absence, Justin. No, Lucinda, you need not come with me. Mrs Mann will look after me.'

Lucinda rose to her feet. 'I think I shall follow your example.'

Justin had risen as soon as Mariah did, but as Lucinda moved to follow her he stepped forwards and caught hold of her wrist.

'I was hoping for a moment of your time, my love.'

Lucinda gazed up at him, seeing the steel in his eyes. She stood where she was, feeling as if turned to stone, waiting for the axe to fall.

Justin waited until the door closed behind Mariah. 'I am sorry Mariah descended on us with no warning. It was remiss of me not to tell you about her. We were close at one time and it is true that I might have married her had she not had the sense to refuse me.'

Lucinda stiffened, schooling her features to remain impassive. 'You do not need to explain. Lady Fanshawe has already told me.'

'Indeed, I wonder whether her version was the truth. No matter. We have more important things to concern us—the child I saw earlier. I think I know the truth, but please give me the explanation you have given my servants.'

'Alice has told them she is my deceased cousin's child.'

Justin's mouth hardened. 'At least you have some notion of decency. The likeness is not so marked that such a story would be immediately seen as false, though some may doubt it and the whispers may start if she continues to stay here.'

Lucinda's cheeks had begun to burn. 'Forgive me. I should not have allowed her to play in the nursery. I thought she would be warm and comfortable in the attic, but it was too confining for her. She was with my old nanny in a cottage in the woods for a while, but she was ill all the time and so...'

Justin's brow creased. 'You brought her here and thought you could keep her presence a secret from me. Tell me, Lucinda, what have I done to deserve such treatment from you? Do you not think you owed me the courtesy to ask if you might bring the child here?'

His quiet tones of reproach took her breath. She hardly knew how to answer him. He was very much the Duke of Avonlea. Tall, handsome and reserved, his disapproval cut her to the heart.

'You have done nothing, Justin. Of course you have not. I was...afraid to tell you at the start, because I knew...that you would not permit me to keep my child here.'

'Was she the reason for your long walks?'

'Yes...' She caught her breath. 'She cried when I was not with her. She had been ill treated, Justin. I swear to you, though, that I did not know that she was alive until the day of our wedding. The blackmail letter...'

'Ah, yes, now I begin to understand. Pray, tell me what happened when you discovered you had a living daughter? You ran away in a panic and then what happened?'

'At first my mother refused to tell me anything. My father gave my child away to the workhouse as soon as she was born, abandoned her to a terrible fate. She was given to a childless couple who afterwards had children of their own—and she was made to work. I saw her carrying slops to the midden.'

'How did you persuade these people to release the child?'

'They did not...' She hung her head, not daring to look at him. 'Angela was thin and desperately unhappy. I watched for a few days and then—I stole her away and, after a while, I brought her here to a cottage in the woods. I thought you could not want me once you knew my secret. It was my intention to ask if you would give me a little money, because I had spent most of what I had. As you know, I have a tiny income of my own and I am prepared to work for what we need, but I needed a decent cottage where we could live until I could support her and a nanny. I should not have asked for much. I thought I might go somewhere and live in seclusion with her, but then—you were angry and refused to allow me to leave.'

'Was my fortune your reason for accepting my offer?' Justin asked. She shook her head, not daring to meet his gaze. He was silent a moment, then, 'What did you hope to gain by bringing the child here? Surely you know what people will say if the truth gets out?'

'I hoped...if we say she is my cousin's child, people might believe us. Could you not allow her to stay here— as the child of my cousin? If you accepted her, people would believe you.'

'Perhaps they might and I might agree—if there were no blackmailer. Do you think he would keep his silence?' His gaze narrowed as she flushed. 'Have you received another blackmail letter?' As she hesitated, he said sharply, 'Come, Lucinda, the truth if you please. I would have no more lies. There have been too many.'

Lucinda swallowed a sob. 'I am sorry. Please believe me, Justin. I did not enjoy deceiving you. I will give both letters to you this evening—if you wish me to stay here. I thought you might prefer me to leave.'

'You are still my wife. I thought I made my position clear the first time, Lucinda. I am not willing to release you from your vows.'

'Angela…my daughter, what of her?'

'I have not yet decided what will be best for her. You must know that she cannot live here as your daughter. If we can convince others that she is your cousin's child, an occasional visit may be acceptable; she might visit us or you her—but you should move her and your nanny into the nursery. Housing them in the attics was a mistake. It must have aroused suspicions. I shall speak to Mrs Mann and explain that the child was brought to you because the woman in whose care you placed her after her mother died could no longer care for her. You were unsure of what to do with her and did not like to use the nursery for your cousin's child until I gave permission.'

Lucinda looked at him uncertainly. She had expected a show of temper, but he was calm, controlled and yet implacable. Her eyes brimming with tears, she made an emotional appeal.

'She needs me—and I love her.'

'I am aware that the child has come to rely on you, but she will be properly cared for wherever she goes, Lucinda. I am not a monster or without feeling, as you seem to imagine. She is your daughter and will be reared as a young lady. One day perhaps she may be introduced into our family as a distant cousin. I make no promises, but if you give me no cause to suspect you of reckless behaviour I shall allow you to see her occasionally. It is a better future than you could provide alone, I imagine.'

He knew that she could not provide a proper home for her child unless he gave her enough money to live independently—and it seemed he was not prepared to do so. Her experience at the cottage in the woods had shown her how difficult she would find life alone with a small child who clung to her.

'Do you think that is fair?' Lucinda asked in a small voice. 'It will be so hard for her to be taken away from her mama.'

A little nerve flicked at his temple, as though he wrestled with his emotions, but his expression did not change.

'She did not have you for the first five years of her life. She will soon grow accustomed to her new situation, which will be better than you could provide alone. Besides, what is the alternative? To live openly with the child would bring shame on a proud family name. You would destroy your own reputation and the child would carry the stigma of illegitimacy for life. Even if you changed your name and pretended to be a widow, someone would discover your secret. The rogue who blackmailed you will never allow you to disappear while he believes he might wrest money from you—or me.

'I shall not allow it. Do you not think you owe me some duty, Lucinda? I did not force you to marry me— but you gave your promise before God. As I recall, you promised to love, honour and obey me. As yet I have seen little evidence that you intended to keep those promises.'

'Justin, forgive me. I did not mean…' She choked on her tears. He did not understand how much it had cost her to deceive him—and he did not believe that she loved him. 'I never wished to hurt you.'

'Your daughter will have a comfortable life and be reared as a lady's daughter—can you promise her as much? Be sensible and consider what is best for all of us. I do not impose this solution as a punishment. For the moment I can think of no other way. Yes, I am concerned for our good name, Lucinda, but that is but a part of the whole. My way means that one day your daughter might have a chance of entering decent society—if your secret were exposed to the world, she must always bear her shame. I do not make the rules in this society of ours. I may find them cruel at times, but they remain whatever I think or do.'

She felt shamed by him. Justin was being so reasonable and what he said was true. He might have raged at her, thrown her out without a penny to live as best she could, but he was offering her the chance to retain her place in society and a future for her child. It was more than most men would have offered after the way she had behaved. Lucinda had wed him of her own accord and without telling him the truth; she had lied and deceived him and yet he was still prepared to do so much for her. Some men might have treated her far more harshly. She could have been sent away to a place of correction and her daughter hidden somewhere that she would never find her again.

Hanging her head, she said, 'Forgive me. I know that I have behaved ill to you—very ill indeed. You have every right to send me away and to disown me. I know that what I have done might have ruined us both.'

'At least you appreciate the gravity of the situation. I had begun to think you lost to all propriety.'

Lucinda blinked hard. A part of her wanted to defy him, to beg or plead, but in her heart she knew that he was right. Had there been no blackmailer her story might have held, but then she would never have known her child lived. Justin was offering her a civilised way out of her predicament; he was being generous, even kind, but although she knew he was right, it was breaking her heart.

'What will happen if I accept your terms?'

'You will continue as my wife. I shall give you your allowance and we shall entertain our friends. You may visit your daughter sometimes, but she must learn to do without you, Lucinda. You have your duty to me and to the family. For the moment there will be nothing of an intimate nature between us. One day I shall need an heir, but in a year or so you may feel able to accommodate me.'

'In a year or so…' Lucinda felt as if he had delivered a death knell. It was to be a cold, loveless union. He had been prepared to forgive her for not telling him her secret, but she had gone too far when she brought Angela into the house. She knew that beneath the icy calm there was a passionate man and that man would need someone to give him the things he did not find in his marriage. He would no doubt take a mistress, as men did when there was no love in a marriage.

He had been in love with Lady Fanshawe once, but she'd turned him down for another. Now she was a widow and something in the way she'd looked at Justin had told Lucinda that she still wanted him. It would be natural if they became lovers—and there was nothing she could do or say.

She had brought this misery upon herself.

'Do not look so distressed,' Justin said in a softer tone. 'You will make friends and perhaps I shall be one of them in time. I shall expect you to give me those disgusting letters, Lucinda. At least I may be able to solve that problem for you—even though you did not trust me to help you with others.'

'I shall give you them after dinner,' she said. 'I—we must keep up a pretence of normality for Lady Fanshawe's sake.'

'Mariah will expect you to call her by her name. She is family, Lucinda. Do not be deceived by her manner. She seems careless, but she is careful of her reputation. Do not confide your secret in her for she would be shocked.'

'I shall be guided by you,' Lucinda replied. 'If you will excuse me, I shall tell Alice to move the child to the nursery.'

'Alice is your maid. The other girl—is she to be the nursemaid?'

'Yes—they were to share the duty.'

'I prefer that they have separate duties. You will tell Alice of the change. Please restrict your visits to twenty minutes twice a day—and it is better if you do not play games. Remember you are the Duchess of Avonlea.'

Lucinda inclined her head and left the room. She felt chastened, but disinclined to weep. Justin had not been unkind. Indeed, he was behaving in a civilised and proper manner. Clearly, he did not intend to banish the child at once. He would make sensible arrangements for Angela and she must be grateful for his forbearance.

Her mind told her to rebel, to take her child and run away—but her heart told her she would regret it all her life. She loved Justin. Perhaps one day he might forgive her. She knew that she could not give Angela the kind of future Justin was proposing for her daughter. If she set up a home with Angela, she could barely afford the wage of her nurse, let alone others to take care of the house. Besides, some people would refuse to let their property to a woman on her own—she might not find anything better than the cottage that had made her daughter ill. Justin was offering to have the girl brought up as a respectable young lady and perhaps sometimes she could have Angela to stay. Her daughter would have a chance in life and might even make a good marriage.

Justin's way was best for all of them. Lucinda knew that she did owe her husband a duty—the duty to be a respectable wife that he could be proud of. If she left him now, it would bring scandal and shame on them both—and his family.

Raising her head, Lucinda went to her room and rang the bell for Alice. At the moment she was too numbed to realise what she had lost. Despite everything, she still loved Justin. She loved the gentle teasing man she had married and lost through her own recklessness. She regretted the lost love that she had cast away so carelessly. One day she might bear his children, but his manner had been so reserved that she knew she could not hope for more. His affection and respect for her had gone and she had only herself to blame.

Chapter Eight

It was not until after dinner that Lucinda had a moment to be private with her husband. Mariah had kept them entertained with stories of her visit to Italy and her journey home through France.

'I was besieged by suitors,' she said, fluttering her long dark lashes at Justin across the dining table. 'Winston left me a fortune, of course, and word had got out. I believe every fortune hunter on the continent was on the catch for me, so I came home to you, dearest Justin. You can protect me from them.'

'I doubt you need much protection,' Justin said, but did not look displeased. 'We have been living quietly, Mariah, but I suppose now that you are here we must entertain more. Your admirers will beat a path to my door. Besides, it is time we gave the summer party.'

'Another custom you have omitted to tell me of?'

Lucinda asked. 'You must tell me—am I expected to provide a theme for that, too?'

'Oh, no,' Mariah chimed in before he could reply. 'We only do that for the balls. We shall eat al fresco, of course. The servants set up tables on the lawns. We have musicians and lots of cold champagne and strawberries. I do hope there is a good crop of strawberries this year?'

'We had arranged a strawberry picking for next week,' Lucinda said, remembering. 'Perhaps that would be a good opportunity for your summer party, Justin—a less formal affair?'

'Oh, no, she cannot do that, can she, Justin?' Mariah asked flirtatiously. 'Tell her that it must be a grand affair as always. I want to invite everyone, let them know that I am home.'

'Lucinda is the mistress of her own home,' he said and looked at her, arching his brow. 'What will you have, Duchess?'

Was he truly asking or merely playing with her?

'If Mariah wants a large homecoming party, perhaps we shall oblige her,' Lucinda said. 'I shall need a list of your friends, Mariah.'

'Oh, I dare say most of them will be here in a day or so,' she said and laughed. 'We always had a house full of visitors when I lived here—did we not, Justin?'

'I believe it suited Father to indulge you.'

'Now you are being a bear again.' She pouted. 'How can you put up with him, Lucinda?'

'Oh, we manage well enough,' Lucinda replied and smiled as she saw her husband discomfited.

'Your papa was always kind to me,' Mariah said and dimpled at him once more.

'My father's health did not improve after you left. He felt himself too old to marry again and blamed me for letting you marry Lord Fanshawe. He thought I should have married you and kept you here.'

'Unfair. It was my choice, of course—though perhaps I did have a few regrets. Had we not argued so much, I might have married you, Justin.'

'You had the knack of putting me in the wrong, Mariah. I do not think you have lost it.'

'We shall not stay to be scolded,' Mariah said and rose to her feet. 'Come, Lucinda, let us retire to the drawing room and leave him to his port. He may join us when he is in a better mood.'

She swept out of the dining room, leaving Lucinda to follow. Only when they were alone did she turn with a rueful smile to apologise.

'Forgive me, darling Lucinda. I was so often the hostess here that I forgot myself. It was for you to take us through. I am so sorry. I did not mean to undermine your authority.'

Lucinda suspected that it was exactly what she had hoped to do, but she merely smiled and shook her head. If Mariah had hoped to cause trouble between her and Justin, she was wasting her time—the damage had been done long before she arrived.

'It hardly matters to me. I have not been used to standing on ceremony, but I think Justin will expect you to remember my position when we have guests.'

'Yes, of course I shall,' Mariah said and smiled at her, all charm and sweetness. 'I would not dream of showing you up in public, Lucinda. Everyone would frown on me.'

Clearly, she intended to concentrate her efforts on Justin. Well, she might find him an easier target than she had imagined.

It was only after she had said good-night to her guest an hour or so later that Lucinda handed both the blackmail notes to her husband. He took them and placed them in the breast pocket of his coat.

'Thank you. Take no notice of Mariah. She is fluttering her wings, trying to pretend nothing has changed—she will come into line if I tell her.'

'Please do not scold your cousin on my account. She is more entitled to be here than I am.'

'You are my wife, Lucinda.'

'Am I?' She tipped her head to one side. He looked so handsome and so proud. Her heart caught because she longed for him to smile at her as he had when they walked together by the river. If only he would take her in his arms and kiss her, but he no longer wanted her. 'If you say so, Justin. Good night. I wish you pleasant dreams.'

'Thank you. I doubt your wish will be granted.'

Lucinda waited, but he did not elaborate. Turning,

she walked up ahead of him, her chest tight with misery. It was obvious that Mariah had him in the palm of her hand. They would most likely become lovers before more than a day or so had passed.

What else could she expect? She had killed any feeling Justin had had for her at the beginning.

Justin looked at the two blackmail notes in the privacy of his study before locking them into a drawer where they would not be found by an industrious servant. It seemed the blackmailer had set an ultimatum. No doubt there would be another note arranging for the money to be placed in a certain spot. When that was in his hands, Justin would be ready. In the meantime he would send for his agents and discover what he could of the person threatening his wife.

Whoever it was must live near enough to Avonlea to know what was going on. He mentally reviewed his neighbours, trying to think who the culprit might be. Unless someone in the house was gossiping about his or her mistress, it would be impossible for a stranger to know that Lucinda had brought her daughter here.

Was one of the maids courting a footman or groom in the employ of the blackmailer? There must be some connection, because the note had not been long in coming after Lucinda brought the child to the house. Could her maid have a follower—or was Mrs Mann a gossip?

Pushing the problem of the blackmail to one side, Justin thought about what he ought to do with the child.

If he arranged for her to be cared for by a worthy couple, they would naturally believe he was her father, but it was better that way. A man might get away with having a love child, but for a woman it meant the loss of reputation and respectability.

Lucinda thought he was being hard in sending her daughter away, but she did not realise how harsh the laws of society could be on someone like her. Had she not married into an important family, she might not have been noticed, but as his duchess she would be the butt of every malicious tongue; she would be condemned, spat at in the street and cut by ladies she was entitled to think her equals. If the papers caught a whiff of the scandal, they would hint at it in such a way that everyone would be laughing and pointing at Lucinda. There would be nowhere for her to hide. Finding a respectable position or a decent home would be almost impossible if she left him.

Justin was not prepared to risk that happening to his wife. It was clear that she placed her child above him. He had thought she might truly care for him and the realisation that she had most likely married him for the comfort he could provide had cut deeper than he would have imagined. Despite everything, she had come to mean a great deal to him and he must protect her even though she hated him for it.

Damn it! He was not sending the child away to hurt her. God knew the look in Lucinda's eyes had made him feel like a rotten swine—but what choice did he have?

If it were up to him, he would say she could keep the child and be damned to the gossips, but it would ruin her and her daughter. No, the child must go away, at least until he could deal with this blackmailer. Perhaps then he might be able to arrange something. There was no reason why he should not take the child of a deceased relative into his home, but she looked so much like Lucinda and if the blackmailer dropped a few hints...

A school might be better than a respectable couple, perhaps. Somewhere that the child would be treated well and yet taught to behave as a young lady of good birth. Lucinda was gently bred and presumably her attacker had been brought up as a gentleman, though his morals were sadly at fault. God damn his black soul! Had he been here at this moment he would have been lucky to escape with his life.

Justin stood up and paced the room, feeling the frustration build inside him. It was little wonder that Lucinda looked at him as if he were one step up from the gutter. She must think him a heartless brute, but that was very far from the truth. Justin suspected that he had this day destroyed his chance of happiness with the wife he had come to care for very deeply. She must hate him for what he was doing, but he could see no alternative.

Lucinda would never forgive him for the way he had behaved—and now Mariah was here, confusing him and making things more difficult.

Mariah was the daughter of his father's best friend.

She had come to live with them after her parents died, because the late duke had been her guardian and the administrator of her father's will.

Justin clenched his fists. It had been such a shock to him when he discovered what his father had done: investing the largest part of her father's estate in a project that had turned out to be almost as foolhardy as the South Seas Bubble.

'How could you invest Mariah's inheritance in anything that risky?' Justin demanded of his father when he told him that not only had he wasted much of his own fortune, but he'd lost more than half of Mariah's money. 'What shall you tell her?'

'She does not need to know the details,' the late duke had said uncomfortably. 'Her lawyer will tell her what she has when the time comes—and in the meantime I shall repay what I can of her losses.'

'You have almost beggared the estate,' Justin replied curtly. 'You will leave the administration of her estate to me in future, Father. Fortunately, I was in charge of my own fortune and my investments have been sound.'

'You will not address me in that manner, sir.'

'Forgive me, Father—but as I see it, Mariah is owed a great deal of money and you cannot be trusted with managing what she has.'

Father and son had quarrelled bitterly over the affair, and even though Justin had been able to restore a part of what was lost through his own investments, she had not received much more than half of what she was due.

It was because of his guilt over her loss that Justin had begged her to marry him. By giving her a home and marriage he had believed he could make up for his father's incompetence. She had refused him, telling him that they should not suit, and then married a man twice her age, a man who had more than enough wealth to make up for any lack of fortune on her side, and she had been spoiled and perfectly happy until her husband died. After that she'd taken herself off to Italy because, she said, she needed a change of scene, and in her absence Justin had forgotten his guilt. Now it had returned.

He frowned as he recalled the way she had taken over at the dinner table. Mariah knew perfectly well that she'd undermined Lucinda's position as hostess. He ought to have reprimanded her immediately, but he felt guilty over the mess his father had made of her affairs.

Lucinda had every right to look at him with disgust. It would serve him right if his wife decided to leave him.

He wondered what had brought Mariah back to Avonlea and why she was flirting with him so outrageously. What could she hope to gain by it?

Lucinda did not weep into her pillow that night. Her heart ached but she knew that she had brought her disgrace and her grief on herself. Justin had behaved with dignity and forbearance in the face of her transgressions. He might have taken Angela away immediately and sent his wife to a place of correction until she had learned her lesson had he wished. He would not be the first husband to act harshly when discovering that he had been betrayed.

The arrival of Lady Fanshawe was, Lucinda felt, a blessing in disguise. Despite the way she flirted with Justin and her tendency to act as if she were the mistress here, Lucinda could not dislike her. She was charming, mischievous and amusing company—and her chatter made Justin smile and lightened the atmosphere, which would otherwise have been frosty.

It would be best to make a friend of Mariah, Lucinda decided. The lady would probably flit in and out of their lives at interludes and it would not do to be at odds with her. In the morning, she rose after having slept better than she had imagined and went along the landing to her guest's room.

Knocking at Mariah's door, she was immediately invited to enter and did so, finding her sitting up in bed wearing an enchanting lace wrap and looking more beautiful than ever with her dark blond curls cascading over her shoulders.

'I thought it must be you since my maid never brings my tray before ten,' Mariah said and yawned. 'I was always lazy and my husband spoiled me. I miss him very much.'

'Yes, you must feel very sad,' Lucinda said and sat on the edge of her bed. 'But you are here now and we shall do our best to spoil you, Mariah. I wanted to ask your advice about the party. I am not accustomed to holding large affairs and I think two heads are better than one.'

'You did very well with your ball, I hear,' Mariah said, her eyes very bright. 'I was told that you were both beautiful and brave—and I think that is true. But let us not waste time discussing party plans. I want to learn more about you and how you came to marry Justin. I must say I felt sure he'd remain a bachelor after I turned him down. And that seemed for the best. Justin has a temper. I do not imagine he is easy to live with as a husband?'

Was Mariah testing her? Lucinda was uncertain, but she merely shook her head and smiled, repeating her words of the previous evening.

'We do well enough together. Ours was a short courtship as we married within weeks of first meeting. I find Justin to be a dedicated and noble husband and I am enjoying getting to learn more about him with every passing day.' Lucinda was desperate to change the subject; she'd promised Justin she would be discreet about them and their marriage and she'd do him that honour at the very least.

'Now, tell me, what would you like to do today? We could go visiting, if you wish? Your friends would learn that you were here and come to visit you.'

'Oh, I called on Lord Lanchester on my way here,' Mariah said with an oddly self-conscious look. 'I dare say he and Jane will spread the word and we shall have callers before you know it.'

'I have had two at-home mornings, but now you are here there will always be someone to receive them so we shall have open house.'

'Are you always as sweet and understanding?'

Lucinda laughed. 'I have not yet made many real friends here, Mariah—though I go visiting once or twice a week and receive people here. Jane and Andrew Lanchester are good friends, but now that you are here I hope we shall be friends.'

'Oh, yes, of course.' Mariah gave her a questing smile. 'I thought you might resent me. I ought to have asked if I might visit rather than just descending on you.'

'Not at all. You must continue to think of this as your home, Mariah—and if there is anything I can do to make things better for you, you have only to ask.'

Mariah toyed with the silken bedcover. 'Andrew said you were lovely and you are. If you become too tired of me you must tell me, Lucinda.'

'I do not imagine that will happen. I think you had a reason for coming here, Mariah. You will stay while you need to—now, are we to go visiting?'

'I should like to walk in the park or ride about the estate—with you, unless you are in a certain condition?'

'I am not carrying my husband's child at the moment. I see no reason why we should not ride or walk, which-ever suits you.'

'Then we shall ride before breakfast. I shall get up

and dress at once and meet you down in the hall in half an hour.'

'Very well, I shall change my gown and join you.'

Lucinda left the room and went back to her own, changing into a velvet habit. However, when she went down to the hall she was told that Lady Fanshawe had sent her apologies and gone out with the duke.

Lucinda bit her lip. Had Mariah deliberately tried to make a fool of her or had she been tempted and acted on impulse?

Deciding that she would ride anyway, Lucinda walked down to the stables, ordered her mare saddled and rode out alone. She had not been to the village in weeks and decided that she would go there now. It was a pleasant morning and her mare was fresh, pulling at the reins until Lucinda gave her her head. It was as she was approaching the church, which stood at the outskirts of the village, that a shot was fired quite close to her, causing the mare to rear up. She hung on desperately, but the spirited animal had been badly frightened and Lucinda was thrown, striking her head against the trunk of a tree as she fell.

'Lucinda, Lucinda darling, please wake up and talk to me.'

Lucinda moaned and opened her eyes. She looked up and saw that Mariah was bending over her, patting her face with a kerchief that smelled strongly of lavender, and Justin was just behind her, frowning.

'Oh, thank goodness,' Mariah exclaimed as she sat

up. 'It was lucky we came this way. Justin heard the shot and thought it odd. He insisted on investigating and thank goodness he did. My poor darling. Are you hurt badly?'

'My head is sore where I knocked it,' Lucinda said as Justin came to offer his hand and help her to stand. She swayed for a moment, but he held her close and his scent was familiar and comforting. She knew a moment of longing, wishing that he would kiss her and tell her she was his love. Of course, he would not. She could not expect it. Tears sprang to her eyes, but she blinked them away. He did not love her; he was simply being kind. 'My horse was terrified by the shot. Did you see who fired it?'

'No, we were too late,' Justin said. He looked white and his mouth was drawn into a thin line. 'This is still my land and if it was a poacher I shall want to know where my keepers were. I shall not stand for this kind of thing. You might have been killed, Lucinda. Are you certain you're not hurt? We should send for the doctor at once.'

For a moment as he looked at her she saw concern in his eyes and was comforted. 'It was just a little tumble, Justin. Please do not trouble the physician. I do not think the shot was fired at me. It must have been a poacher— or one of your keepers shooting game for the table.'

'My keepers would not be foolish enough to scare your horse,' he said and looked grim. 'I shall have this investigated, Lucinda. I can only apologise for what happened and beg you to forgive me.'

'It was not your fault,' Lucinda replied. 'I should have asked one of the grooms to accompany me, but thought it would be safe to ride alone here.'

'And so it should be. I give you my word this will not happen again.' He looked stunned, as if the realisation of what might have happened had shocked him to the core. Lucinda smiled at him shyly, warmth spreading through her as she realised that he was truly concerned for her.

'Do not worry, Justin. I am only a little bruised.'

'You are still trembling. I must get you home.' He touched her cheek with his fingers.

'It was merely an accident,' Mariah said. 'You make too much fuss, Justin. Should we all ride on together now—unless you would rather Justin returned and fetched the governess's cart for you, Lucinda?'

'Of course, I shall do so,' he said. 'Lucinda should not attempt to ride after a fall like that—and I shall send for the doctor.'

'Please do not make a fuss,' Lucinda said. 'I am perfectly capable of riding back to the house, if you will help me mount?'

'If you are sure, you can ride with me,' Justin said. 'Mariah can lead your horse. I fear you might turn dizzy and fall, Lucinda.'

'So much fuss,' Mariah said and pouted. 'I do not recall you insisting on taking me up before you when I fell, Justin. You told me to get back on at once.'

'You did not bang your head. It was only your pride that was hurt,' he said and offered his hand to Lucinda. 'Please do as I ask.'

Lucinda gave him her hand. She did not want another cause for dissent between them. His hands were strong as he put her up on his horse, then, as he mounted behind her, his arms came round her and held her close to his chest. The warmth of his body and the comfort of being held moved her and she had to blink hard to hold the tears at bay. A fierce longing swept through her and she knew how much she was missing by their estrangement. She wanted Justin to carry her up to her room and lie beside her in her bed, to hold her and touch her and kiss her. She loved him so much and it hurt to know that he was merely being kind, behaving as a gentleman ought. The smell of horses and musk and his own scent mingled in a heady mix and made her heart race as she leaned back against him, relaxing as she had not in days.

She could have ridden forever with his arms about her. It seemed but moments before they reached the house and Justin was dismounting, letting her slide down into his arms. He held her for a moment or two longer than was strictly necessary, gazing down at her. She thought he would kiss her or say something—perhaps tell her he loved her and had forgiven her—but Mariah's voice broke the spell.

'I am hungry. Riding always gives me an appetite. Shall you join me in the parlour, Justin?'

'Perhaps, after I have seen Lucinda to her room.'

'No, I am perfectly able to walk upstairs. I shall lie

down for a little while, Justin—but I do not need the doctor, just a tisane from Mrs Mann.'

He stared at her for a moment as if he would protest, then inclined his head. 'Just as you wish, my love. I shall come up a little later and see how you are.'

Lucinda thanked him, turned away and walked up the stairs. Her eyes filled with tears. If only he meant it when he called her his love! She blocked out the pain; she could not face her unhappiness now, wanting only a warm soothing drink to ease the pain at the back of her head. She took off her habit and sent Alice to fetch her a drink, then slid under a light cover. When her maid brought the tisane she drank it and was soon asleep.

Lucinda did not know that Justin kept his word to look in on her an hour later, because she was sleeping.

Justin finished giving his keepers their instructions and walked back to the house. He was still reeling from the shock it had given him to see his wife lying so still on the ground. She'd been unconscious for a few moments and he'd feared she was dead. In those first terrible seconds Justin had understood what he might have lost. The realisation that he loved Lucinda was a blinding revelation that left him unable to do more than stand and stare while Mariah patted her cheek and begged her to open her eyes.

His relief once he'd known she was alive had been overwhelming. Yet still he'd stood there like a statue until Lucinda moved; then, he'd given her his hand, drawing her to her feet and holding her close. He'd accused her of trembling, but in truth he thought it was he who had been close to collapsing. Justin was too shocked by the depth of feeling her accident had roused that he did not know how to express it. So this was love—an emotion he had never experienced, a pain that encircled his heart and made him want to die. For had she died, how could he have lived?

Was he mad? How long had this feeling been there? Had he loved her from the beginning and not known it? Was that why he had felt such anger when she deceived him? He'd hidden behind his pride of family, but in truth he'd been hurt by her deceit, feeling that she could not care for him. Suddenly, the matter of the child seemed so much less important. He was unsure how to protect his wife from scandal and yet to banish her child seemed unnecessarily cruel. Justin realised that he must give the matter more thought.

Looking in on her she slept, Justin felt his throat close with emotion. He would ask the doctor to call in the morning, though he believed she had been lucky.

He had been lucky. She was still alive. He had a chance to make amends. Somehow he must heal the breach between them because he could not bear his life if she did not smile at him.

It was nearly time for tea when Lucinda entered the drawing room. She discovered that Jane and Andrew Lanchester were already there together with Justin, Mariah and another gentleman she did not immediately recall having met before. He was about the same age as

Justin, handsome in a girlish way with dark brows and light hair, his mouth redder than normal for a gentleman. His eyes rested on her as she entered for a moment, then flicked away almost guiltily. It was only after a moment's reflection that she remembered he was Lady Morgan's nephew. She had hardly spoken to him at the ball, but he'd stared at her most oddly.

'Lucinda, Duchess,' Andrew said and rose with alacrity, coming to take her hands and lead her to a chair next to the fireplace. It was such a warm day that no fire had been lit, but the chair was comfortable and warm because he had been using it. 'I was most distressed to learn that you took a tumble this morning.'

'Oh, it was nothing very much, but Justin thought I should rest,' Lucinda said with a smile. 'I am glad to see you here and Jane, too—I am not much acquainted with your friend, though I believe we met once.'

'Oh, Royston,' Andrew said in a dismissive tone. 'No, you would not have seen him about because he has just returned from his most recent trip to Devon.'

'My uncle has been ill,' the young man said, coming forwards to bow over her hand. 'He asked me to attend him and so I did. I believe he may have been a friend of your father, Duchess—Sir John Marston.' The look in his eyes sent a chill down her spine; it was so knowing, almost mocking.

'Yes...' Lucinda felt her throat close as she looked at him. It had not occurred to her at the dance, but now she could see the likeness between the uncle and nephew and it made her feel as if she were suffocating. That was why he'd stared at her so strangely. He knew! He knew her secret. 'I—he may have known my father.'

'And you. He spoke well of you, Duchess. He was most interested to hear of your marriage.'

His words held a veiled threat. Lucinda stared straight through him. 'Thank you, Mr Royston. I—I trust your uncle is well?'

The words were a civil lie. She wished his uncle anything but well. She could scarcely contain her anger and her distress.

'He died last week. I inherited his estate—such as it was—and all his papers.'

Lucinda could not look at him. Did he know that his uncle had raped her? Did he know that she had born an illegitimate child and that the child was staying here in this house? She was certain that he did—the knowledge was in his manner, in his eyes and the faintly insolent tone of his voice.

'I am sorry for your loss, sir.'

'I came to tell Mrs Mann,' he replied. 'Her cousin worked for my uncle for many years. I believe there was some concern that she might need to find other employment. However, I have reassured her that she is welcome to remain where she is. I may not visit the estate often, but for the moment I have no intention of parting with it.'

Why was he telling her all this? Lucinda could not

but feel that he was conveying some secret message—
that his polite conversation held a threat.

Tea was brought in at that moment. Mariah offered
her services, but Lucinda declined, saying that she was
quite well enough to resume her duties. She poured tea
for her friends and passed their cups to the maid who
waited on hand to assist her, feeling proud that her hand
did not shake.

Could it possibly have been Sir John Marston who
had sent the blackmail letters himself? The thought
made her cold inside—would it cease now that he had
died? Or was the blackmailer in this room?

She was conscious that Mr Royston was watching
her, his gaze narrowed and calculating. Had he discovered her secret through his uncle—had he then taken
it upon himself to blackmail her? How could he have
known that her child was in the house? Of course, Mrs
Mann might have mentioned it to her cousin in idle
gossip. How right Justin was to fear careless talk. Mrs
Mann had meant her no harm, but an innocent line in a
letter had given this man all he needed to continue his
blackmail. It was clear to her then that her husband's
plan for her child was the best solution, even though it
would cause her grief.

Lucinda saw too easily what had happened. Mrs
Mann had written to her cousin and told her of the wedding. Sir John learned of it from his housekeeper. Had
he blackmailed her the first time—or had his nephew

been privy to his secrets even before he died? Had they plotted it together?

Lucinda's thoughts went round and round in her head. Her friends were laughing, talking of the summer weather and the parties to be held locally, but their chatter was a muted blur.

She looked at Mr Royston, meeting the challenge of his gaze steadily. Why had he come here today? Was it to warn her that he knew of the blackmail and wanted his money?

The visit seemed to go on for much longer than was usually felt polite. For Lucinda it was sheer torment. She was relieved when Mr Royston at last took his leave, though she was sorry to see her friends follow soon after.

'Thank goodness he has gone,' Mariah said as soon as the three of them were alone. 'He makes my skin creep.'

'You mean Mr Royston?'

'Of course.' Mariah laughed. 'He was always coming here before I was married, snooping about and spying on us. He asked me to marry him once and I turned him down. Even if he had a fortune—which he doesn't despite inheriting his uncle's estate—I should never accept an offer from him.'

'I had met him only once previously at our ball,' Lucinda said, careful to hide her feelings. 'He had not called on us before. I wondered why he'd chosen to visit now.'

Mariah laughed carelessly. 'Oh, I suppose he knows Winston left me a fortune and thinks I might be fool enough to let him have it to gamble away.'

'Is he a gambler?' Justin asked, looking thoughtful.

'I know his uncle was a terrible gambler. He was ruthless when he was on a winning streak, but I've heard he lost too much at the tables and was forced to retire to the country some months back.'

'In financial trouble?' Justin arched his brows. 'Where did you hear that, Mariah?'

'Oh, somewhere,' she said airily. 'If you will excuse me, I must go upstairs. I have some letters to write before dinner. Perhaps you would frank them for me, Justin?'

'Yes, of course,' he said and stood up as she rose and left. When the door closed behind her, his gaze turned to Lucinda. 'You were distressed when Royston spoke of his uncle. Will you tell me why?'

She hesitated, tempted to keep her thoughts to herself for a while, then raised her head to meet his gaze. 'Sir John Marston was my father's closest friend—or so I thought until the night he...attacked me.'

'It was he that...?' Justin swore beneath his breath. 'The damned rogue! Do you think the nephew knows what happened?'

'I think Mrs Mann may have written to her cousin with the news of our wedding, as was only natural...' Lucinda faltered as she saw his frown. 'It would have been innocent gossip, Justin. Somehow Sir John learned of the wedding and then...'

'He decided to blackmail you and had his letter taken to your room on our wedding day.' Justin's eyes glittered with contempt. 'But then he became ill and died recently. The new letter must have come from his nephew. I had noticed slight differences in the hand. Yes, I think I have it clear. Royston must have tried to copy his uncle's writing to fool you.' He was silent for a moment, thoughtful. 'I must question Mrs Mann. I need to know who delivered these letters and when another arrives I shall interview the messenger.'

'Another?' Lucinda was alarmed, the colour leaving her face.

'Of course. There will be a letter instructing you to place the money somewhere secret—which you will do after showing the message to me. I shall watch to see who collects the package and have him or her followed.'

'What will you do then?'

'You may safely leave that to me, Lucinda.'

'Yes, Justin, if you wish.' She looked at him awkwardly. 'I am so sorry to give you so much trouble. You must be wishing that you had never met me.'

His expression hardly altered as he answered. 'There have been moments when I have felt it might have been better for us both, but there is no point in looking back. You are my wife and we must make the best of what we have.'

The regret in his voice and the barely held expression

of pain in his eyes struck Lucinda to the heart. She saw now that she had wronged him terribly by accepting his offer of marriage, without first telling him of her situation. Turning her head, she hid the tears that stung her eyes. She had asked Justin several times if he wished her to leave, but he had made it clear that he preferred her to stay, for the sake of his family name.

'Yes, I know I have behaved badly towards you,' she said in a small voice. 'Have you decided what you wish to do concerning Angela?'

'The servants believe that she is your cousin's child,' Justin said. 'She must certainly go to school soon—a school for the children of gentlefolk who cannot be with their offspring. I have heard of a very good place in the south of Devon. There she will be cared for properly and learn her manners so that one day you may bring her here as your guest. We may even find a suitable husband for her. Whatever, she will want for nothing.'

'You are…generous.'

Justin's gaze narrowed as he looked at her 'What else can we do, Lucinda? You must know I cannot allow you to keep the child here whilst that man is at liberty to ruin you?'

'I suppose you cannot,' she said. 'Excuse me, Justin. I should go up to change for dinner.'

'Listen to me, please.' He caught her arm as she would have passed him. 'Do not look so miserable, Lucinda. I can promise nothing at this time but—if it becomes possible—in time we might take her into the house as the child of your cousin.'

'Do you mean that?' Her voice caught, a faint spark of hope making her look at him eagerly. 'She is happy enough with Alice in the schoolroom—but if she must go so far away and live with strangers...' Her voice caught again and she could not go on. 'Forgive me, I shall need a little time to accustom myself...'

'Lucinda, I am not a monster. I do not wish to hurt you. Believe me, if there were any other way...'

'Yes, I know you are not to blame. Had I been honest with you at the start, this would not have happened.'

She broke away from him, walking quickly to the door and up the stairs towards her own apartments. It would break her heart to part with Angela, but she loved Justin, too, and she knew that she owed him the respect due to his name and position in society. He was trying to protect her from her own folly. She ought never to have brought the child here. Had she found herself work as a seamstress and let Justin divorce her, the harm would have been so much less. To leave him now and expose her shame to the world would be wilful cruelty and she could not do it—even though she must suffer another parting from her darling daughter. Angela would be safe and well educated, and perhaps one day they might spend a little time together.

Justin swore as the door closed softly behind her. He was angry with himself for hurting her yet again—but what else could he do? Royston had a vicious tongue and a vast circle of friends. If he chose to ruin Lucinda, he could do it simply by letting a few hints drop about the similarity between the child and Justin's bride. Nothing need be confirmed; innuendo would be enough to bring shame on both Lucinda and the proud name of Avonlea.

If it were only his name that would suffer, he would say be damned to the gossips and let them do their worst—but Lucinda would bear the brunt of society's censure. Had the child looked less like his wife he would have acknowledged her as his love child; a man in his position might be bold and ride out the storm—but Lucinda had risen high from lowly beginnings and the spiteful tabbies would take pleasure in knocking her down. He had to protect her somehow.

Justin would make further inquiries about the school and in a few weeks he would take the child there himself and make certain she was cared for in the appropriate way. He wished the girl no harm for he had seen she was sweet and beautiful and she was his wife's daughter. Justin must and would do all he could to make her life happy and comfortable.

In the meantime he must exercise his thoughts in the matter of Mr Royston. The man could not be allowed to get away with threatening Lucinda, but this business must be handled with care. Sir John Marston had been a gambler and, if Mariah were to be believed, there was probably little of his estate left for his nephew to inherit. If Royston was also a gambler, it might be possible to find a way of ensuring that he was willing to disappear and cause no trouble for Lucinda or Justin.

First he had to discover if Royston was responsible for the blackmail. However, he did not imagine the man would wait long to claim what he clearly thought was his by right—almost an inheritance since the information had come to him from his uncle.

Justin was right in thinking the blackmailer would not wait long before making his next move. Mrs Mann had declared that she knew nothing of any unpleasant letters delivered to the duchess's apartments and instructed the maids that any letters delivered by hand were to be given to her before being taken up to Lucinda's room. Since Alice knew nothing of this arrangement, having been excluded by the housekeeper, a letter was taken straight to Mrs Mann two days later in the morning. She went immediately to Justin's library, the maid following her close behind. A description of the messenger was given. He had been kept waiting at the back porch for an answer, which Justin supplied after taking one glance at the distinctive script.

'Yes, this is what I wished for,' he said with a curt nod as he tore open the plain seal of wax and read the instructions. 'You may tell the messenger there is no answer, Milly.'

'Yes, your Grace,' Milly said and hesitated, then, 'If your Grace pleases, I know the lad.'

Justin had risen, prepared to follow the boy to his master. Now his gaze narrowed intently. 'Who sent him?'

'I do not know that, sir—but he is Farmer Jenkins's second son and the Jenkins family farms land that belonged to Mr Royston.'

Justin held back the exclamation of triumph that rose to his lips. He nodded his head, waited until the girl had gone before looking at his housekeeper thoughtfully.

'Milly has been useful, Mrs Mann. You may give her an extra two shillings in her wages this month.'

'Thank you, sir. Do you wish me to continue to intercept the duchess's letters?'

'For the time being—but only those that arrive with no franking. I wish to save my wife the distress of reading spiteful letters, Mrs Mann. However, I have no intention of censoring her letters from friends.'

'Yes, sir. I understand. I must say that whomever it is deserves to be punished for distressing her Grace. The duchess is very young, sir, but everyone likes her—and I know she has tried hard to do what is expected since you returned and reminded her of her duties. It was simply that at the start she did not know what was expected of her.'

'Quite. Thank you. You may go, Mrs Mann.'

Justin frowned as the housekeeper left. Had she been reproaching him for his neglect of Lucinda at the start of their marriage? Was there an atmosphere in the house? Servants picked up on these things and if Mrs Mann had taken Lucinda's side he must have been harsher than he'd realised.

Remembering the look in his wife's eyes when they'd

spoken of the best thing for the child, Justin felt a stab of pain. How could he hurt the wife he loved so cruelly? Yet what else could he do? The question went round and round in his head. Surely there must be another way—something that did not cause Lucinda so much grief. She did not deserve to be punished for something that was not her fault.

It had surprised Justin that Lucinda should accept Mariah into her home with both warmth and kindness. He had known at once that Mariah had intended mischief, at least a flirtation, and possibly an affair—and if she could manage it, an estrangement between Justin and his duchess. Whether she had hoped to wed him herself after a decent time had passed he did not know, but she had certainly resented another woman in what she thought of as her home.

However, he had seen a change in Mariah these past few days. She seemed to have ceased her attempts to upstage Lucinda and, instead of trying to put her in the shade, seemed almost to champion her—as if Lucinda's sweetness had won her over.

Justin felt a savage cut of grief surge through him. He knew an urgent longing to run upstairs, take his wife into his arms and beg her to forgive him. Had he not believed it was impossible he would have allowed her to keep the child, because he wanted her to have everything that would make her happy. He missed that shy smile she had once saved for him, which he saw now only rarely.

A little voice at the back of his mind told Justin that it might be achieved if he were willing to put his seal of authority on the child as her cousin's daughter and be damned to the gossips. It would take courage and determination, but it might be done if he wished for it—but first he must be certain that Royston could not ruin Lucinda. Innuendo and gossip was one thing, proof another.

A plan began to form in his mind—one that might make Royston careless and thus trap him into making a mistake. For the moment he could tell only one person. Everyone else must believe that the child had gone away to school.

A grim look on his mouth, Justin went upstairs to speak to Alice. His wife's maid would need to be willing to help her mistress and keep a secret or his plan would not work.

Chapter Nine

It was the morning of Jane Lanchester's fête. At least, it was in reality the church fête held every year at this time, but Jane was the mainstay in running it. Jane decided on how many stalls there should be, what entertainment could be got for the pleasure of the villagers, in particular the children. Lucinda had agreed not only to open the fête, but also to purchase and present the small prizes for the children's games and races.

She rose early that morning and spent the first hour or two in walking to her friend's home to discuss last-minute arrangements with her and to help set up some of the stalls. The fête was held in Lord Lanchester's large park and it was there that the stalls had been set up. All manners of things were on sale, ranging from beautiful cakes and sweets made by the village women, and also some from Jane's kitchens.

'I like to make sugared fruits, brittle toffee and

marchpane treats for the children to buy with their pocket money. I dare say they cost more to make than the halfpenny we charge for a paper twist of sweets. However, that hardly matters. I would gladly give them away, but the money goes to the church fund. We must not forget that the church needs money and the fête is primarily for that purpose—though I love to see the children's pleasure.'

'Well, they may win a prize of sweets, also little gifts like a peg doll or a tin whistle,' Lucinda said, looking about her with pleasure. 'I shall enjoy opening the fête, though I wish...' She ended on a sigh.

'What is it, dearest?' Jane asked, looking at her with concern. 'Sometimes you seem so unhappy.'

'I should like to take Angela to the fête. She has never been to anything of the kind and it would be good for her to mix with other children.'

'Why can you not bring your cousin's child? I am sure there is nothing wrong in that,' Jane said. Her eyes narrowed as she looked at Lucinda's face. 'What is it— she isn't...oh, Lucinda, is it so?'

Lucinda nodded, for she knew that Jane had guessed the truth. 'Yes. My parents lied. They gave her away and I did not find her until a few months ago, soon after my wedding. I dare not tell anyone, though Justin knows.'

'Will he allow you to keep her?'

'Only until he can make arrangements for her welfare. She is to go to a good school until she is older, when she may be allowed to visit—and her future will be arranged, either as a governess or a decent marriage to a sensible man.'

'Oh, Lucinda, how wretched for you,' Jane said, all ready sympathy. 'You will never see her—at least very seldom.'

'It is breaking my heart,' Lucinda said and blinked hard. 'Yet I know it is the right thing for her—and Justin is considerate to do so much for us.'

'I know many would think so, but I feel it is unkind to separate you.' Jane touched her hand. 'If you should need help, I am always here for you, my dear friend.'

'At one time I did think of leaving and taking her,' Lucinda admitted. 'I could not do it, Jane. It would hurt and shame Justin. No, it is not to be thought of. I must bear it—and so must she, though I know it will distress her.'

'You are very brave,' Jane said. 'If you ever wish to visit her without asking Justin, come to me and I shall arrange it.'

'Perhaps we could—but he might hear of the visit and be angry. No, it is not to be thought of. I have shamed and hurt him enough. Please, may we speak of the fête?'

'Yes, of course. Forgive me.'

The conversation was turned. Lucinda had arranged to spend the day with her friend, helping to get everything prepared for the fête. After a light lunch they changed their gowns to be ready for the afternoon.

Lucinda was nervous as the time for her speech grew close, but she held her head high as she went up to the little dais and took her place. Everyone had been laughing and talking, but there was a respectful silence as she stepped forwards.

'Ladies and gentlemen, friends,' she said in her soft sweet voice. 'I am so happy to be here with you today and to open your fête for you. I am, as many of you know, the very new and inexperienced wife to the Duke of Avonlea. However, I am a very simple person and I enjoy simple pleasures. The fête is meant for everyone to enjoy and I hope that it will be embraced by all: ladies, lords and village folk, and especially the children. There are races and games for the children and lots of little prizes for them. I shall enjoy presenting these prizes and hope that all the children will enter. I am certain that they may all win something. As for the rest of you, we are here to raise money for the church and I hope everyone will give something—and that those amongst us that have money to spare will give generously. There is also a prize of a pig for the tug of war, which the duke will present as always, and a barrel of beer for the archery contest. I declare the fête open, so please enjoy yourselves.'

A round of applause greeted her as she stepped back and then somewhere music started as a fiddler began a merry jig. An organ grinder was also playing a loud tune, his monkey performing tricks for pennies, and the seesaws and swings were soon in full swing. People moved from stall to stall, trying to guess how many beans were in a jar, throwing balls at an Aunt Sally and shooting arrows at a target. Children were running, taking part in games of jumping and throwing, ball games, and blind-man's buff and many other forms of amusement. The smell of roasting suckling pig and hot pies was drifting on the air, and children were bobbing for apples and sucking gingerbread and large sticky humbugs purchased from the stall that sold all manner of treats.

It was a warm afternoon and the scent of roses and honeysuckle seemed to drift above the other enticing smells whenever a breeze blew from the direction of Jane's precious gardens. Busy applauding the children and presenting prizes, Lucinda had no chance to regret that she had not been able to bring her daughter. When she suddenly saw the child playing with others at a game of fishing with little rods for trinkets out of a glass tank, she felt a shock of pleasure mixed with apprehension. Alice and her sister Marie had brought the child; they had not asked her permission, nor had they told her of their intention. Had they done so she would have refused, much though it would have hurt her to do so. However, now that the child was here, she could not bring herself to send her away.

As yet she had seen nothing of Justin and did not know if he meant to put in a brief appearance before the end of the afternoon. She could only hope now that he would not, but her hopes were dashed as a little later she saw him walking towards her, a look of disapproval on his handsome face. Her pulses raced at the sight of him. She loved her husband so very much and she hated to be always quarrelling with him.

Please let him not be angry again, Lucinda prayed silently. It had been a happy day and she did not wish to argue with him. He had Mariah on his arm and she guessed that it was their guest who had prevailed upon him to visit. Lucinda had asked if she would come, but Mariah had not known if she could be bothered.

'These fêtes are all the same,' she'd said in a bored voice. 'One is obliged to attend if one is opening the thing, but otherwise they are sorry stuff.'

Now she was here and Justin with her—and he had seen Angela with Alice and her sister. Lucinda braced herself. He would not scold her here, but she would feel his displeasure.

'Duchess—Lucinda.' Andrew Lanchester's voice cut into her thoughts. 'What a splendid afternoon. Are you enjoying yourself? But I need not ask. You have been wonderful with the children and much admired. Ah, here comes Justin and the lovely Mariah. I shall tell him what a success his duchess is with the common folk.'

'Lucinda,' Mariah said before he could speak. 'You look flushed, dearest. Have you been playing games with the children? Everyone is singing your praises, telling us how good you are with them, and how much you are admired.'

Lucinda's flushed cheeks might have been due to another reason, but she smiled and said, 'You are right to think that I enjoy seeing children enjoying themselves, Mariah. I know the fête is to raise money for the church, but it is good to see children happy, do you not think so?'

'I suppose so,' Mariah replied, still looking bored.

Andrew smiled at Lucinda and then offered Mariah his arm. 'Come, my lady, will you not allow me to show you some of the delights of the fête? Perhaps I could buy you a bag of toffee or some such delight?'

Mariah raised her brows. 'Really, Lanchester—do you imagine I should want sticky toffee?'

'Perhaps a cup of iced lemonade in the house?' he said and drew her away, leaving Lucinda alone with her husband.

Justin looked at her oddly. 'What did you mean by bringing Angela here?'

'I would not have done so without asking your permission, Justin. I fear that Alice acted on her own impulse. I will, of course, have a stern word with her. I will instruct her to take Angela back to Avonlea.'

'I dare say it has done no harm. Most people don't seem to have made any connection between you two as yet—but should spiteful tongues begin to wag it would be a different matter. I believe I shall take her to the place I told you of next week.'

Lucinda blinked hard, her nails curving into her palms. 'If you think it best, Justin.'

'Pray do not look at me as if I am a monster,' he said stiffly. 'You know we have no choice for the moment.'

'Yes, of course.' Lucinda struggled to control her distress, though the tears were burning behind her eyes. 'Excuse me, Justin. I believe Jane needs me. I shall see you this evening.'

'Perhaps one day she may visit us—and sooner than you imagine. I shall speak to you at home. Please come to the study before dinner.'

'Yes, if you wish.' Lifting her head, Lucinda walked away. She wanted nothing more than to hide away and weep.

How proud and beautiful Lucinda looked. Justin frowned. Mariah was right to say that everyone was praising her. If only he could cast aside his own doubts and show Lucinda how deeply he had come to care for her.

He blamed himself for the breach between himself and his wife. Justin was not an unjust man and the hurt look in her eyes when he'd spoken of taking her child to school had struck him to the heart. Yet what else could he do? If he allowed the child to remain rumours might start and it only needed a few words from Royston for a tale to spread. Only if he could catch Royston out would he be able to protect his wife from the man's spiteful tongue.

Royston would be careful not to let Justin know of the blackmail—but he might not be as careful of another. His brow furrowing, Justin glanced towards Andrew Lanchester standing in the sun and laughing with Mariah.

Could he trust Lanchester with Lucinda's secret? He was certain that Jane Lanchester knew the truth, but he believed she would not have confided in her brother. Alone, Justin might find it difficult to trap the blackmailer, but with Andrew's help a plan might be worked out. It might mean that Andrew Lanchester would not think quite so highly of Lucinda—but that was surely a small price to pay. He would not disclose the secret to another, of that much Justin was certain.

Yet perhaps he would be wronging Lucinda by revealing her secret to a man she liked. Justin swore beneath his breath. It was not his secret to reveal. He must ask for Lanchester's help, but without revealing Lucinda's shame—not for his pride's sake, but for hers.

Glancing about him, Justin saw that his wife was not to be seen. He frowned, wondering where she had gone and why she had left the fête when she had seemed to be enjoying herself so much.

Lucinda took sanctuary in Lord Lanchester's beautiful summerhouse. She sat on a padded couch and bent her head, burying her face in her hands. Justin's harsh words had brought her almost to tears, but she had been determined to smile and carry on with her duties—until that hateful man had come up to her as she stood watching the egg-and-spoon race.

'How charming and innocent the children look,' Royston purred in a voice so soft and low that only she could hear. 'And your daughter is enjoying herself so much. I wonder that your husband allows your shame to be seen—unless he truly believes the lying tale you have put about in your household.'

Lucinda stared at him, feeling all the warmth and pleasure of the day drain away as she saw his spiteful gaze. 'I do not understand you, sir. I think you are mistaken. I have no daughter.'

'You may fool others, but you cannot deceive me,' Royston said. 'My uncle confessed his sin to the priest as he lay dying. I stood outside his bedchamber and listened, and then I looked through his things and found the evidence I needed. He had written down the date of your wedding and details of your daughter's whereabouts, which he meant to sell to you for ten thousand pounds. However, he died before he could send the second letter. You surprised him when you ran off and found your daughter without his help.'

'You are a liar, sir. I have no idea of what you speak.' Lucinda was trembling inside, but she held herself proudly.

'My uncle no longer needs your money to clear his gambling debts—but I have been cheated of my inheritance by his folly and I intend to recoup my losses from you. The price is now twenty thousand. Each week you delay will put the price up by five thousand pounds. If I were you, I should follow the instructions in the letter I sent or you will be very sorry.'

Lucinda had no idea what he meant and she was too distressed to ask. Lifting her head defiantly, she said,

'Again, I say you are mistaken. You have no proof of your assertions, sir.'

'That is where you are mistaken, Duchess. I have the sworn testimony of the doctor who delivered the child—and of a servant who took the child from the room.'

Lucinda swallowed hard. 'It is only the word of paid servants against mine. I shall simply deny whatever you say.'

'Such a story does not need to be proved,' Royston replied. 'A word here and there and your reputation is destroyed. People love a scandal and they will laugh behind their fans. Some will cut you, others will sneer at you—and you will find it impossible to make friends with respectable ladies.'

'You have a spiteful tongue, sir,' Lucinda replied with dignity. 'If you wish to tell your lies, you must do so—to my husband. He will know how to deal with you. Please excuse me now.'

'You would do better to pay me, Duchess—or your pride will take a tumble.' He hesitated then, 'I could have shot you, you know. The day you took a tumble from your horse. I fired into the air to scare the beast—but had I wished I could have killed you and none the wiser. I make a formidable enemy, Duchess, remember that.'

She walked away from him, seeking privacy. How could he say such a wicked thing? Now the tears fell, her shoulders shaking as she wept bitter tears. Justin would send her child away as soon as she told him of Royston's threats.

'Duchess—Lucinda.' Andrew Lanchester's voice made her bring her head up. He came to her and sat on the bench beside her, reaching for her hands and holding them firmly. 'You were happy and now in such distress. Tell me, who has upset you so? If it was Justin, I shall speak to him and—'

'No, it was not Justin,' Lucinda caught back a sob of despair. 'I cannot tell you—it is too shaming. You would turn from me in disgust.'

'Believe me, I shall not. Have you killed someone?'

Her eyes flew to his, seeing the teasing look. 'Nothing quite that dreadful, but...I am being blackmailed by a rogue who threatens to destroy me socially and thereby ruin Justin's good name.'

'May I ask the name of this rogue?'

'Mr Royston.' Lucinda clasped her trembling hands before her. 'His uncle—Sir John Marston—raped me when I was sixteen. He came into my bedchamber one Christmas and forced himself on me. He then threatened to ruin my father if I told anyone. I had a child, which was taken from me at birth. I believed her dead, but on my wedding day I was told she lived and offered the chance to find her for ten thousand pounds.'

'Good grief! No wonder you ran away as you did.' Andrew stared at her for a moment, then captured her restless hands and held them. 'Sir John is dead, so that must mean his nephew discovered your secret and is now blackmailing you in his uncle's place—am I right?'

'Yes.' Lucinda looked at him. 'Have I disgusted you?'

'Royston and his uncle disgust me, as do all creatures of that sort—you remain what you always were, Lucinda—beautiful, innocent and lovely of nature.'

'You—you are too kind…'

'Does Justin know?'

'Yes. He intends to send my daughter to a good school next week, though I may be allowed to see her when she is older. Yet I think it will not be enough. Royston demands twenty thousand pounds and the price goes up each week I delay payment.'

'The devil he does!' Andrew looked angry. 'The damned fellow—to threaten you so. I shall make it my business to teach him a lesson he will not easily forget.'

'No!' Lucinda caught his hand. 'Justin says he will deal with the man. He might not wish for your help in this matter.'

'My dearest Lucinda, I would not for the world interfere between you and Justin, but if he knows of this he must act instantly. Believe me, this man will not trouble you again.'

'What do you mean to do?'

Andrew smiled. He stood up, gave her his hand to help her to rise and then handed her a clean white kerchief. 'Dry your face, my dear friend, and do not ask. Believe me, this ends here. Go back to the fête and do not give this horrid business another thought. I thank you for giving me your confidence and I shall rid you of this anxiety.'

'You make me feel much better,' Lucinda said. 'But please do nothing that would bring trouble to yourself or Jane.'

'You need not fear for me,' Andrew replied. 'Leave the matter to me and forget it, Lucinda.'

'Thank you. I do not know what else to say, sir.'

'You need say nothing more. Go and find my sister and enjoy the afternoon, Duchess.'

'Yes, I shall, thank you.'

Lucinda walked away from him. He had been so kind. Yet how could he force Mr Royston to keep her secret? She feared that threats would only make the man more spiteful.

Had she been privileged to see the subsequent meeting between the two a little later that afternoon, Lucinda would have been very surprised indeed. She might have expected threats or even an offer to pay the blackmail demand, but the cordial invitation to supper and cards would have baffled her.

She made an effort to enjoy the rest of the afternoon, and when she went down to the library before dinner that evening she met Justin with an air of calmness that belied the torment in her mind. Ought she to tell him what Royston had said to her—and should she confess that she had confided her secret to Andrew Lanchester?

'Lucinda, my dear,' Justin greeted her kindly. 'I wanted to tell you how pleased I am with what you did at the fête. I may have been a little harsh earlier, but in sending the child away I am acting for your sake as much as mine. Believe me, for the moment it is for the best.'

'I shall never believe that it is for the best. She will be unhappy and so shall I—but I do accept that you are doing what you think right. You have not been harsh, for you might have sent Angela away immediately, but you gave me a little time to accustom myself to the idea and I am grateful.'

'Would you wish to accompany us when I take her to school?'

'I think that might make it harder for us both. I believe it will be better if Alice goes with you and I say goodbye here.'

'If that is your wish.' Justin frowned. 'Perhaps if this matter of blackmail is settled, you may visit her and have her here during the holidays.'

'You are very kind.' Lucinda took a deep breath. 'I should tell you that Royston threatened me at the fête this afternoon—the price has now gone up to twenty thousand pounds and will continue to rise each week unless I pay him.'

'Royston spoke to you this afternoon?' Justin looked astonished. 'The devil he did! Why did you not tell me at once?'

'I was too distressed...' Lucinda hesitated, then, deciding that honesty was best, 'Royston fired the shot that made my horse throw me. He told me that he could kill me if he wished and I believed he would do it. I went to the summerhouse to think and was in some distress when Andrew Lanchester found me there. He asked me what was wrong and—and I told him the truth. He vowed that he would deal with Royston and that I should not be troubled again.'

'Lanchester said that?' Justin's brows rose. 'I wonder that you cared to share your secret with him, Lucinda.'

'He—he has been very kind. I thought my secret might give him a disgust of me, but he says it has not. He blames Sir John and Royston—and I think he means to give Mr Royston a thrashing.'

'As if that would help,' Justin said and frowned. 'I had wondered if I should confide in him—indeed, I meant to ask if I might disclose a part of your secret, because I think this matter needs to be handled delicately and two of us might do it easier than one. What you have told me about Royston firing that shot means he is more dangerous than I had thought.'

'Forgive me for pre-empting you. I was feeling very distressed and he was so kind…'

Justin looked thoughtful. 'I must just hope that he does not do anything foolish. If we did not have guests this evening, I would ride over there and tell Lanchester what is on my mind. As it is I must wait until the morning and hope no harm is done in the meantime.'

'I am truly sorry.'

He shook his head. 'It was not your fault. I have handled this affair badly from the start. Had I been kinder and more understanding you would have come to me instead of confiding in your friend. I allowed my pride to come between us, Lucinda—and for that I ask you to forgive me.'

'He will do nothing to harm us, Justin. Andrew is your friend, too.'

'Yes, I know it.' His expression eased. 'I know he has a hot temper. I just hope he will consult me before he does anything precipitate.'

'You are not angry with me? I thought it best to tell you. I can't bear there being any more secrets between us.' She gave him a tentative glance, tears hovering, but not falling.

He hesitated, then reached out and touched her cheek with his fingertips. She caught her breath, looking up at him wonderingly. There had been anger and hurt on both sides, but the look in his eyes made her lips part as her breath came faster.

'I am glad you did, Lucinda. I wish for no more lies between us. You must tell me the truth—even if I am annoyed I prefer it to being kept in the dark.'

She smothered a sob. When he looked at her that way all the reasons why she loved him came back to her: his teasing smile, his gentleness and care for her when they were courting, his quick mind and so many other things that could not be put into words. She blinked hard, holding back the foolish tears.

'Yes, I thought you would wish to know, but I feared it would make you angry again.'

'Have I been such a bear?' Justin asked, a new softer note in his voice. 'I am truly sorry, Lucinda. I did not mean to make you unhappy.'

Her heart raced as he bent his head to kiss her softly on the lips. It was a sweet kiss, tender and gentle, but without passion. Her heart caught and she longed to throw her arms about his neck; she wanted him to take her in his arms and love her. He had not been to her room since that night when he had kissed and touched her, but refrained from making love to her, and she feared he no longer wanted her as a man wants his wife, but at least he was being kind to her.

'I think my unhappiness is my own fault,' Lucinda replied as he drew back. She blinked away her tears. 'I should have been honest with you at the start. You might then have withdrawn your offer and much distress would have been avoided for us both.'

'Lucinda…' Justin looked white about the mouth. 'I must ask you again to forgive me. I should prefer not to quarrel with you.'

'I do not wish for an estrangement between us. Perhaps we may do better in the future. Now, I think we should greet our guests. Mariah will be down and it would be rude to leave her to greet everyone alone.'

Raising her head proudly, she walked away, leaving Justin to follow.

Justin looked at the regal way his wife carried herself. She was every inch the proud duchess he'd told her he required—why then did he feel so hollow and empty inside? Why did he regret that look of trusting innocence that he'd seen in her eyes when he'd courted her? Lucinda had trusted him then, which, after the way her family had treated her, was surprising. She had been willing to be his true wife despite all that had happened to her. Perhaps she ought to have told him the truth before they wed. Had she done so, Justin realised now, he would still have wed her. It was his foolish pride and her deceit that had made him react so badly.

Had he lost her?

It was clear to him that Lucinda regretted her marriage and that, of course, was his fault. She had been—despite all that had been done to her—a sweet, gentle and loving woman. Her father and grandmother had failed to break her spirit, but he with his bitter tongue had destroyed the very thing he loved most.

She would never, could never, forgive him. He had hoped that they might find a way to be happy together, but now he was uncertain of the future. Ought he to allow a separation after all? Was he being grossly unfair to Lucinda to insist that she remain his wife? She was unhappy. Her words had made her regret abundantly clear.

Had she fallen in love with Andrew Lanchester? The thought filled him with conflicting emotions; he felt anger and jealousy, but most of all an unbearable sense of loss. Justin was pretty sure that Lanchester felt the warmest emotions for Lucinda, even though he had flirted gallantly with Mariah at the fête. The man's ready acceptance of Lucinda's secret and his willingness to help her was proof, if Justin had needed it, of Lanchester's feelings.

Justin had hoped that in time they might find a kind of happiness together—but if she loved Andrew the case was altered.

Despite what he had once said to her, Justin did not suspect Lanchester of trying to seduce his wife. Andrew was one of the most honourable of men. He would never do anything underhand or dishonest.

Justin was correct in his assessment of his friend's character and would have been much astonished if he had been privy to Andrew's thoughts that night.

'You are too good for me this evening, Royston.' One of the gentlemen seated round the table in the private parlour of the country inn threw in his cards. 'I've never seen such a prodigious run of luck.'

'Nor I,' Andrew remarked carelessly. 'Yet I am not ready to give you best yet, sir. I shall raise my stake and hope to recoup some of my losses. What say you, Hendricks?'

'What will you raise?' Sir Philip Hendricks asked carelessly. He flicked open a beautiful enamelled snuff box and took a pinch of the strong mix, placing it on the back of his hand before taking a sniff. He glanced at his pocket watch. 'It is not above three in the morning, too early to call it a night. Ah, I see, you raise two hundred, Andrew. Yes, I'll take you—and raise another three. Come, Royston, how do you fancy your luck against us?'

Mr Royston took a sip of his wine, a strange wild expression in his eyes as he pushed forwards a huge pile of golden guineas. He had been drinking steadily, his face flushed, as he grew more and more reckless. His luck had held all night and at least three other gentlemen had withdrawn, complaining that the luck was against them.

'I'll see the both of you,' he said. 'Unless you wish to raise again, Lanchester?'

Andrew pushed forwards a pile of gold coins. 'Five hundred,' he said without a flicker. 'And I'll raise another three hundred.'

'Too steep for me,' Hendricks said and threw in his cards. 'I should throw in your hand, Royston. Your luck must have turned.'

'I'll raise you by a thousand,' Royston said and pushed a pile of coins into the pot. 'And I'll see you, Lanchester.'

Andrew smiled as he turned his cards over, revealing nothing more than three tens. 'I give you best, sir,' he said pleasantly, but then, as Royston sat forwards eagerly to draw the pot towards him, one thin, strong hand reached out and gripped his wrist. 'Your cards first, sir.'

'Oh, you can't beat these,' Royston said with a confident smile and turned over three aces.

'As I thought,' Andrew said and turned over Hendricks's cards, revealing two aces and two kings. 'Since when did we play with a pack with five aces? I discarded those aces and Hendricks picked them up and so I knew that you either had a royal flush or were bluffing—but it appears that instead you were cheating.'

'Cheating?' Royston's face went white, then red. 'How dare you accuse me of cheating? I had two aces from the start and then acquired a third. If anyone is cheating, it must be Hendricks.'

'Why is this in your sleeve, then?'

Andrew inserted two fingers beneath the frill at Royston's wrist and withdrew a card. He turned it over to reveal a king. A gasp of disgust issued from the lips of the men watching.

'Damned cheat,' Sir Michael Jones muttered. 'I lost four hundred to him a week ago.'

'I knew no one could be that lucky,' another gentleman muttered. 'Give us our money back, Royston.'

'No…' Royston rose to his feet shakily, his hand trembling. 'It is a lie. Lanchester planted that card on me. I've never cheated in my life.'

'I've been watching you all evening,' Andrew said and rose to his feet. 'Are you calling me a liar, sir?'

'You are a damned liar. I did not cheat.'

'Then how is it that there are five aces in the pack?' Hendricks asked. 'You are a cheat and a liar, sir—and I for one shall never play cards with you or invite you to my house.'

'When news of this gets out you will be ruined,' Andrew said, still in that pleasant tone. 'If I were you, I should leave England as quickly and quietly as you can.'

'Damn you, you'll meet me for this!' Royston said. He made a lunge at Andrew across the table. 'I swear I'll kill you.'

'I should be only too pleased to teach you some manners,' Andrew said. He glanced at Hendricks. 'You will be my second—and you, Jones?'

'Certainly,' both men agreed with alacrity. 'We shall arrange it for tomorrow at dawn. Ask your seconds to call on us this afternoon, Royston. It is too late to fight now and we're all a trifle drunk.'

'We shall meet at my estate tomorrow morning at first light,' Andrew said. 'I shall arrange for a doctor to be present, also a pair of Manton's best pistols—which you or your seconds will be at liberty to inspect. I think I should warn you that I was a crack shot in the army, but no doubt you are proficient with the pistols yourself?'

'I can acquit myself well enough,' Royston said. He looked round the table at the men gathered there. 'You all think I cheated, but it is a damned lie. Lanchester is the cheat here, but none of you will believe me.'

'I suggest you take yourself off before I am tempted to give you a thrashing, sir,' Hendricks said. 'You have insulted one of the finest men I know. I would take his word above yours any day.'

'I do not know why you've done this.' Royston paused at the door and threw Andrew a bitter look. 'I'll get even with you, if it takes me the rest of my life.'

'We shall settle our score tomorrow,' Andrew said. 'Shoot straight, Royston. I never miss.'

Royston looked sick, went out and slammed the door after him.

'The snivelling rat,' Sir Michael said. 'I've suspected he was a cheat before this—but how did you know, Lanchester?'

'It was his manner. He was nervous, sweating—and I thought I felt something on the corner of one card.' He retrieved an ace from the pack and ran his finger over it. 'There, tell me, is that not a pinprick?'

'Marked cards. He must have slipped them in when it was his turn to shuffle the pack,' Hendricks snarled. 'I thought his luck had changed recently. For weeks he did nothing but lose, then suddenly he started to win every hand. Had to be something havey-cavey about that, don't you know.'

'Well, he has been exposed for the cheat he is,' Andrew said calmly. 'I trust we can make certain this rogue is never allowed to enter decent company again.'

'Best way to do that is to kill him,' Sir Michael said. 'Bound to be some fools that will believe his story.'

'Not when I've finished with him,' Hendricks said. 'Best to wound, but not kill, Lanchester. You don't want to have to make a bolt for France until the dust settles.'

'It might be worth it for the pleasure of seeing him dead,' Andrew said, causing his friend to look at him in a puzzled way. 'But I dare say you are right. If he shows,

I will put a ball in his shoulder and hope he learns his lesson.'

'He'll more than likely make a bolt for it,' one of the other gentlemen said. 'Cheats are usually cowards...'

Chapter Ten

'You've done what?' Justin stared at Andrew in disbelief. 'Why on earth did you provoke him? If you kill him, you may have to leave the country for a spell.'

Andrew shrugged carelessly. 'I have friends in Paris and Spain. I shall not let the possibility of an extended holiday weigh with me.'

'Had you waited, I had intended to offer him a bribe to leave the country. I thought we might catch him picking up the blackmail money and threaten him with prison.'

'It might have worked, but Royston is a cheat and a liar. He might have taken your money and come back for more.'

'Not if we scared the life out of him,' Justin said grimly. 'However, your plan may be better. He is ruined and will not be welcomed in most houses. Besides which, he may well run rather than meet you.'

'Hendricks said the same, but I think he will show. He is a fair shot and will try to best me if he can—without my testimony he might bluff his way back into society.'

'I would back you against any man I know,' Justin said and frowned. 'I've played a hand or two of whist with Royston myself and did not notice anything amiss.'

'I dare say he became desperate,' Andrew said, looking at a spot beyond his shoulder. 'I shall certainly shoot to wound rather than to kill—but if my aim should be a little off we shall at least be certain he will never trouble the duchess again.'

'I'm still not convinced this is the best way to deal with Royston, however. It was possible to get away with a duel to the death in our grandfathers' days, Andrew, but it is frowned upon now. Indeed, you may find yourself up before the beak just for taking part in the affair.'

'It is a price worth paying, wouldn't you say? At least this way no scandal attaches to you or the duchess.'

'You have my gratitude—but we shall say nothing to Lucinda or Miss Lanchester of this.'

'Certainly not. No point in upsetting the ladies.'

'Then I shall say thank you for your help, my friend. I know I have no need to mention that Lucinda's name must be kept out of this affair.'

'None at all. It is the reason I undertook the business myself. Royston might have been wary of you.'

'Very true. Lucinda told me she had confided in

you—and I had meant to myself, once I had her permission. Her secret…well, least said the better.'

'I just wish I had the opportunity of addressing Sir John,' Andrew said. 'He would not have found me so accommodating as to offer him a chance to live.'

'Had she told me his name sooner, I should already have given the man the thrashing he deserved. For a man like that hanging would be too good.'

'She is blameless,' Andrew said. 'How anyone could be so cruel as her father…?' He shook his head and smiled. 'It is beyond me. I dare say you are proud of her courage in all this, Justin. I should be were she my wife.'

'Would I be right in thinking you admire Lucinda?'

'Greatly,' Andrew replied promptly, looking him in the eyes. 'Had I met her again before your wedding I might have asked her to marry me—but I know that she loves you and I am honoured simply to be her friend.'

'You are a man of honour, Andrew. We are both lucky to have you as a friend,' Justin said. 'I should like to be present at the duel—at least I should like to observe it without Royston being aware.'

'If you wish. However, it might not be wise to let him see you. He might think it was all a plot to trap him.'

'Very well. I shall remain out of sight, but I wish to know what happens.'

It was decided between them that Justin would go to the agreed spot and wait hidden so that he could watch the proceedings without being seen. After that the two men left, shaking hands in a cordial way.

Only after Andrew had gone did it occur to Justin to wonder why Royston should think it a plot. He had after all been caught red-handed—or had he? Had Andrew somehow engineered that showdown?

No, it was not possible. Andrew Lanchester was the most honourable man alive. He would never falsely accuse a fellow gentleman of cheating or plant a marked card on him. Certainly not! It was a rogue thought and must instantly be dismissed—though a man might go to extreme acts for a woman he loved. Justin would have preferred to catch the rogue picking up the blackmail money and given him a good thrashing himself, but perhaps this way would work just as well.

'Why are you so kind and generous to me?' Mariah asked as she and Lucinda walked together in the gardens that morning. She bent to pluck a yellow rose and hold it to her nose, inhaling its scent. 'You do know that I came here intending to make trouble between you and Justin?'

'At the start I thought you might feel a little put out at finding another woman as the mistress of your home.' Lucinda smiled at her. 'I could hardly blame you, though you had your chance to wed Justin, I believe?'

'He never loved me,' Mariah said and laughed. 'His papa made a mess of administering my fortune. My guardian's unwise investments lost much of what was left to me. Justin did his best to repair the damage, but he could not restore all I had lost. It was no matter since my husband's fortune is more than even I could spend—and most of it invested in solid blue chips, which provide me with a generous income.'

'Oh…I thought Justin was in love with you then.'

'Yes, I suspected you did,' Mariah said and smiled. 'I wanted you to think that—I wanted to hurt you, Lucinda, but I'm sorry now if I did.'

'You did not,' Lucinda replied. 'You could have taken nothing from me that I had.'

'But you are in love with him, aren't you?'

'Yes, I love my husband. I am not sure how he feels about me.'

'He loves you, of course. Why else would he have married you?' Mariah's gaze narrowed. 'There's something wrong between the pair of you, isn't there? I've sensed it more than once. Justin is always meticulous about family matters, of course—but he is not usually as sharp tempered as he has been of late.'

'There are things that have tried his patience,' Lucinda replied. 'Do not ask, Mariah, for I cannot answer you.'

'I love secrets. If it were anyone but you, I should ferret them out, Lucinda, but I do not wish to distress or harm you. I have come to think of you as a friend and I shall miss you when I leave.'

'Must you go? This is your home for as long as you need it, Mariah. I am certain Justin would say so.'

'Yes, possibly—but I cannot stay forever.' Mariah

blushed. 'I needed somewhere to hide while I considered my position. I have received a proposal from a man I find attractive, but the man is a gambler, reckless and possibly a rogue. He may want me for my fortune rather than my person.'

'No, how should he?' Lucinda looked at her in surprise. 'Have you spoken to Justin about him? Did you want his advice?'

Mariah laughed prettily. 'Yes and no. My head says that I should ask Justin to investigate his circumstances, but my heart tells me to run to him, to throw caution to the winds and marry him. I am tired of being a widow. I want to be loved and petted again. What would you do in my place, Lucinda?'

'I am not certain what to tell you. Normally I would say follow your heart, but if he is a reckless gambler it might be unwise. He could ruin you and break your heart, Mariah. You are beautiful. If you wait for a while, you will find someone who loves you.'

'I dare say he may break my heart in the end,' Mariah agreed. 'But would it not be worth it for the glorious fun I should have first?'

'Perhaps, I cannot say.' Lucinda looked at her anxiously. 'I should not wish to see you cheated or made miserable. Please ask Justin for his advice. I am certain he will know what you should do.'

'He would no doubt tell me to forget the rogue and marry one of my very worthy and boring suitors.'

'No, you are unjust. I think he would advise you to

wait—until you can marry with a whole heart to a man you both respect and love.'

'I think I shall go to London soon,' Mariah said. 'Would you come with me, Lucinda? I should like you to meet Sebastian and give me your opinion of him.'

'Go to London with you?' Lucinda was uncertain. 'I am not sure of Justin's plans...'

'Do you always do exactly as he says?' Mariah pulled a face. 'How very boring for you both. You should tease him a little, Lucinda—make him aware that he cannot always have what he wants.'

'Do you think so?'

Lucinda was thoughtful as Mariah chattered on. Perhaps because of her feelings of guilt she had been too meek—and perhaps that was why Justin found her so boring that he had never returned to her bed. She had thought it was because he was disappointed in her, but perhaps he simply found her dull.

She was not sure what she could do about it, unless she took the very daring step of going to his room and demanding her rights as his wife.

No! He would think her shameless. Yet unless one of them made an effort this sterile marriage would continue and Justin would not have his heir.

Aware that she was soon to lose her precious daughter, Lucinda dreaded the empty life ahead of her. She had all the material comforts she needed, friends and a busy life—but what was any of it worth without someone to love?

If she had Justin's child, she would at least have a part of him to lavish her affection on.

'So, shall you come?' Mariah asked, breaking into her thoughts.

'Perhaps—if you delay your departure for a week or two.'

'Very well,' Mariah said and linked arms with her. 'I am in no particular hurry. It will do Sebastian good to kick his heels a little longer.'

Justin reached the appointed spot a few minutes before the hour. He was the first to do so and found himself a place where he could see everything and not be seen by climbing into a tree. From his vantage point, he would be able to witness the duel and hear what went on without Royston being aware.

He had settled himself in the branches when the first party arrived. Andrew and his seconds, a doctor and an independent witness were the first to arrive. For a moment Justin thought the plan had failed for it was striking the hour and Royston had not shown. However, before the church clock finished its strike a small party of horsemen cantered into the clearing and dismounted.

'I was uncertain of the exact place,' Royston said. 'I would not have been tardy for this meeting, my lord.'

If he had been on edge or nervous the previous night, he had recovered his usual arrogance. Watching, Justin frowned as the two men were offered pistols and Royston's second chose a pistol for him. They were loaded and checked by the independent witness, who then asked if they were certain they wished to continue.

'Of course,' Royston said. 'It is a matter of honour. I am not a cheat and I mean to clear my name.'

'We continue,' Andrew said a trifle grimly.

They were asked to stand back to back and then to take twenty paces forwards.

'On the count of twenty you will turn and fire,' Hendricks said. 'I shall begin the count now. One, two, three, four...'

Justin watched as the men took their measured steps. He was aware of tension amongst the seconds, then, as Hendricks spoke the number nineteen, Royston turned and fired. His ball struck Andrew in the back of his left shoulder, causing him to stagger. On the count of twenty he turned, lifted his arm to fire, but Royston turned and fled without waiting for the shot.

'The damned coward,' Hendricks said. 'He fired too soon, Lanchester. Are you much hurt?'

'Not so very much,' Andrew replied faintly, clutched at his left arm, sank to his knees and then fell flat on to his face.

Hendricks and the doctor bent over him. Justin shinned down the tree and ran to them. He saw the startled look on the other men's faces but ignored it.

'Is he alive?'

'Yes, still breathing, your Grace,' the doctor said.

'I have my chaise close by,' Justin said. 'Take him to my house. I shall follow once I've dealt with Royston.'

'To your house?'

'Do you want to upset Miss Lanchester by taking her brother home half-dead? My people will know what to do. I have other business.'

Ignoring their startled looks, Justin caught Andrew's horse, leaped into the saddle and set off in pursuit of Royston. The man had run like a scared rabbit and left his horse behind in his panic. He could not get far. Justin was determined that the man would not get away with what he had done this night. A duel was one thing, but Royston had fired early. Had his shot not gone wide, he would have murdered Lanchester.

The man must be apprehended and punished for his crimes. Andrew's plan had misfired for there was bound to be scandal now, but it could not be helped. Royston could not be allowed to escape.

Lucinda was woken by the noise downstairs. Pulling on a silk wrap she went down and discovered that the butler and a footman were arguing with several men in the hallway.

'What is happening here?'

'Forgive us, Duchess,' a gentleman she vaguely recognised as Sir Michael Jones said apologetically, 'but your husband bade us bring Lord Lanchester here rather than upset Miss Lanchester. He has been wounded in a duel, you see.'

'Wounded?' Lucinda stared in astonishment. 'Lord Lanchester—how dreadful. You must bring him upstairs at once. Melkins, the best guest chamber, if you please—and a doctor, we need a doctor.'

'I am a doctor, your Grace,' one of the gentlemen said. 'I was there in case of some such thing, but we never expected to see such treachery. Lord Lanchester was shot before the count ended and it is a mercy he is not dead.'

'Who shot him?' Lucinda had a shocking thought. 'It was not the duke?'

'No, madam. Your husband appeared from nowhere and took charge when Mr Royston shot Lord Lanchester and then ran before his lordship fired. Shockingly bad form,' Sir Philip Hendricks said. 'But there, the man was a cheat and it was only to be expected.'

'Mr Royston fought a duel with Lord Lanchester?'

Lucinda could not hide her shock as she followed the men upstairs. She waited outside the best guest chamber until Sir Michael came out to her.

'Is there anything more I can do for you, sir?'

'I think we should all like some brandy, ma'am,' Sir Michael said apologetically. 'It is too shocking to disturb you like this, but the duke insisted it was for the best and sent Lord Lanchester back in his chaise.'

'Where is my husband?'

'He went in pursuit of the culprit, which I must admit none of us thought to do, ma'am. We were all stunned by what happened. No one but an utter rogue would fire before the count finished.'

'Perhaps a very frightened man might,' Lucinda said. She felt a spasm of nerves in her stomach. Justin had gone after Mr Royston and might be hurt—and she had a feeling this awful affair was all her fault. 'Have you any idea of the reason for this duel, sir?'

'I believe it may have been a matter of cheating at cards. Lord Lanchester discovered Royston was cheating at the tables. He denied it and called Lanchester out—and now we know why. He hoped to murder him and get away with it.'

'Is Lord Lanchester very badly wounded?'

'The doctor will tell us that, ma'am.'

'I shall have brandy sent up,' Lucinda said. 'Please make yourselves comfortable. I expect my husband will return soon.'

Pray God that he did and unhurt!

Hurrying away to stir the servants into bringing refreshments for their visitors and tea for herself, she bumped into Mariah to whom she told everything and Mariah declared she would have brandy herself rather than tea.

'What a kick up,' she said, her eyes gleaming with excitement. 'Poor dear Andrew. I would never have thought it of him—and for Justin to have gone haring after the rogue, well, it beats anything.'

'I pray he will return safely,' Lucinda said. 'Come and have your brandy in my sitting room, Mariah. I do not think I shall sleep another wink until I know the outcome of this business.'

It was more than an hour before the doctor declared himself satisfied with Lord Lanchester's condition, by which time Justin had returned alone.

Moments after his return, he was met by his wife and an excited Mariah, who declared that she wanted to know everything before she retired to her room.

'There is little more to tell,' Justin replied. 'I knew of the duel—believing Royston to be a rogue, I went to observe it—though I took no part in the affair. Royston arrived at the last second, appeared to be prepared to go through with it, then fired on nineteen, an instant too soon. When Andrew swayed, but did not fall, and turned to take his shot, he panicked and ran. I told them to bring Andrew here rather than frighten Miss Lanchester, and took his horse to pursue the rogue. However, I must have missed him somehow, for I could not find him.'

'I am glad of it, Justin,' Lucinda said. 'Had you done so he might have shot you too. If he was prepared to murder Andrew, he would not balk at killing you.'

'I dare say you are right, my love,' Justin agreed with a smile. 'As a magistrate I shall offer a reward for his capture. If I have my way, he will hang for attempted murder.' His smile died. 'Andrew isn't dead—is he?'

'The doctor has managed to retrieve the ball and repair his wound,' Lucinda replied, 'but I dare say he will have a fever. He was still unconscious when I went in to make sure he has all he needs. Alice volunteered to sit with him this first time—and I am sure Jane will come as soon as she knows he is here.'

'I am certain she will,' Justin said. 'Perhaps you would like to write to her yourself, my love?'

'I shall go in the chaise and fetch her as soon as I

have dressed,' Lucinda said. 'Jane may pack a bag and stay with us until her brother is able to go home. I am certain she would wish to nurse him herself.'

'Poor Andrew,' Mariah said and looked thoughtful. 'I am perfectly willing to take my share of the nursing, you know. My darling Winston said I was the perfect nurse. I shall take a look at our patient now and tell Alice she may have a little rest.'

'I am sure Jane will be grateful for your help,' Lucinda said. She looked uncertainly at Justin as Mariah walked away, obviously getting ready to prepare herself for the role of nurse and comforter. 'Do you think Royston will come back?'

'Not unless he wishes to face trial for attempted murder.'

'Justin—why were you there? If it was a duel because of a game of cards...or was there more?'

'I am certain there was more,' Justin replied and frowned. 'Andrew has not confided in me, but I think you may be certain that he managed the affair somehow—and that his motive was to rid you of an enemy.'

Lucinda's blood ran cold. 'Do you imagine he meant to kill Royston?'

'I am not precisely sure, my love. It would have made a clean ending, would it not?'

Lucinda shuddered. 'How very horrible this is.' She was trembling and he reached out, drawing her into his arms. She pressed her face to his chest, inhaling the familiar scent she loved.

'Yes, these things are most unpleasant,' Justin said and kissed the top of her head. 'I do hope this has not interfered with your plans, my love? I thought it best to bring Andrew here until he recovers. Miss Lanchester should not bear the burden alone.'

'No, that would be too bad,' Lucinda agreed. 'I had no particular plans, Justin.'

'Ah, did you not? Mariah spoke to me last evening of a trip to London. I collect that the idea was not of your making.'

'Mariah has a problem to solve. She wanted my advice, though I told her I am not the best person to give it. She should properly ask your advice, Justin, but seems reluctant to do so.'

'No doubt she already knows my answer,' he said and smiled oddly. 'Should you wish to visit London or Paris I shall take you when I return. I am leaving on a trip this afternoon.'

'Oh…yes,' Lucinda faltered, her throat catching. 'The school…'

'I shall not take Angela away just yet. I wish to make inquiries about a school much nearer to Avonlea. If it is suitable, you would be able to have her with you on weekends. If we can silence Royston, I may find a governess for her so that she can stay here as your cousin's child—though she may have to go away for a little time, just until I am certain that rogue cannot harm you.'

Lucinda stared at him, hardly daring to believe her ears.

'Do you mean that you will take her into our family?'

'As your cousin's child—yes. I fear we must keep her true birth a secret, but I am not such a brute as to deny you your daughter, Lucinda. At first I thought she must go away, but then I realised that would be too cruel. I have spoken with Alice. She is prepared to care for the child until we can have her here and she will never betray your secret. Indeed, she is willing to swear in a court of law that the girl is your cousin's child. It may not be all you would wish, but it is the best we can do if you are to be accepted by society. Believe me, if I could I would cast convention to the winds and allow you to keep her as your daughter—but both you and our children might suffer for it.'

'Shall we have children?' Lucinda asked in a small voice.

'I most certainly hope so,' Justin replied and smiled at her. 'I shall come to your room soon and then we shall begin again. It is my hope that we shall find contentment together, Lucinda.'

'That is my wish too, Justin.'

Lucinda inclined her head, left and went upstairs to change into a carriage gown of striped linen. She looked at her reflection as she tied a cherry-red bow on her bonnet. Her cheeks were pale, but her eyes were bright with the tears she refused to shed. Justin was being kind to her and he intended to put an end to the breach between them—but she could not convince herself that he truly loved her. He merely wanted heirs for the sake of a proud name and family.

* * *

Jane Lanchester was shocked and burst into immediate tears. It took a moment for her to recover herself, but then she raised her head and smiled.

'Forgive me for an excess of sentiment,' she said with a brisk toss of her head. 'I just cannot bear the thought of losing my brother. I was so relieved to have him back from the wars. However, he would be annoyed if I gave way to emotion. I shall pack my bag and some things for him and come. Have you time to wait or shall I order the carriage?'

'Naturally I shall wait. I am so sorry to be the bearer of this news, Jane. I would not have had it happen for the world.'

'As if you could have prevented it,' Jane said and blew her nose hard. 'Andrew has a temper and I know there have been other duels. He was once arrested and it was only because Justin spoke up for him that he avoided being tried for breaking the peace, which was all they could have charged him for since the affair ended with both men firing in the air.'

'It would have been better if it had ended that way on this occasion,' Lucinda said. 'But we waste time. I should help you to pack.'

'Andrew's man will put up some things for him,' Jane said. 'I shall be but a moment. My maid will send over anything I forget.'

'As you wish,' Lucinda said and went to the parlour window to gaze out. She had been staring fixedly at a bush without truly seeing anything when she had the strangest feeling that she was being observed. She then concentrated her gaze on the garden, but could see nothing untoward, though the uneasy feeling remained until Jane returned carrying a small bag. 'You have been quick, but anything else you need can be fetched. We should go at once. The doctor plans to visit again later this morning and I am certain you would wish to be there.'

'I shall be glad to hear his opinion,' Jane said. 'We need wait for nothing more.'

'Come, then, for I know you must be anxious.'

The two ladies went out to the waiting carriage and were soon bowling along at a swift pace towards the Avonlea estate. Once inside the house, they parted, Jane to her brother's side and Lucinda to her own bedroom, where after a few moments to compose herself, she removed to the nursery. She must make the most of her time with her daughter. Justin had promised he would allow the child to live with them if a scandal could be averted, but that was not certain and she might soon have to part with the child for a time.

'He has a fever,' Jane said when Lucinda went to the door and asked about Andrew's health later that day. 'He has been wandering in his mind, saying all sorts of strange things. It is as well that I am here to nurse him, for the maids would undoubtedly be shocked.'

'Oh…' Lucinda looked at her warily. 'What on earth can he have been saying?'

'He thought I was his mistress and tried to kiss me,'

Jane said and laughed. 'Oh, and he said how beautiful your eyes were, Lucinda—though he called you his duchess and other things…just foolish nonsense, of course. I shall not tell him when he comes out of the fever for it would be sure to embarrass him.'

'Well, I am glad he has such a sensible sister to care for him. Shall I have a tray sent up or will you come down to eat?'

'Mariah says she will sit with him while I have nuncheon. I shall come down in a little.'

'You must do whatever you wish. This is your home and Andrew's for as long as you both need it.'

'You are very kind.' Jane frowned. 'I still do not understand this business, do you? Why my brother fought a duel over a hand of cards—and why your husband should have been there, though not one of his seconds.'

'Gentlemen do such odd things, do they not?' Lucinda dismissed Jane's concerns, but felt a pang of guilt since she was perfectly certain that Andrew Lanchester had fought the duel for her sake. She was not sure whether he had intended to shoot Royston or merely ruin him in the eyes of polite society, but Royston had been too clever for him—or perhaps too frightened to wait and take his chances like a man.

Recalling the feeling of being watched as she stood at the window of Jane's parlour, Lucinda wondered. Justin had said Royston had disappeared. He clearly believed the man had made a run for it and was probably either onboard a ship or heading for the coast. Supposing he was wrong? Supposing Royston had lingered in the vicinity...

Yet he must know that his reputation was finished. He might just have recovered from cheating at cards, but to shoot too soon and take foul advantage in a duel was beyond the pale. Royston would scarcely be received in society again and, if Andrew Lanchester were to die, he might be hanged for his murder.

After nuncheon, Lucinda persuaded Jane to take a walk with her. They did not go beyond the private gardens close to the house and Lucinda was not conscious of any uncomfortable feeling of being overlooked. She kept Jane in the fresh air for more than an hour and when they returned to the house Justin had left on his business trip and strangely the house felt empty.

Chapter Eleven

In the morning Andrew confounded everyone by declaring that he was well enough to go home and would not be persuaded to keep to his bed another day. He took a courteous leave of Lucinda and asked that Justin would visit him as soon as he returned.

Mariah decided to accompany Jane and Lord Lanchester to their home. Jane had invited Mariah to stay for a few days.

'My brother is chafing at being confined to the house,' she explained. 'You amuse him, Mariah. I heard him laughing when you sat with him—and he needs someone to entertain him. You have such a lovely reading voice and you play cards so well.'

'We played for shillings, but it did seem to please him,' Mariah agreed and looked at Lucinda. 'You will not mind if I go? I dare say Justin will be home soon.'

'Yes, I dare say he will,' Lucinda agreed and smiled.

'Of course you must go and stay with your friends, Mariah. You do not have to stay and bear me company. I have plenty to do and Justin will be home later today.'

'We'll go to London soon,' Mariah promised and kissed her. 'And I shall tell Justin he is a fool to think of sending the child away—there is simply no need.'

Lucinda blinked back the tears that rose to her eyes. 'You must do nothing of the sort, Mariah. You do not understand.'

'I must thank you for your hospitality, Duchess,' Andrew said and took her hand in his left hand, because his right arm was still supported in a sling to save his shoulder. 'I hope we have not been a trouble to you?'

'How could you think that—after...?' Lucinda could not continue. 'I am grateful, but you should not. You really should not...'

'I hope that I have not made things worse,' he replied seriously. 'Please do not forget to ask Justin to call on me as soon as he returns.'

'I shall not forget.'

Lucinda went outside to bid her friends farewell. If she had felt lonely before, it was nothing to the despair that settled over her now. Was this what her life would be in the future? Justin had been kind to her recently, but still he made no attempt to come to her bed and his indifference hurt her. Even if he eventually came to her in the hope of an heir, it would not be because he loved or wanted her.

Blinking back her tears, she decided to fetch her

cloak and go for a walk. It was a long time since she had bothered to walk anywhere other than the gardens; she had come to enjoy the exercise on those visits to the cottage. She felt restless and without Justin the house seemed too big and empty.

Justin arrived half an hour after Lucinda had gone out. He asked for his wife at once, but no one seemed to know where she was until one of the footmen said that he thought her Grace might have gone out for a walk.

'Where are our guests?'

'They all left this morning, your Grace. Lord Lanchester had recovered and insisted on removing to his own house—and Lady Fanshawe accompanied them. She is to stay for a few days.'

'Damn!' Justin muttered loudly enough for the footman to look startled. 'I thought she would at least have Mariah's company.'

He strode back out of the house and walked in the direction of the woods. Lucinda had walked there often when he'd left her and gone off to London. With any luck he would find her before too long. He was hungry and tired after a frustrating journey, for the school was unsuitable. It would not do for his wife's child; the pupils were neither properly educated nor cared for, as he would expect. Justin had come to a decision; keeping the child here and engaging a governess was risky and might lead to some gossip, but he had decided that he was willing to take the risk—but he must tell Lucinda of his decision as soon as possible. She must make the final decision, because she had the most to lose.

Although Justin had walked for an hour before giving up and returning to the house in the hope of finding his wife in her parlour, he saw no sign of Lucinda. He enquired of his housekeeper whether she had returned and was told her ladyship had left no instructions for dinner.

'It is most unusual—this is the day we decide the menus for the week, my lord.'

'I dare say my wife had other things on her mind,' Justin said. 'You will please tell her that I am home and request a few moment of her time as soon as she returns.'

'Yes, sir. Her Grace has seemed a little down of late, my lord.' Mrs Mann hesitated then, 'We all admire her, sir. It was such a charitable thing she did, taking that poor little mite in after her cousin died. I mean, I've heard the cousin was not wed and that is why the little girl might not be able to stay here—but it does seem a shame.'

'Where do these rumours start?' Justin asked, arching an eyebrow. 'The child is perfectly legitimate, but an orphan. I have been making enquiries about good schools, but we may decide to engage a governess. That must be for my wife to decide, however.'

'Well, there, such a wicked tale,' Mrs Mann said and looked pleased. 'Had I known I would have scotched the rumour immediately. I shall do so at the next opportunity.'

'Please do,' Justin said with a curt nod. 'I should not wish any scandal to attach to the girl.'

'No, your Grace, certainly not. It was a misapprehension and I shall make sure the staff know the truth.'

Feeling satisfied he had taken the first positive step in installing little Angela into his home Justin returned to the issue of Royston. He must be dealt with. He could not allow the rogue to harm Lucinda. Justin had begun to understand just how much his wife's happiness meant to him. He knew that he could not expect her to love him or confide in him, as she once had, but perhaps he could make something of their marriage at last.

Where was she? Lucinda had not yet returned to the house or his housekeeper would have told him. Perhaps she had gone to visit Jane Lanchester, though it was a fair walk and she had only parted from them this morning.

Unable to stay in the house another moment, Justin left and walked down to the stables. He would pay a courtesy call on Andrew and see how he was faring. Surely Lucinda would be home by the time he returned.

Justin returned in time for tea. There was still no sign of Lucinda. He knew that she had not visited Jane Lanchester, for they had asked if she had come with him. He frowned as he turned away from the parlour where Lucinda liked to sit in the afternoons and went upstairs.

Her maid was laying out Lucinda's evening gown when he entered the bedchamber. She turned with a smile, which faded as she hastily made her curtsy.

'I thought it was my lady, sir.'

'I was told she went walking. She said nothing to you?'

'No, sir. My lady seemed sad this morning after her friends left. She fetched her cloak and went out, your Grace—but she took nothing more with her. Her reticule is here and I do not think she went visiting for she did not change into a carriage gown.'

'Please tell her I should be pleased with a few moments of her time before dinner.' Justin nodded curtly and left to go to his own room.

He did not recall Lucinda ever staying out this long before. Had she been in such distress that she had done something foolish? Remembering his fears when she disappeared soon after their wedding, Justin told himself not to let his imagination run away with him. Yet the thoughts went round and round in his mind until he was sure his head would burst. Had he made her so unhappy? He had told her he wanted to continue their marriage and then treated her as though she'd done something wicked—when all she'd done was to love a child—a child who had been cruelly treated. He should have admired her courage and made her understand that he blamed the man who had shamed her, but that she was blameless in his eyes.

Oh, God, how he wanted and loved her. He had been

such a fool, allowing his temper to get the better of him, putting his pride before his love for her—before her needs and her happiness. How could he have been such a brute?

Justin knew full well that his friend was in love with Lucinda, but his instincts told him that Andrew would do nothing about it unless she went to him in desperation. At the moment he was recovering from the duel he'd fought—the duel Justin should have fought for Lucinda's sake. Had he been able to find Royston that day he believed he might have killed the man. A ball through the head and his body left to rot with no one the wiser, but the rogue had disappeared.

Suddenly, Justin's blood ran cold. Royston was at large, in debt if all accounts were to be believed and in fear of his life. Supposing he had taken Lucinda in revenge for the loss to his reputation? Andrew's intentions had been good, but he had inadvertently made the situation worse.

Lucinda had not left him. She had been abducted.

Pacing his bedchamber, Justin felt a growing certainty that wherever Lucinda was, it was not of her own free will. He was sure that she had been kidnapped.

What was he to do? Sit tight and wait for a ransom note or look for her?

He had come up to change for the evening, but now abandoned the idea and went back to his wife's room. It was empty, her fashionable gown still lying on the bed where her maid had left it.

He went downstairs and enquired if any of the servants had seen her since she went out that morning, but the answer was the same. No one had seen her since early that morning. His chest tight with fear, he sent for his bailiff and set up a search while there was still time before the light faded. Someone on the estate must surely have seen something!

As Lucinda opened her eyes she was aware of a pain in the back of her head. She put up a hand and felt, but there was merely a bump; the blow to her head had not broken the skin. Whoever hit her had wanted her alive. She had been wearing her emerald ring and her pearls, both of which she still had—so the motive was not theft. The only person who could gain anything from her capture was Royston. Where was he and what was his next move?

Sitting up as her eyes accustomed themselves to the gloom, she discovered that she was in a bedroom. A faint light showed through windows at which there were no curtains. It was sparsely furnished with just the bed, a chair and table, and one bedside chest—a servant's room, perhaps, though it looked too spacious. Once a guestroom, but now almost empty.

What kind of a place was this? She put her feet to the floor and tried to stand, but swooned and fell back against the pillows. The blow to her head had knocked her unconscious and she was aware that she felt rather sick. She supposed that she ought to rest for a while longer, but it was already late in the day and her servants would wonder where she was—or would they simply think that she'd taken up her old habit of walking for most of the day?

She'd never stayed out this late before. Even Mrs Mann would start to think it strange, but whom could she tell? Justin was due to return that day, but would he realise what had happened?

What a careless idiot she was! Lucinda felt vexed with herself. Justin would return home and might think she had broken her promise and left him because of what he was planning to do. He might not bother to look for her and when the ransom note arrived he would be furious with her for causing more scandal. After all, why should he care about a woman who had caused him nothing but trouble? Tears stung her eyes. She loved Justin so much despite their quarrels and it was all so hopeless.

She tried putting her feet to the floor once more and discovered that she could now stand without fear of falling. Her feet were bare. She looked for her shoes, but could not see them. Had they fallen off as Royston carried her here—or had he taken them so that she could not escape?

The thought made her tingle. If she could escape and find her way back home, it would save Justin the tiresome task of paying her ransom.

Walking softly to the window, she looked out. She appeared to be in a house set in large secluded gardens. Could this possibly be Royston's own house? Somehow she did not think it. She would swear that it was an empty house, abandoned by its owner and left to decay. The woodwork about the window was rotting and, from what little she could see in the rather poor light afforded by a moon half in shadow, she thought the walkways and once smooth lawns had been neglected for some time.

Where could she be? She had no memory of having been brought here. Was she close to Avonlea or had she been conveyed some distance in a carriage?

How careless she'd been to let herself be captured so easily. Lucinda tried the window. It opened perfectly well, but there was nothing she could catch hold of and she did not fancy leaping to the ground below. She would either break a limb or her neck, which was why the window had not been secured.

Hearing a sound outside her door, she hastily closed the window and turned as the door opened and a man entered. He was carrying a lantern and his gaze went first to the bed and then to the window.

'Mr Royston,' she said, lifting her head proudly. 'I suspected my abduction must be your work. What do you hope to gain from such wickedness, sir? Surely you would have done better to leave the country?'

'Yes, that is what your husband and friends would like,' Royston said, his top lip curling in a sneer. 'Well, madam, you have mistaken your man. I do not yield so easily. Lanchester tricked me. He planted that card on me. It was he that fed me the cards and then he accused me of cheating. I dare say he meant to kill me in the duel, but I was too clever for him.'

Lucinda felt chilled. 'Forgive me if I take leave to doubt you, sir. Lord Lanchester is one of the most honourable men I know.'

'His word will be believed before mine, I know. I am ruined and I must flee to France or perhaps Italy where I may take an assumed name, but for that I need money—and your husband will pay for me to live comfortably abroad.'

'My husband is from home,' Lucinda said. 'What makes you imagine he will pay for my release?'

'He was desperate enough when you disappeared before, Duchess,' Royston sneered. 'If ever I saw a man at his wit's end it was Avonlea. We met out riding and I even offered my help to search for you, but he refused me. He loves you despite the fact that you bore an illegitimate child. You should have paid my twenty thousand when you had the chance, madam. Now the price for your return and my silence is fifty thousand.'

'No! That is foolish talk. How could anyone pay such a sum? The duke will not pay. He will set agents to find us—and when he does you will be arrested. I fear that you will hang, sir, unless you relent and allow me to leave now. If you do so, I shall be silent and allow you to evade the law.'

'You will not escape so easily. Your husband would see me dead if he could for daring to blackmail you. Avonlea is a proud man and he will not allow me to escape—but if I have money I can go beyond his reach.'

'I beg you to reconsider, sir. If you will but allow me to return home, I shall find the ten thousand pounds your uncle demanded and say nothing of this affair to my husband.'

'You waste your breath, Duchess.' Royston laughed unpleasantly. 'I imagine Avonlea is searching high and low for you—but he will never think of looking here, for he does not know this place belongs to me. I shall leave him to fret for a while. When he is desperate enough he will pay my price.'

'I fear you will be sadly disappointed. My husband will not pay.'

'Then you will never leave this house alive,' Royston said. His eyes glittered in the lantern's glow and Lucinda shivered. 'If I am to die, then you shall lead the way, Duchess. I promise that I would put a ball through your head rather than let you go without payment.'

Lucinda swallowed hard. 'You must lower your price. No one could pay so much for a ransom.'

'Your husband is wealthy beyond most men's dreams. He will find it somehow,' Royston said. 'I wish you sweet dreams, Duchess. Do not think of jumping from the window. You would not like the consequences.'

'I am hungry—do you intend to starve me?'

'I have no food here. The plan presented itself when I saw you walking alone and acted on impulse. I shall bring food in the morning if you behave. Again, I bid you good-night.'

He went and closed the door behind him. Lucinda retreated to the bed. The moon had gone behind the clouds completely and the room was in darkness. She felt her way round the wall until her knees touched the bed and then sat down, wrapping her arms about her body.

Royston was ruthless. She was certain he meant exactly what he said. He would see her dead rather than let her go—unless Justin paid the price.

How could anyone find that much money at a moment's notice? It was impossible. Even his estate could not be worth such a fabulous sum, could it?

Cold, tired, hungry, her head aching, Lucinda lay down on the bed. She could not escape tonight, but perhaps in the morning when he brought her some food...

'She has been gone all night,' Justin said. He ran his fingers through his thick locks with an air of desperation. 'I said nothing yesterday, because I still hoped she might return—but now I must ask if you know anything, Andrew? Did she say she was leaving me? Did she confide in you or Jane?'

'She was a little quiet when we left her,' Jane replied for her brother who was frowning. 'I think she was in some distress, but she said nothing to us. What makes you think she might have left you?'

'She knew I was enquiring about a school for her child and I think she did not wish to part with her.'

'It would distress her to part with the child, but I know she would not leave you—unless, has the child gone, too?'

'No, she is in the nursery, which is why I fear that

she may have been abducted. I've had men searching the grounds all day in case there has been an accident.'

'Abducted?' Jane was startled. 'Who would do such a thing?'

'Royston.' Andrew looked grim. 'This may be my fault. I intended to settle this business, but I believe I've made things worse, Justin. Forgive me. We must search for her in your woods and I'll send for the agents we used last time—but I fear Royston is out for revenge.'

'Will he be content with a ransom do you think?'

'He is a scoundrel and a wastrel, but I do not think he would harm her—unless he feared for his life.'

'He must already know that his life is forfeit. He was ruined when he fired at you before the count ended—but abduction is a hanging matter. If the law takes him, he will die at the rope's end.'

'Then he has nothing to lose and that makes him more dangerous. You must arm yourself, Justin, and if you get the chance shoot to kill. I shall certainly do so.'

'Your shoulder must still pain you,' Justin said with a quick frown. 'I beg you not to put yourself out over this, Andrew. I came in the hope that Jane might know something, not to ask you to join the search.'

'My shoulder is stiff, but it was little more than a flesh wound after all. I should never forgive myself if I sat at home while you searched alone. I believe I may have pushed Royston to this desperate act. I acted without sufficient thought.'

'Why?' Mariah was looking at them from the doorway, having overheard them. 'What did you do that was ill considered?'

'Were you listening at the door?' Justin frowned at her. 'I thought you had grown out of that trick, Mariah.'

'It is just as well I haven't,' she said. 'If you are looking for a place that Royston may have taken Lucinda to, I may be able to help you.'

Three pairs of eyes looked at her in surprise and she smiled, looking like a cat that had devoured the cream.

'That odious man was accustomed to paying me attention before I was married—well, I happen to know that he has an old derelict house not far from here. It belonged to an elderly aunt of his. Royston inherited it, but the house was in such terrible repair that he never bothered to open it up after she died. He cannot sell it as it is and it would cost a fortune to put right.'

'How do you know this?' Justin demanded.

'You know I am always curious about old houses,' Mariah said. 'I came across the property when out riding some years ago and could not resist having a look round. It had been empty for two years or so then and the doors were not locked, some of them hanging from their hinges. I went in to have a look and Royston found me there. He tried to take advantage, but I struck him across the face with my riding crop and escaped. I think he has never quite forgiven me, though he afterwards spoke of it as a jest and begged my pardon.'

'You should have told me at the time. I would have thrashed him,' Justin said. 'Where is the house?'

'It is Lady Ridley's old house. You must know it, Andrew?'

'Good God, yes!' Andrew looked struck. 'Royston asked my father if he would buy it years ago. It lies between our estates, Justin, in that piece of no man's land that neither of us wants. There is a large garden, but no other land. Father told him he was not interested.'

'We should go there immediately,' Justin said and then recollected himself. 'If you are certain you feel up to it?'

'Yes, of course. I shall show you the way. Allow me to put on my coat and fetch my pistols. Jane, pray ask the groom to saddle my horse.'

'And a horse for me,' Mariah said. 'I shall come with you. I am as good a shot as any of you.'

'You most certainly will not,' Justin told her. 'We shall take two of your grooms, Andrew. Royston will undoubtedly make a fight of it.'

'And who will he shoot first? I imagine it might be Lucinda,' Mariah said, her words bringing a dreadful silence. 'He will not suspect me. Allow me to try something. I am very fond of Lucinda and I think in this case guile might win out over brute force.'

'I think you should listen to her,' Jane said. 'Mariah is not a fool—if she has an idea that might help, you should at least listen…'

Hearing a door slam downstairs, Lucinda ran to the window and looked out. She saw Royston leave and a moment or two later he mounted his horse and rode off, presumably in search of some food for them both. Looking about her, Lucinda sought a weapon. She must be ready to attack him when he returned. Her gaze moved over the chest, bed and chair, finding nothing so handy as a candlestick with which to strike him. She picked up the chair, but knew that it was too heavy for her to wield as a club. Holding it by the back, she smashed it against the wall and heard a cracking sound. One of the legs had cracked, but not broken. It took her three efforts before she was able to wrench the stout wooden leg free, but she looked at it with satisfaction when it was finally in her hand. Now she had something to protect herself with.

When he entered the room with her food she must run at him from behind the door and strike him. He was much stronger than she so her plan would only work if she had the element of surprise. She ran to the bed, arranging the bolster under the cover to look as if someone were lying there.

Now she was ready.

A short while later she heard a door open below and stiffened, her nerves tingling as she waited for Royston to climb the stairs to her door. Hearing sounds, she knew he was outside now. He was trying the door, but it did not open. She heard an exclamation of annoyance and then a voice called out.

'Lucinda, are you in there?'

It was a woman's voice. Mariah's voice! Lucinda's heart leapt with excitement.

'Yes, I'm here. Royston has gone for some food. Be careful. He may return at any moment.'

'Stand back. I'm going to shoot the lock out.'

'Yes, all right. I'm out of the way.'

The noise of the shot was terrifying, but the lock shattered and was pushed wide as Mariah rushed in. She saw Lucinda and the weapon she held and laughed, her eyes bright with excitement.

'I might have known you would not give in tamely,' she cried. 'Justin and Andrew are outside. I persuaded them to let me come in first, because I thought Royston might shoot you if they burst in here fully armed.'

'Oh, Mariah,' Lucinda said. 'How reckless of you. Royston is quite lost to all sense of decency and would not hesitate to shoot either of us if cornered. We must go quickly before he comes and finds that you have found me.'

'I am not frightened of that little rat,' Mariah said. 'Besides, I have the pistol left to me by Winston. I would as soon shoot him as look at him.'

Lucinda shook her head. 'You might not think it such an adventure had you been hit over the head and locked up all night with nothing to eat. Really, we must go.'

She went ahead of Mariah out of the room down the landing to the head of the stairs. However, before she was halfway down them Royston entered through the door Mariah had left wide open. His pistol was in his hand and he pointed it at Lucinda.

'So your husband has found you. Where is he?'

Royston demanded with a snarl. 'He may think himself clever, but you will not leave here alive.'

Lucinda saw his finger move on the hammer and knew that he was preparing to fire. She screamed just as two men rushed in at the door and then, hearing Mariah's warning shout from behind, dropped down to crouch on the stairs. Two shots rang out. Royston's body jerked as both found their mark—one through his forehead and the other into his back.

Glancing round, she saw that Mariah was holding a small pistol with a silver handle, its barrel still smoking. Andrew Lanchester had also fired, his ball hitting Royston squarely in his back. Shivering, Lucinda struggled to her feet and walked unsteadily down the stairs past Royston's slumped body to the bottom, where she stood swaying until Justin ran to take her into his arms.

'Is—is he dead?' she asked in a faint voice as Andrew examined Royston's body.

'Perfectly.' Andrew said from behind her. 'I'm not sure whether it was my shot or Mariah's that did him, but he will certainly not trouble you again, Duchess.'

'Thank you,' Lucinda whispered, looking at Justin with tears hovering on her lashes. 'Take me home, please. I cannot but pity him, though there is no doubt he was a hateful man. I believe this will come as a terrible shock to Lady Morgan. We must think of some story to tell her that will not reveal the depth of his infamy.'

'Do not distress yourself,' Justin told her with a gentle smile. 'You may leave all this to me. Mr Royston would most certainly have been hanged had Andrew not shot him. Mariah's name must be kept out of it for the sake of propriety.'

'Oh, nonsense,' Mariah said, coming down the stairs, her eyes bright with excitement. 'I am certain it was my shot that stopped him shooting you, Lucinda. I do not give a damn whether it was improper or not. I'm a damned fine shot and I do not care who knows it.'

'You certainly are,' Andrew agreed and laughed. 'I would give you the credit, Mariah, but I think Justin is right on this one. Best not to involve you. I may have to appear before the beak for murder, you know.'

'No such thing,' Justin said. 'I have friends who will know how to handle this discreetly. You saved my wife's life. I am more grateful to both of you than I can express. I shall vouch for you, Andrew—and as for you, Mariah, I am merely thinking of your good name.'

'I think you should attend to Justin,' Lucinda said, gave a little sigh and fainted.

When she opened her eyes, Lucinda was lying on a *chaise longue* in her parlour and Justin was sitting by her side, waving a burnt feather under her nose.

'Oh, that is horrid,' she said and pushed his hand away. 'Please desist, Justin. I am quite recovered.'

'Are you, my dearest one? I am relieved to hear it. We were beginning to worry about you.'

'Have they all gone?'

'Yes, I managed to send them off, though Mariah wanted to stay and nurse you. I told her it was merely a faint and you would be perfectly fine when you had recovered your senses—you are, aren't you?'

'Perfectly. It was merely a little faint. I am sorry to have made you anxious, Justin, but I am famished. I ate nothing after breakfast yesterday and I suddenly felt very weak.'

'My poor love. You have been treated shamefully and not just by Royston.' Justin reached for her hand, taking it in his own. 'Do you think you can forgive me for my unkindness? I must tell you at once that I have decided against sending Angela to school. She will stay here with us and I shall employ a governess to teach her, her lessons. When she is older she may go to a finishing school for a year or so, but this will be her home. I shall make a settlement on her so that she will have her own marriage portion and we must hope that she will make a good marriage one day.'

'That is truly generous. I did not expect so much and you have made me so happy, Justin.'

'I fear we must keep up the pretence of her being your cousin's child, though I have taken Mariah into our confidence. After her bravery and loyalty today I feel sure that she will not spill your secret.'

'Of course, Mariah must know the truth. She has become a true and dear friend to me and I know I can trust her with my life. As for Angela, I shall gently explain that she must call me aunt or ma'am. If she is loved and happy, she will soon become accustomed to the idea.'

'Yes, it is a small price to pay. I should have accepted it from the start, but I fear my pride was hurt because you had not trusted me. I do hope you can forgive me and give me a chance to show you how much I adore you.'

Lucinda's heart began to beat faster. As she looked into his eyes she caught her breath, hardly believing what she saw.

'Do you?' she asked, a faint flush in her cheeks. 'I thought you might be disappointed in me after—you did not come to my bed a second time. I know that I failed you, but I shall try to do better.'

'You have not failed or disappointed me,' he told her and took her hands as her gaze dropped. 'Look at me, Lucinda. I did not come to you because I thought you found the physical side of marriage not quite to your taste—that you needed a little time to accustom yourself to the idea, because of what you had suffered at the hands of that brute.' His frown deepened. 'Oh, that I had known sooner! I should have liked to thrash him for you, dearest. Indeed, I think I should have broken his neck with my bare hands.'

'He is dead,' Lucinda reminded him softly. 'He can no longer harm us—unless we allow him to come between us.' She reached up to touch his cheek. 'I have lain alone every night and wished you would come to me. I thought I had given you a disgust of me…'

'Never!' He caught her hand and pressed a kiss to the palm. 'How could you think it? I love you. I adore you. I burn for you, Lucinda—but when I touched you that night you held back. You did not touch me and I thought…but I have been a fool. You were young and shy and knew nothing of love, only of brutality. I should have shown you, taught you how to respond. You must never be afraid to tell me what will please you.'

'Do you think…?' Lucinda faltered and looked at him shyly, but with a glimmer of eagerness in her eyes. 'Do you think we could begin tonight?'

Justin laughed. 'If you feel well enough?'

'I am perfectly well, but, Justin—I truly am very, very hungry.'

'Are you, my darling?' He smiled and stood up, reaching for the bell. 'In that case I shall have supper served at once.'

'It is but three in the afternoon…'

'But I did not sleep last night and I should like to go to bed rather early this evening…'

Epilogue

'Are you too tired to go out again this evening?' Justin asked.

They had been exploring the sights of Paris, finally able to enjoy their long-overdue honeymoon, spending the morning on the river on one of the little boats that plied its trade up and down the Seine. The previous day they had driven out to the wonderful palace of Versailles and before that had visited various museums and gardens, besides being invited to a grand ball on their arrival in Paris. 'You have seemed a little sleepy at times recently, Lucinda. Are you certain you are not ill?'

'I am perfectly well,' she replied. 'I believe I may be with child, Justin. I recall being very sleepy when Angela was first on the way, but I did not wish to raise your hopes too soon only to disappoint you. I have missed my courses twice now, so I am fairly certain, but—'

She got no further for Justin took her hand, raising it to his lips to kiss it. 'Is it indeed so, my love? Would you like to rest for the remainder of the day? Should I take you home to Avonlea?'

'Certainly not,' Lucinda said and laughed. 'I have an appointment with a doctor who was recommended to me. I may have more certain news then, my love. I am perfectly sure that he will tell me I am quite healthy and the tiredness is natural. We shall continue our visit and say nothing to anyone for the moment—though I may rest for an hour or so in the afternoons if my doctor advises it.'

'You will certainly rest on your husband's advice,' Justin said and his eyes smouldered with passion as he looked at her. 'I intend to take good care of you—and I shall brook no argument, Lucinda.'

'I meant to offer none,' she said and laughed softly. 'I enjoy being made a fuss of, Justin, but I do assure you that I am perfectly well—and there is no reason why you should not rest with me for the time being. Only when the child is advanced some months shall I have to rest alone.'

'You are a minx, Lucinda,' he said. 'A beautiful, charming, adorable minx—and I love you. I'm not sure if I've told you how much?'

'If you have not, you may do so when I return from the doctor this afternoon…'

'And so, my love,' Justin said softly as he lay by her side, looking into her eyes. 'I am to be a father, then?'

'Oh, yes, the doctor was sure, though it is early yet, Justin, but he says my symptoms are clear indications. Many women experience sleepiness in the early stages.'

'You are not feeling ill? Do not ladies in your condition feel sick in the mornings?'

'Many suffer badly with it,' Lucinda said. 'As yet I have not—and since I hardly felt it at all with Angela I do not suppose I shall this time.'

'And you are quite sure you wish to continue with the visit?'

'Quite sure, my dear love,' she said and touched his cheek. 'I am enjoying my first visit to Paris and am relishing the chance to have you all to myself for once! You have become quite besotted with Angela and I find myself quite jealous. Now, put your concerns from your mind, my love—and kiss me. It is quite two hours since you told me how much you love me. I have a fancy to be told again.'

'And so you shall, my love,' Justin replied and obliged her in a way that brought nothing but pleasure to them both.

* * * * *

A sneaky peek at next month...

HISTORICAL

IGNITE YOUR IMAGINATION, STEP INTO THE PAST...

My wish list for next month's titles...

In stores from 2nd March 2012:

❑ The Mysterious Lord Marlowe – Anne Herries

❑ Marrying the Royal Marine – Carla Kelly

❑ A Most Unladylike Adventure – Elizabeth Beacon

❑ Seduced by Her Highland Warrior – Michelle Willingham

❑ Reynold de Burgh: The Dark Knight – Deborah Simmons

❑ The Bride Raffle – Lisa Plumley

Available at WHSmith, Tesco, Asda, Eason, Amazon and Apple

Just can't wait?

0212/04

Don't miss *Pink Tuesday*
One day. 10 hours. 10 deals.

PINK TUESDAY
IS COMING!

10 hours...10 unmissable deals!

This Valentine's Day we will be bringing
you fantastic offers across a range of
our titles—each hour, on the hour!

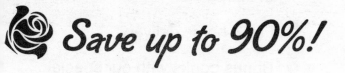

Save up to 90%!

Pink Tuesday starts
9am Tuesday 14th February

MILLS & BOON Book Club

2 Free Books!

Join the Mills & Boon Book Club

Want to read more **Historical** stories? We're offering you **2 more** absolutely **FREE!**

We'll also treat you to these fabulous extras:

- 🌹 **Books up to 2 months ahead of shops**
- 🌹 **FREE home delivery**
- 🌹 **Bonus books with our special rewards scheme**
- 🌹 **Exclusive offers… and much more!**

Treat yourself now!

2 Free Books!

Get your free books now at
www.millsandboon.co.uk/freebookoffer

Or fill in the form below and post it back to us

THE MILLS & BOON® BOOK CLUB™—HERE'S HOW IT WORKS: Accepting your free books places you under no obligation to buy anything. You may keep the books and return the despatch note marked 'Cancel'. If we do not hear from you, about a month later we'll send you 4 brand-new stories from the Historical series priced at £3.99* each. There is no extra charge for post and packaging. You may cancel at any time, otherwise we will send you 4 stories a month which you may purchase or return to us—the choice is yours. *Terms and prices subject to change without notice. Offer valid in UK only. Applicants must be 18 or over. Offer expires 31st July 2012. **For full terms and conditions, please go to www.millsandboon.co.uk**

Mrs/Miss/Ms/Mr (please circle)
_____

First Name
_____

Surname
_____

Address
_____

_____
                         Postcode

E-mail
_____

Send this completed page to: Mills & Boon Book Club, Free Book Offer, FREEPOST NAT 10298, Richmond, Surrey, TW9 1BR

Find out more at
www.millsandboon.co.uk/freebookoffer

Visit us Online

0112/H2XEA